BEYOND THE WINTER KINGDOM

AURELIA JANE  KEL CARPENTER

Beyond the Winter Kingdom

Aurelia Jane and Kel Carpenter

Published by Raging Hippo LLC

Copyright © 2025, Raging Hippo LLC

Cover by Book Brander Boutique

Chapter Spreaders by Manuela

Photography of Lylith Sammons, courtesy of Cody Sammons

Edge Design by Samaiya Art

Kel Carpenter and Aurelia Jane do not support AI artwork, cover designs, or writing. All artwork and cover designs are commissioned by working artists, and AI was not used to write this book.

About the Authors

Kel Carpenter and Aurelia Jane are the hilarious team behind the international bestselling book, Reject Me.

They pride themselves in being absolute weirdos, spending hours on the phone coming up with detailed worlds, and laughing about crazy ideas for torturing characters. While they believe they each have the personality of a rabid badger, people still seem to like them okay.

They share a love of coffee, snarky t-shirts, and tacos. Best friends and work wives, Kel has the audacity to live in Maryland while Aurelia lives in Texas, but they try to see each other as much as possible.

instagram.com/kelandaureliabooks

patreon.com/kelandaureliabooks

tiktok.com/@kelandaureliabooks

The mind is its own place, and in itself
  Can make a Heav'n of Hell, a Hell of Heav'n.

John Milton, *Paradise Lost*

To our therapists, Alexis and Jenn,

We may pay you to listen to our crazy asses, tells us why we are the way we are, and you have the absolute audacity to call us out on our bullshit, but you haven't fired us as clients yet and we thank you for that.
May your pillows always be cold.

AN IMPORTANT NOTE FROM THE AUTHORS:

We are both aware that AI runs rampant nowadays, both in art and writing. These authors would like to make it clear: we were around before AI was used to write books. We will be around long after the next fad appears too.

We are also aware that the use of em dashes—this fancy little thing on each side—has been flagged by readers as inherently AI. As one of these authors has spent fifteen years as an editor, she is well-versed in their use according to the rules of CMoS, section 6.85. That's the Chicago Manual of Style for all you non-publishing folks. These authors wanted to make sure that all readers know that *we know*, and we don't care what AI is doing. Fuck AI. You can take our em dashes—and ellipses—from our cold, dead hands.

Thanks for coming to our talk.
As you were.
Happy Reading!

Aurelia & Kel

CHAPTER 1

VARECK

"You're a godsdamned menace!"

My mate's voice pierced the hazy fog of sleep that still enveloped me. I frowned, rolling onto my back. Sunlight streamed through the open curtains, and the room was a comfortable temperature. It was perfect for the lazy morning I planned to spend in bed with Meera.

There was just one problem.

She wasn't here.

"She's downstairs," Corvo said as I bolted upright. He loafed in front of the dying embers of last night's fire, enjoying the warmth. I was so used to him popping in and out, it wasn't surprising for him to show up here. "Not happy either, by the sounds of it."

I slipped out of the bed, then paused. My favorite pair of fur-lined leather trousers was already on my body, as was a black shirt with rolled cuffs. I raised a brow in an unspoken question.

"Figured you'd want to go running downstairs, and not everyone wants to see you swinging your junk around like a sad balloon animal."

My jaw tightened. "Prior to your insult, I was going to say this was oddly considerate of you."

Corvo's tail flicked. "Ew, Vareck. Don't make it something it's not. Meera bothered me about clothes. I saved myself the trouble when I knew you would inevitably ask for the same favor before chasing after your lady friend."

"And there's the asshole we all know." I rolled my eyes, donning the socks and boots at the end of the bed. A dark cloak lay over the back of one of the chairs. I tossed it on, barely tying the damn thing before I was out the door.

Crash.

My pace quickened as I sped toward the commotion. I took the steps two at a time, then turned toward the hall. My breath halted when my gorgeous mate came into view. Fiery red hair, curvy form, and pissed off glowing green eyes.

"Tell me who hired you," she demanded, her voice laced with persuasion.

"Stop trying to compel me, lass. It's just wasting your power."

"Tell me!"

"I can't! You know—" The black-haired fae ducked as she threw a dish at his head. If not for his quick reflexes, that would have hit its mark with impressive force. "For fuck's sake. Can you calm down so we can talk about this like reasonable folk?"

"Calm down?" Meera repeated. She'd gone deathly still.

I winced. He didn't seem to realize that he'd committed the greatest of sins.

He told a woman to calm down.

I hoped he was praying to whatever god he believed in because he was going to need it.

"My fucking sister is missing, you prick!"

"Now, now, Meera. There's no need for name-calling."

I recognized the leprechaun without question, and I could easily understand her wrath considering the circumstances surrounding their last meeting, but his name had escaped me. Larry? Lachlan? No, that wasn't it.

"Name-calling is the least of what I'll do to you if you don't tell me what I want to know."

Slowly, the bearded man stood to his full height, trying to inch backwards while placating her. "You know I can't do that—"

That was also the wrong thing to say.

Meera grabbed a butter knife and chucked it at him. Assassin, my woman was not. However, the knife spun in his general direction before the flat length hit his chest and clattered to the floor.

"Really?" he said, arching an amused eyebrow.

Meera let out a battle cry that more closely resembled a wailing banshee before she launched herself at him.

That was when I decided to intervene.

"Come back here, you coward!" she called when he bolted away with surprising agility for his size.

Unfortunately for the leprechaun, he ran in my direction and realized his mistake too late. I lifted my forearm as he plowed into me, catching him on the throat. Before he could react, I pivoted, slamming him against the hallway wall.

"Logan?" I muttered under my breath. "Luke? No, that's still not it."

"*Lucian*, you pompous fuck." He narrowed his eyes at me but valued his life enough to keep his hands up in surrender.

"Ah! That's it. But she called you Lou."

They both cast me confused glances before returning to their feud.

"Oh, thank the gods yer here!" another voice said. Farris came around the corner, relief etched on his face. "He showed up an' she lost it!"

"I'll handle it from here, friend. My apologies." I tried to be as diplomatic as possible, and it seemed to give the innkeeper a measure of peace. He grabbed his broom, sweeping broken shards of plates and glass, glancing at us warily.

Meera didn't spare the other man a glance, her gaze focused on the leprechaun I had pinned to the wall.

"How'd you even find me?" she asked, placing her hands on her hips.

"I suggest answering her," I said, using my forearm to hold him in place by the throat.

A guilty look flashed across his expression. "The necklace. I put a tracking spell on it. Then I paid a witch for a temporary portal to get here."

"What the fuck?" we said in unison.

"In my defense, I was only looking out for you—"

"Tell the truth," Meera snapped. "Or I'll have Vareck squeeze the life out of you."

He tried to twist his neck a little to give him room to breathe, but I held firm, pressing my arm into his throat a fraction more. He exhaled in resignation. "I wanted to be able to find you if I ever needed to."

Meera clicked her tongue. "How self-serving of you," she said, acid filling her tone.

"You wouldn't have known your sister was missing if I hadn't."

"You're right," she agreed, face still impassive. "And because she's my sister, I don't need you or your stupid contracts to find her. Since you didn't get the hint before, consider this my resignation. I will never take a job from you again."

"Meera, lass—" he began in a charming, honeyed voice that had no doubt worked on plenty of women before.

The details Meera had told me about her job as a bounty hunter returned to me.

"Contract?" I repeated.

Once I accept the contract, I'm bound to it.

I can't talk about the job.

That includes who my broker is . . .

Then there was the other conversation. The one in the library when Lou had brought the necklace. Her instant animosity toward him.

I had asked if they knew each other, and she'd only answered with, "You could say that." But she never explained how. He was a criminal, and she'd even called him one, but Meera still knew him. While she was a bounty hunter, Meera never gave me the impression that she'd gotten mixed up with the wrong people apart from one person.

Her broker.

My forearm pressed into his throat and then angled upward, lifting him a few inches off the floor while he started to cough and grab onto my arm in the hopes I wouldn't crush his windpipe. "You're the one who hired her to kidnap my nephew."

Meera didn't confirm or deny, but I didn't need her to. I knew her contract prevented her from revealing who hired her, even in our current situation. Apparently, inadvertently saying she'd never take a job from him again was a workaround to the magic that bound her to silence.

"Tell me where he is," I growled, my jaw muscles tensing.

"I don't know—"

"Who paid you for him?"

Lou shook his head slightly. "Can't." He tried to take a breath but struggled. "Contract."

I pulled a dagger from my belt, aiming the blade at his gut. "You'd better figure out what you can say, and you'd better do it quick."

"You really don't wanna do this," the leprechaun wheezed through gritted teeth and a slowly shrinking windpipe. Despite the position of power I held over him, he didn't seem afraid, only wary.

"Oh, I very much do," I ground out. "Give me one reason why I shouldn't."

"Because we have dibs on killing the fucker first," an unfamiliar female voice said, cutting in.

Lou closed his eyes and groaned. Meera and I turned to see a group of crazed redheads that had entered through the front door of the inn, but that wasn't what caught me off guard.

Meera's mouth fell open in shock. "Mom?"

CHAPTER 2

MEERA

My parents and four brothers burst through the door, looking ready to fight their way out of hell. My mother held Babe, her trusty metal baseball bat, propped against her shoulder. While my brothers often did the shakedowns when people attempted to screw my family over, they had to learn from somewhere—and it wasn't our father.

In all of the nine realms, Molly Wylde was one of the greatest forces to be reckoned with. As if we didn't even exist, she ignored me and Vareck entirely when she stormed over and shoved the end of the bat under Lou's chin in a violent threat.

"I'm gonna beat you within an inch of your life, you manipulative, lying twat!" Her blood-red hair was frizzy and disheveled. She had a murderous, crazed look in her eyes right until she glanced over at me and her face brightened. "Oh, hello dear. I'm so glad you're safe," she said softly, cupping my face with her free hand before she returned her ire on Lou. Her tone increased again to a rage-driven decibel. "You have fucked with my family for the last time, leprechaun. After I bleed you dry, I'm going to bathe in what's left of you." The way she oscillated is what made her all the more intimidating. The men in my family were predictable. Mostly. The women, not so much.

"I think that's a bit dramatic," Lou whispered, despite Vareck's hold on him.

My eldest brother, Atlas, elbowed our dad in a friendly way, and a small grin curled up one side of his mouth. "I told you if we followed this shady fuck we'd find her."

Fearghal and Darroch fist-bumped each other and then recrossed their arms, standing like ominous bodyguards.

Cadoc, the second eldest, stood next to my mom, twirling a knife in his palm. Copper bracers circled his wrists. His vicious gaze was focused on Lou. If he was surprised or even happy to see me alive, you couldn't tell.

I stood there in shock. "You're all here," I said slowly, looking between each of them. "In Faerie."

"Bloody realms!" Farris yelled, coming out of the kitchen. He dropped the broom pan he'd retrieved, letting it clatter on the floor as he pressed his palms against his face. "There's more of ya! Get out before ya break everythin'!"

The poor innkeeper was ignored, even by me.

"Why are you here?" I asked, finally regaining my ability to string my thoughts together in a coherent sentence.

"Saving you," Darroch said with a huff, as though it were obvious. "What's it look like?"

My father knocked him upside the head with an open palm. "Don't be a knob."

I tossed my arms out. "Hello! Can I please get a real answer? It's not that I'm not happy to see you, but I'm confused about how you showed up here, of all places. At a tavern. In Warwick."

"Of course, darling," my mother said with a smile. She jammed the end of the bat into Lou's jaw. I cringed when his teeth clanked loudly. "You've been gone for over ten days, and none of us had heard a thing. Sadie went missing while she was trying to find you, so we hired this dolt to find her."

"Of all people, you hired Lou?" I said, jutting my thumb at my broker. "After all the shit you gave me for taking jobs from him?"

"We hired him because you work for him," Cadoc said in a low voice, glancing over and meeting my gaze for the first time since he showed up. I wanted to shrink beneath the weight of his stare. Of all my brothers, he was the most reserved. Not because he didn't have thoughts or feelings on things, but because Cadoc watched. He studied people and the world around him the way an editor did a manuscript. Everything was part of a game—a piece on the board that he played. That's not to say he didn't love me or Sadie, or our family. He was just . . . different. Something in his brain was wired in such a way that Cadoc viewed the world the way a predator did prey.

"You went missing, kiddo. And then your sister did as well. What else were we supposed to do? We couldn't just sit back and wait." My father came up to me, wrapping a thick arm around me in a hug. He smelled of coriander and whiskey. Home. I closed my eyes for a brief moment, letting his presence settle me. I hugged him tight before letting go. He filled me in before I could ask more questions. "Like Cadoc said, we hired Lou because you take jobs from him. We suspected that if we hired him he would lead us to one or both of you. We planned to follow him—"

"Then we'd find you and kick his ass," Darroch interjected with a deep nod. Dad liked to provide context, which on occasion, was needed. Darroch, however, was more likely to handle things like Sadie or I would—which is to say we got to the point. Quickly.

Lou sighed, clearing his throat as best he could against Vareck's forearm and my mother's bat. "And if it didn't lead to Meera?" His tone was low and graveled. It sent a shiver down my spine. Despite the pain in his voice, there was something else in it too. Something unafraid, and perhaps even a little angry. Lou might be a leprechaun, but I sometimes wondered if he was more than that.

Atlas sniffed, lifting a shoulder. "We were going to beat your ass anyway. This only ends one way for you." How very typical of my brother. Where Cadoc was reticent, Atlas was outgoing. If a golden retriever could be a grown man, Atlas was it. The guy had an upbeat demeanor, even when beating the shit out of someone.

Lou grumbled something unintelligible beneath his breath, and I ran my hands through my hair. "This is a lot to process right now."

"We just explained it." Fearghal said. He lifted a brow, making the white scar that ran down the left side of his face stretch. Most people grew out of the 'look mom, no hands' phase. Unfortunately, my brother was not one of them. The many scars that decorated his skin were a testament to his adventurous nature. "What all is there to process?"

"Um . . ." I laughed nervously. So, so much. Having just spent a blissful and euphoric night having the best sex of my life. Finding out Vareck was my mate when true mates weren't a thing anymore. Not knowing what any of that meant for my future—*our* future? Running into Lou and learning Sadie was gone. My family showing up in Faerie, at the tavern where Vareck fucked my brains out, no less. Let's see. Where to start?

Vareck cleared his throat, and I turned to him for help,

pleading with my eyes to find the right words. He placed his free hand on the small of my back. It was at that moment that each one of the Wylde clan also took note of him in a more serious manner.

Atlas' grin sharpened.

Cadoc's stare flattened.

Darroch and Fearghal exchanged a wary but knowing glance.

My mother? She looked him up and down, a twinkle in her eye as she gave her approval with a wink and a coy smile. "Handsome man. Strong too." She patted his bicep on the arm that held Lou pinned. "Good job, love. Is he coming to dinner?"

Darroch wasn't nearly as impressed. His brows lowered as he assessed the king of Faerie, oblivious to who he was standing in front of. "Who the fuck is this guy?"

I shot him a dirty look before answering. "Um, Vareck, this is my mom and dad, Molly and Conor." Their lips parted. A part of me suspected that at least my parents knew damn well who he was, even if my brothers were ignorant. I cleared my throat, continuing the introductions as though I hadn't noticed the recognition of his name. "Mom, Dad, meet Vareck. We're . . . sort of . . . seeing each other?" I immediately winced, knowing I'd chosen the wrong words, but not knowing what the right words should have been. Either way, phrasing it like a question didn't help. The heat of Vareck's gaze made my skin warm. While his expression was unreadable, his eyes burned.

"Seeing each other is a bit of an understatement," he said quietly. His anger was restrained, but it was unmistakably present.

"What does that mean?" Cadoc responded coolly.

"Pretty sure it's biblical," Fearghal stage-whispered to Darroch.

For fuck's sake.

Corvo jumped onto the counter by Farris and licked his paw. The innkeeper scowled at him but said nothing. "It means she just pissed him off by not admitting they're mates." I glared at Corvo, and if he could've shrugged, he would have. "What? It's true. When have I ever lied?"

"Mates? Hope this isn't a shotgun marriage situation," Atlas joked. Maybe he was joking? Sometimes it was hard to tell where my happy-go-lucky brother ended and the protective bear of a man took over. My mom and dad exchanged a quick look that didn't escape me, but before I could clarify, the damned cat kept going.

"Might as well be now. They did spend all night fucking." Of all the times he had to interject into a conversation, this one was undoubtedly the worst. I closed my eyes, hearing my heartbeat in my head as all hell broke loose. The inn was filled with the cacophony of my brothers shouting over each other, going on about killing more than a leprechaun today, and who the hell did this douchebag think he was screwing their sister, and whatever else the hotheaded fools thought made them sound intimidating.

My mother whirled around to face my brothers, then pointed at Cadoc and Atlas. "Do you know who this is? Have some fucking manners! I know I taught them to you. I expect this shit from Darroch and Fearghal, but you two get your act together!"

"You can't be serious, Ma! C'mon, this guy is fuc—" Fearghal interrupted, right before Cadoc punched him in the arm. "Ouch!"

"I see where you get your charm," Corvo muttered.

Cadoc turned, finally refocusing on his surroundings.

"Okay, but is no one going to address the fact that the cat is talking?"

Corvo hissed at him. "Who you calling a cat?"

"What the hell else would we call him?" Darroch whispered. "He's literally a cat. Just hissed and everything."

Vareck growled, the rumble in his throat reverberating over my skin before he shouted. "Everyone sit down and shut up!" The entire room tensed, staring at him with wide eyes. He looked at my mother, politely inclining his chin, adding, "Please."

He removed his forearm from Lou's neck, pointed a finger in his face and grabbed him by the collar as he dragged him to a large rectangular table. "You included. One move to escape and you're dead."

Farris muttered, reminding us we were at his inn. "Oh good. Yer all stayin', then? We're really doin' this?"

"I'm so sorry I broke your dishes, Farris," I said, grimacing as my family pulled out chairs. The sound of the legs scraping against the wooden floor cut through the silence. I took the seat next to Lou, leaving an empty one next to me, but I had a feeling Vareck wasn't going to sit.

With a crease between his brows, Farris looked around at a table full of angry redcaps. He finally sighed in resignation. "Can I get ya' anythin'? It's not on the house."

Vareck held out his hand to shake the innkeeper's, clasping it firmly. "I'll cover the damages. My apologies."

Farris nodded, releasing Vareck's handshake, speaking softly before his gaze jumped over every redhead in the room, myself included. "It's not you I'm worried about, yer majesty."

I felt my shoulders tighten the moment the words came out of his mouth.

"Did he just say 'your majesty'?" Darroch whispered

harshly to my dad, and my father nodded, then rubbed at his forehead with his eyes closed.

Vareck paused. "You knew who I was when we checked in?"

Ferris chuckled, rolling up his sleeves and evening out the crease of the fabric. "Of course. My wife an' I traveled to Brumlow for yer coronation, an' once more when ya' opened the castle to commoners. Lovely event that was."

I could feel six pairs of eyes burning into me. My mom could barely hide her smirk. My dad remained stoic, but open-minded. It was my idiot brothers who had a different reaction. Each of them leaned back in their chairs, arms crossed. Cadoc's fingers were twitchy, and he started twirling one of his knives.

"Oi!" Farris shouted, shaking a hand at Cadoc. "Put that away an' stop breakin' my inn!"

"No," Cadoc replied in a flat tone, without taking his eyes off Vareck.

I forced a smile for Farris' sake. "They'll behave themselves," I said, hoping my assurance would placate him a little bit. The wary look he gave me suggested he didn't trust me either. "Do you think we could get some of that tasty venison stew you made? And maybe a pitcher of ale?" Farris turned for the kitchen, muttering his incoherent response.

Lou put his hands on the table. "Well, this seems like a family affair. As nice as it's been, it would only be polite if I saw myself out."

Vareck grabbed his shoulder, shoving him back into the chair while he and my brothers spoke in unison. "Sit the fuck down."

Lou held hands up in surrender, keeping his seat. "Hard to argue that," he muttered.

"Won't stop you from trying, though, will it?" Cadoc asked, keeping expert control of his blade. Lou watched it with concern. "If you didn't need your tongue right now, I'd be happy to help you part ways with it."

Darroch uncrossed his arms, leaning an elbow on the table as he gestured to Corvo and then me. "So we're going to ignore the talking cat, and the fact that Meera is boinking the king of Faerie?"

"Again with the cat insults," Corvo muttered.

"Boinking?" I repeated at the same time. "What are you, twelve?"

Darroch glared. "You're my baby sister. Saying your name and the word 'fucking' in the same sentence when it's in reference to—"

Atlas kicked Darroch under the table. "You're being a dick. The talking cat, nor Meera's . . ." He glanced at Vareck, grimacing. "*Friendly* relationship with the king matters right now." I didn't have to look at Vareck to know that the situation had just gone from bad to worse, and that was before Corvo started cackling like the Wicked Witch of the West.

"There's nothing *friendly* about our relationship." A warm palm settled on my shoulder despite the apathetic tone of his voice. Vareck gave me a tight squeeze.

Kill. Me. Now.

I leaned back in my chair while rubbing my temples. "This is a nightmare. That must be it." I pinched myself, but nothing happened. The silence was overwhelming. I pinched harder a second time, my nails breaking the skin. "Fuck me. This can't be real. Maybe I'm dead. This must be hell. Explains why Lou's here."

"Excuse me?" he asked, having the audacity to sound offended.

"Afraid not," Corvo chimed in. "Hell is warmer. Two suns and all that."

"But the cat *is* talking," Fearghal said. They just couldn't let that one go, could they?

"We're in Faerie," Atlas rolled his eyes. "I'm surprised the furniture isn't breaking out in song and dance. A talking cat is the least important thing right now." I gave him a tight smile, silently thanking him for trying to get this conversation back on track.

Corvo came down from the counter and sauntered over to the table, hopping into my lap. He balanced himself precariously before curling up. "Says I'm not important. Peasants."

I stroked him absentmindedly, hoping he would help calm me. Granted, his loudmouth was part of what stressed me out, but if I pretended he was more like a therapy cat, maybe my heart rate would slow down.

My father took a deep breath, sitting up straight in his chair. His short red hair was just as messy as my mother's. He looked like he hadn't slept in weeks, and a sudden pang of guilt stabbed at me. His daughters were missing. Of course he'd be worried and losing sleep. "Atlas is right. We found Meera. Now we find Sadie." He turned his attention to the leprechaun. "So where is she?"

Lou sighed loudly. "I don't fucking know where she is. That's why I came to Meera."

I scrunched my nose and let out an annoyed harrumph. "Just when I think you can't go any lower, you take a job from my family to find my sister and me, and then you try to hire me to find her."

"You're the best, lass. Everyone knows." He glanced at my brothers. "Even though they act like you need saving, they know it too."

"And *you* are the worst."

Vareck squeezed Lou's shoulder, pressing his fingers into the muscle. "Tell me more about the tracking spell on the necklace."

Lou scratched his beard, stretching his neck. "I'd rather not."

Cadoc flipped the knife up and caught it by the tip. He lifted a brow, angling his gaze toward Lou's groin so he understood what was going to happen unless he cooperated.

"Fine," Lou threw his hands up. "Point made. It's not complicated. Just a simple tracking spell. Nothing more. Just as I said. Believe me or don't, but it's true that I wanted to keep an eye on you. Make sure you were safe"—he shifted his gaze toward the king in a once-over—"all things considered."

I snorted with a huffed laugh. "Please. You didn't want to lose a valuable asset."

"Both things can be true, lass." Lou shrugged, the expression on his face unchanging. "But the king came for a trinket to nullify your powers, and it doesn't take a genius to see the danger in that. You might think I'm the worst, but I'm not soulless."

My mother and father both clenched their fists, and my mother's voice shook as she asked, "*He did what?*" Aw shit. As much as I hated that cursed necklace, I understood Vareck's reasons for putting it on me. Reasons we didn't have time to go into with Sadie missing.

"It's not like that, Mom, I swear. He wasn't trying to hurt me. It was the opposite, actually." I pointed at my brothers as they opened their mouths. "And before any of you speak, *don't*. You don't know the full story."

"What exactly is the full story?" Lou asked. "'Cause

from where I stood, it didn't look good when you told him not to do it, demanded it in fact, and I watched him put it on you anyway."

"Says the asshole who sold him the necklace to begin with."

"I'm a businessman. It wasn't personal, and I already told you I had a tracking spell put on it so I could find you. You act like I'm some heartless con man."

"You said it, not me," I replied.

"She wasn't wearing the necklace when I found her," Vareck said, cutting in. I didn't miss the anger radiating from him. "How'd you know we were here at the inn?"

"I tracked the spell to Warwick. Got a portal. Then started asking questions about a curvy ginger. It wasn't hard. You two practically left a trail of destruction behind. Made quite the impression on Irene."

At the mere mention of her name, I clenched my teeth. "Of course you know that lecherous quim."

He made a show of fanning himself after my insult. "A bit harsh, isn't it, lass? That's my cousin you're talking about. Not all leprechauns know each other. Don't be a speciest." He tutted, shaking his head in mock disappointment.

My mouth fell open. "I'm not! I'm saying it because you're both untrustworthy snakes, and *she* wanted me to work at her brothel." Vareck's features hardened, and he turned his neck to the side to crack it.

Lou patted his pocket, looking for a cigarette, but came up short. "And? What's your point? She's a businesswoman. Prostitution is the oldest profession. Can't blame her for wanting to add a spicy redhead to her lineup."

I placed my hand on Vareck's trying to comfort him, but

it didn't work. Vareck dug his fingers into Lou's shoulder again, pushing him further down in the chair.

"Correction, Lou. She tried to force me into it."

Lou winced under the pressure of Vareck's harsh grip. "She neglected to mention that."

Farris came back with a tray full of stew, utensils, cloth napkins, and several pewter mugs. He set it all down, adding a big basket of fresh baked bread. "It's water for ya'. I'm not givin' a bunch of angry redcaps ale. Ya' all look close enough to battlelust as is." Then he left again, though I noticed him hovering near the bar top by the kitchen door. Eavesdropping, perhaps, or just staying close by to make sure we didn't destroy everything.

Corvo sat up on my lap, scenting the air. "Oh, I wouldn't say no to a good venison stew." He reached his paw up and dipped it in my bowl, catching a piece of meat with his claw before he pulled it onto the table with a splatter of gravy. Instead of being grossed out and scolding him, I let him eat. Better he was occupied with food given his penchant for making situations worse.

Atlas sniffed softly, cracking his knuckles after the innkeeper had retreated to the safety of his kitchen. "I'd like to know more about this Irene."

"And where we can find her," Darroch added with a single nod.

Vareck waved them off. "It's taken care of."

Cadoc tilted his head at the king. "Is she dead?"

Vareck's brows lowered, sensing the challenge. "No."

My brother pursed his lips. "Then it's not 'taken care of'." Cadoc looked at me with judgment. "This is the poon you mated yourself to?"

A piece of meat came shooting out of Corvo's mouth. "He called you a poon!" He nearly choked on his laughter, almost rolling off my lap. Vareck glared at his familiar, then took a deep breath.

"For once, I agree with your brothers," my dad said, and my mother rolled her eyes.

I sighed, long and loud. The testosterone in the room was too much. "Cadoc, stop being a dick. Lou, just . . . fuck off. Dad, not now, *please*. Sadie should be our focus, right? If she was looking for me, it would stand to reason she would have come to Faerie. I couldn't tell her about the contract, but she figured out a lot about my work without me saying much."

My dad took a moment, then released a breath, conceding. My mom dipped her head, giving me a gentle nudge with a look of hope. "Do what you do best, dear. We'll be quiet."

I pressed my lips in a tight smile, thanking them for dropping it, and then began to center myself. Reaching for my power, I searched for the gold line that would lead me to my sister. Energy flooded me. My surroundings blurred as I pushed everything I had into finding her. I heard the muffled comments from my brothers about the vibrant shade of green my eyes had turned. I felt the soft vibrations of Corvo's purring on my lap as my hand rested on the soft fur of his back. Seconds passed. Maybe minutes. I saw nothing. Not even a flicker. When I let it go, my voice quivered. "I have no path."

My mom choked out a gasp, covering her mouth with her hand. A sheen of tears threatened to spill. "Does that mean she's dead?" Never in my life had I seen my mom scared. It nearly broke me.

"I could only be so lucky," Lou grumbled.

A short whistle sounded as Cadoc's knife flew through the air at a remarkable speed. Vareck's reflexes were swift as he moved his hand out of the way. Lou grunted, leaning forward slightly. He reached for his shoulder. "What the fuck," he growled, wrapping his hand around the hilt of the blade.

"Leave it where it is." Cadoc pulled another knife from his side and began twirling it. "Or I'll pin your hand to your chest with the next throw."

"Do it anyway," Fearghal egged him on. "Just for fun."

Cadoc ignored him, pointing the blade at Lou while he spoke, his voice menacing and low. "You'd better hope she's alive, leprechaun. If we find her otherwise, your luck will have run out. Nothing, and I mean *nothing*, in this world or the next will save you."

"Meera? You have no path. What does that mean?" my dad asked, his arm wrapped around my mother's shoulders as they waited for me to answer.

I shook my head. "It doesn't mean she's dead. She's just not in Faerie, or . . ."

"Or what?" my mother said quickly.

I took a breath. "I can't track to realms I haven't been to before. I've only been to three."

"I thought you could track between realms," Cadoc interjected, and the hope in his voice pulled at my heart.

"I can. But I don't get a direct path. It's more like a feeling? The direct path appears when I'm in the same realm as what I'm tracking. All it means is that Sadie isn't in Faerie."

"But you should feel a path to her, right? Something," my mom urged. "If you don't feel a path at all?"

I sighed. "She might be in a realm I've never been in. Or she's in a realm that doesn't have passage between it and

Faerie, so I won't feel that nudge here. I need to go back to Earth and see what I can pick up from there."

My brothers all cursed at the same time. My dad swallowed thickly, and his eyes lost focus the way they did when he was thinking. No doubt, he was mapping out risks and possibilities. Finally, he refocused and looked at me. "We have no choice. If Meera can't find her when we're back Earthside, then we search the realms."

I tucked a curl of my hair behind my ear, nodding in agreement. "We'll need a witch for portals. Amelia might be able to help us—"

"I'd leave her out of this one," Lou said quietly. When I met his gaze, there was a stern crease to his brow, and a hardness etched in the lines around his eyes I'd never seen before. He gave the most subtle shake of his head.

"Why is that?" Vareck asked, covering him in shadow as he stood tall behind Lou's chair.

Lou didn't bother to turn around, and he answered without missing a beat. "Amelia's prices are steep, as of late. And she doesn't accept coin."

I chewed on my bottom lip. Amelia was the only witch I really knew well enough to ask.

Vareck cleared his throat. "Kaia knows where portals are located in every realm, and where to find a witch that can help if needed." Despite being in pain, Lou smiled as soon as he heard Kaia's name. "But this won't be easy. Not every realm has a portal to the other eight. There will be a lot of back and forth. It could take weeks. Even months."

"She may not have weeks," I said, fear causing my chest to constrict.

My family looked at each other, sharing a silent conversation before my mother spoke. "Then we're all going."

Corvo's ears perked up. "Oh, this is like a family vacation!"

I poked him in the side, and he let out a small chirp. "No! That's not what this is, and also, you aren't invited."

"Rude," he muttered quietly, narrowing his golden eyes at me.

"Before we start realm hopping on a whim, we need to know a few things," Vareck began. He picked up one of the cloth napkins Ferris had dropped off at the table and he tossed it at Lou. "Clean up. You're bleeding on the floor."

"Because I have a knife in my shoulder," Lou said through a clenched jaw.

"Should have kept your mouth shut," my father said. "Lucky it wasn't Molly who got to you first."

Lou took the cloth and tried in vain to wipe the blood and prevent it from dripping onto the floorboards.

Vareck stood by me, gently placing his hand on my shoulder in support, grazing his thumb in a soothing back and forth motion. "First things first," he began, directing his question to Atlas. "You said you knew if you followed Lucian, you'd find Meera."

"That's right."

"Did you go to anyone else before hiring him?"

"Sadie's ex."

"Jared?" I asked in surprise, not expecting my voice to squeak as I spoke.

Darroch chimed in with a slight chuckle. "Yeah. Him. Fearghal and I went to his place to see if Sadie was there making another mistake. He gave up some information that saved his skin. Told us he'd seen Sadie at the Witching Hour about to beat up a leprechaun, claiming he knew where you were. Gave us a perfect description of our friend here." He winked, giving Lou a wicked grin.

I stared at him deadpanned. "Was this information given under coercion?"

He shrugged. "Define coercion."

"You're such an idiot." My nostrils flared as I exhaled a harsh breath. "How do you know he wasn't lying just to get out of an ass-kicking from you two? You could have wasted valuable time if Jared had lied to you."

"A few other patrons confirmed it, Meera. We're not stupid," Fearghal huffed.

I pinned Lou with a dirty look. "Funny how you didn't mention this earlier."

Lou tossed the bloodied napkin on the table. "Sadie held an axe to my throat, and contrary to what they heard, I told her I *didn't* know where you were. I did, however, tell her I knew you were with the king. I obviously didn't lie," he said, flicking his eyes to my brother, then back to me. "Then Amelia dragged her off after she broke the rules and pulled a gun. That was the last I saw her. If you hadn't been so busy throwing dishes and chairs at my head, I *would* have told you that."

I patted Corvo's leg, gently nudging him to get off so I could stand. He reluctantly complied, hopping onto the empty chair next to me and curling back up. I looked at Vareck. "I have to go to the Arcane District. Start where she started and see what I can find." He rubbed the back of his knuckles down my cheek.

"I'm coming with you," he said softly, and I heard my brothers chortle in an annoying harmony.

"I don't think she needs you to come with us, *bud*," my brother said with a snicker. "The Wyldes protect our own just fine."

"Darroch!" my mother shouted. "That's the *king of Faerie*. You'll mind yourself and shut it, *now*."

"I'm sorry," I whispered. "They mean well . . . for temperamental assholes."

"Darroch, is it?" Vareck said, keeping his formidable stance, but clearly at the end of his patience with my brothers' antics. "While I appreciate your enthusiasm in protecting Meera, I wasn't suggesting I accompany her. I *will* be with her. She's my—"

"Okay, that's enough of that," I interjected with a nervous laugh, standing up and putting a hand on Vareck's chest. I widened my eyes at him in a desperate attempt to keep him quiet, pleading with him not to say the words he was about to say. A frown creased between his brows; his icy blue eyes darkening as though a storm were brewing. Despite his obvious displeasure, he remained silent.

I knew we'd have to talk about the whole mate thing, but I wasn't going to have that conversation in front of my family.

After an intense silence, he inclined his head. "We shouldn't all go to the same place. We have to split up."

"What do you suggest?" Atlas and my dad asked, almost in unison. They were often so much alike.

"Meera?" he said, turning to me. "You know your sister best."

"Okay . . ." I blew out a breath, running through scenarios in my mind. I had to think like her. Where she would go, and what she would do. She'd be on a murderous rampage, so I knew she had her axes and bracers on her. Maybe her gun. Unless someone took them from her during capture. If she was captured. "If she comes back before we find her, the first place she is going to go is home, and then the gym."

My parents looked at each other, then nodded in agreement. My mom snapped her fingers harshly, grabbing my brothers' attention like she was training a pack of dogs. All four of them straightened their backs, listening. "Fearghal. Darroch. You run the gym while we're gone."

"What? No—"

"No arguments," my dad interjected, pointing at the two of them. "Meera's right. She'll go there if no one is home, and we need to keep the family business running."

With reluctant mumbles, a chorus of "yes sir" ended the conversation.

"The rest of us should split up in the Arcane District," I suggested, and chewed at my thumb nail while I considered further. "We start at the Witching Hour and decide which direction we go from there."

"And what do we do with our Lucky Lou here?" my mother asked, angling her head toward him as though he were yesterday's trash.

"Your family and nicknames," Lou muttered with an annoyed shake of his head.

Vareck assessed the leprechaun, considering our options. "He may be of some use still. He'll need to be escorted to the dungeons."

"I'm going with him," Cadoc said. His tone didn't leave room for pushback, though it didn't appear that Vareck had planned on disagreeing. On the contrary, the twist of his lips made it clear he rather liked the idea.

"Done. Corvo," Vareck started, and the cat opened an eye, peering at him with displeasure. "I need you to get Drayden."

Lou audibly groaned, mumbling something that sounded suspiciously like "not again."

The cat made a sour face, his whiskers bunching up as he muttered mockingly. "Corvo, do this. Corvo, do that.

Corvo, I need clothes. When is it ever, 'Corvo, let me adore you?' Or 'Let me feed you fresh fish, Corvo.' Never."

Then he popped out of the room.

Atlas and Fearghal jumped out of their chairs, staring at the spot where Corvo had just been. "What in the nine realms!"

"You get used to it," I said, shrugging. "Mostly. It's when he shows up in the weirdest places that throws you off." Which reminded me, I still wanted to talk to him about why he was at Irene's last night.

"Who is Drayden?" my mother asked, reaching over for a piece of bread and using it to soak up the stew before she took a bite. It had to be cold by now. I wasn't even sure she was truly hungry, or if she was just stress eating. We had that in common.

"After Kaia, he's next in command," Vareck answered, and Corvo popped back in the room, appearing on the table near a bowl of stew.

"He'll be here shortly," he said, dipping his paw in and grabbing another piece of meat.

"Fucking great," Lou muttered, shifting in his chair. He looked like he was going to be sick, and it had nothing to do with the knife embedded in his shoulder.

"Not your favorite person, I take it?" He shook his head.

"Drayden holds a grudge longer than anyone I know," Vareck said fondly. "And Lou is at the top of that list. How long has it been now, Lucian? Twelve years?"

"Thirteen."

I snickered. "You always said you thought thirteen was a lucky number."

"Beginning to reconsider that, lass. My luck might be running out." Lou glanced at the stone hearth, rubbing his palms over his pants in an anxious gesture I'd never seen from him before. Then the flames began to hiss and spark.

CHAPTER 3
VARECK

The fireplace crackled. A loud pop rent the air, sending embers flying.

Lucian startled at the sound, his already pale complexion turning ghostly. A slight smirk pulled at my lips as Drayden walked through the flames and into the tavern.

Eyes like burning coals surveyed the room, his impassive face gave nothing away.

"Drayden."

"Vareck," he responded in an apathetic tone. "You sent the cat?"

I snorted, thrusting my chin toward Lou. "I need you to pyroport that one back to the castle."

Drayden arched a dark brow. "If you needed an errand boy, you should have called—" He paused when his gaze settled on the leprechaun. The twitch of his lips indicated his feelings on the matter had shifted. "Well, if it isn't Lucian Devlin."

"Oh, he knows your full name? That's serious. Is there

anyone you don't know?" Meera asked, eyeing the leprechaun. "Genuine question."

"Know is a bit of a stretch," Lou started.

"I do believe I promised to kill you if we ever crossed paths again."

"Ah," she hummed. "That makes more sense."

"You're really not helping here, lass."

"I wasn't trying to." Meera assessed Drayden, then asked, "Out of curiosity, what did he do to piss you off?"

Drayden tilted his head casually, but the movement was stiff. I had handed him easy prey in the form of Meera's broker, and the predator wanted nothing more than to attack. "Yes, Lucian, do tell us what you did." The mocking tone sounded almost playful, but I knew better.

"I didn't do anything," Lou insisted.

Meera snorted. "Unlikely," she muttered under her breath, earning a glare from the leprechaun before he turned back to Drayden.

"I told you that then, and I'll say it again now. You have no proof—"

"Which is the only reason you're still breathing. I can rectify that."

"Enough," I commanded, shutting down the oncoming bloodbath that was sure to happen at any moment if I let it. "Drayden, I need you to put him in the dungeon. *Alive.*" I emphasized my point, punctuating the last word to make myself clear.

A cold chill nipped at the air. Drayden didn't like my restriction, but I wouldn't budge. We needed him alive for the time being.

People often thought my presence was hard to be around.

As a dark fae and fury, I possessed the abilities of both.

Add the burden of a royal crown, and the trifecta left many fae uncomfortable in my vicinity.

Drayden was another beast entirely.

Not even I knew what he truly was. I didn't ask, and part of me didn't want to know. Power rolled off him like an oncoming storm. There was an air about him that was distinctly different. *Other.* Even before my sister's death, Drayden was quiet—until he wasn't. Now, whatever darkness existed in him before had completely taken over. He was a living, breathing shadow of a man. Once a legend, now the stuff of nightmares.

If not for who he was to Maeve, I would have feared him to be my enemy. After all, he was going to be king. Everything about his future changed the day my sister was killed. Alas, while he wasn't easy to read, Drayden had proved his loyalty. I was his king now, but Maeve had been his everything. She was the only one he would have left my side for. I appreciated him, though I wasn't sure he had the capacity to care. When she died, he was left hollow. Empty. There was a time when he'd asked me to put him out of his misery but I couldn't bring myself to do it, even if it would have been a mercy.

"Now wait a minute," Lucian began. The set of his jaw betrayed the first real trace of fear that he'd shown today. "I haven't done anything or broken any laws. You have no right to imprison me."

Meera laughed heartily. The sound called to something inside me and sent goosebumps over my skin.

"Apparently, Meera disagrees," I said, suppressing the sudden desire to wrap my arms around her and pull her close.

"Oh for fuck's sake. She's biased—"

"You're dangerous. A criminal," Darroch interjected.

"Again, you have no proof."

"You took advantage of a desperate woman, repeatedly putting Meera in danger for your own greed," Atlas added.

"First, that's not a crime. Second, as you pointed out, she's a woman. Not a child. No one forced her hand."

Meera's nostrils flared, her cheeks turning red. "As much as I would *love* for you to be locked up, I concede to your point. I make my own choices, stupid as they may be at times."

I groaned, frustrated that this was even a conversation. "You're responsible for Damon's abduction. That's more than enough."

"Ah, see, I didn't take anyone. That was Meera. Again."

True to his form, Corvo chose to stop playing in the stew and comment. "Yeah, but you aren't a beautiful redhead he's fucking, so you're out of luck."

Several of Meera's brothers made a choking noise. Cadoc paused what he was doing to stare me down like he wanted, and planned, on killing me.

Meanwhile Meera reached out to give Corvo ear scratches and coo at him like he was a baby. "Aw, you think I'm beautiful."

Fearghal snorted. "Of course. *That's* your takeaway."

"Jealous no one calls you pretty?" she asked, raising a brow at him in challenge. The entire Wylde family groaned as she and Fearghal traded insults.

"You may not have taken my nephew with your own two hands, leprechaun, but you orchestrated it. Conspiracy to kidnap royalty is also a crime." Lucian's expression changed, dual lines creasing between his brows. He was cornered, and he knew it. I turned back to Drayden. "No torture. Dungeon only. Corvo, go with them."

My familiar slowly narrowed his golden eyes. "Why I gotta be the babysitter?"

"How is the cat going to protect me?" Lucian demanded at the same time.

"Excuse me, sir, I am a *god*," Corvo scoffed.

I rolled my eyes. "The cat isn't for protection."

"Again. Who are you calling a cat?" Corvo sneered. He flicked his tail in my direction, added, "You're the only pussy I see here."

Meera snorted, then slapped a hand over her mouth, like that could somehow take it back.

I grabbed my familiar by the scruff and lifted him until we were eye level. "I know you aren't hangry since you've been eating stew for the last half an hour. Go take a nap and quit being an asshole."

"Animal abuse!" he cried out, pawing at me with his eyes closed. "I feel violated!"

Was he serious right now?

"Vareck!" Meera plucked him from me and cradled him against her chest. "You can't grab him like that. You'll hurt him," she scolded.

Scolded me. Not the cat that tripped her out my bedroom window. Me.

"He's fine. He's a god, remember?"

"He's a fucking cat. What's wrong with you? Don't grab him by the neck," she snapped. To add insult to injury, Corvo started purring against her breasts, snuggling closer before flashing a sly grin over his shoulder at me. Fucker.

"Have your lover's quarrel later," Drayden said, then he looked at Lucian and snapped his fingers. "You. Up. I don't have all day."

"I'm not a dog," the leprechaun replied distastefully.

"No shit," Meera said, still petting Corvo and holding him to her chest. "Dogs are loyal."

Drayden glanced at Meera, and while his mouth remained pressed in a firm line, the corners around his eyes crinkled. "I like her."

"Glad I have your approval," I deadpanned.

"His approval isn't the person's you need," Cadoc said in a flat tone.

A hand darted out, smacking him in the back of the head. Mrs. Wylde pursed her lips at her son. "Stop being a misogynistic asshole and act like the man I raised you to be. This isn't the eighteenth century. He doesn't need anyone's approval except Meera's."

"Exactly." Meera pointed at him sternly. "I don't need your approval, or anyone else's. I can make my own choices, thank you very much."

"Debatable." Cadoc scoffed, then pointed toward Lucian with a blade in hand. "If not for that particular *choice*, we wouldn't be here."

"Let it go," Mr. Wylde said, voice dropping low.

I knew Meera wouldn't appreciate me fighting her battles for her, especially where her family was concerned, but it was a hard thing to stay quiet while my mate was trading jabs with her brother.

"What's that saying about stones and glass houses?" Meera said acidly, arching an eyebrow.

"I know better than to live in glass, so my point still stands."

Conor Wylde's hand clapped down on Cadoc's shoulder, knuckles white from the strength of his grip, but Cadoc didn't flinch, nor did he look away from Meera and the stare down they had locked into. "All right, that's enough. Your sister gets the point. We need to focus on the matter at hand, and that's getting Sadie back. You two can fight about her profession and associates later."

Meera huffed, rolling her eyes. "There's nothing more to talk—"

Lucian's chair erupted into fire, effectively breaking the tension and cutting Meera off. He leapt to his feet, eyes narrowed at Drayden. While the other man hadn't moved an inch, the red glow of his eyes was the telltale sign he was behind it.

"Hey!" Farris yelled from behind the bar. "Put it out! Now!"

The flickering orange flames blinked out of existence, like they were never there to begin with. The only proof that remained was a single wisp of smoke and a pile of ash where the chair had been.

"I'll pay for it," I told Farris.

"Mhmm," he mumbled under his breath. He sent a scathing glare at Drayden before disappearing in the back.

"Start moving, or next time it will be you I light on fire," Drayden told Lucian in a bored voice. He turned his back on us and started for the fireplace, not caring that everyone was staring.

"That'll be hard to do, seeing as I'm fireproof you feckin' gobshite," he called after him.

Drayden glanced over his shoulder, a cruel smile gracing his mouth. "I enjoy a good challenge."

I sighed. It would have been better to have taken Lucian to the castle myself, but it would have delayed our departure immensely. Unfortunately, the only person that could transport people within the realm was Drayden.

"He really doesn't know when to quit, does he?" Corvo said to no one in particular. "Even I don't fuck with the surly one, and I'm a—"

"We get it, you're a god," I cut him off. Corvo let out a harrumph and muttered something about not getting the respect he deserved.

"That's our cue," Meera said, putting Corvo down and brushing the fur from her shirt. "Let's get moving." She clapped twice and started for the door.

"I'm still going with them," Cadoc said, sheathing his blade. He thrust his head toward the fireplace.

Molly Wylde frowned, looking between her son, Meera, and Lou. "Are you sure that's a good idea?"

He shrugged. "All the other bases are covered. I'm more useful extracting what information I can from the shady fuck."

"I've already told you everything," Lou said dryly.

Cadoc flashed a smile that was all teeth. "We'll see about that, won't we?"

"Drayden?" I asked. While King, there were only two people—three if you counted my mate—who I couldn't command. The first was Kaia, who would have my balls if I tried. The second was Drayden, who would have my head.

A suspended moment passed when all of Meera's family got to their feet.

"He can come."

"Greaaat," Lou drawled. "Just what I need, another sociopath along for the ride—and all you're sending is a fucking cat to make sure they don't kill me."

"Actually, I'll meet you there. Fur and fire don't really mix, if you know what I mean."

"Can I travel with you?" Cadoc asked, glancing at the fireplace with caution.

Corvo shook his head. "No can do. I can't teleport living things. Just me, myself, and I."

"What happens if you do?" Meera crossed her arms, looking at him curiously.

"I'm not sure, exactly. Tried it once. We never saw Kevin again. Well, that's not entirely true. We did find half his face in a litter box in the east wing about a week later. Scared the shit out of me. Literally." With that, Corvo teleported out.

Meera's eyes snapped to mine. "What?"

I waved her off. "He was the royal accountant. Trust me, it wasn't a loss."

"Fuck my life," Lou muttered.

Meera snorted as Cadoc grabbed the leprechaun by the arm and started dragging him toward the fireplace.

"You ever pyroported before?" Drayden asked.

"No, but there's a first time for everything," Cadoc replied. "Sounds better than the litter box."

"Don't kill him." I called as they stepped into the flames. "Drayden, do you—"

A dark laugh cut me off. I wasn't even sure which man it belonged to, and that made it all the more concerning.

CHAPTER 4

MEERA

"I'd say it was nice knowing him, but it really wasn't," Darroch said with a shrug.

I'd known Lou since I was a teenager. He carried an air of confidence everywhere he went, but the moment Drayden arrived, all that bravado began to crack. "What exactly is their history?" I asked Vareck after they'd pyro-ported from the room. "I've never seen Lou look genuinely worried before. Not even when Cadoc stabbed him."

Vareck had a slight smile as though he was pleased by that fact. "Drayden was certain Lou stole Amoret's amulet, and Lou was telling the truth. We never had concrete proof. The interrogation was intense. If Kaia and I hadn't stepped in the last time they were alone together, the leprechaun would be dead. Without a confession or any hard evidence, I chose to exile him. To say Drayden was displeased would be an understatement."

Fearghal scoffed. "Seems like letting that one live was a mistake, *your highness*." He curved his thumb toward the spot where Drayden had been. "Why couldn't you be with the other guy instead? He seemed like a nice bloke."

I smacked his arm with the back of my hand, leaving a slight sting on my skin. "You *would* pick the guy with serial killer vibes."

"I don't execute or imprison my people without cause, Fearghal. Perhaps when you grow up, you'll understand that."

I snorted, my other brothers laughing at Fearghal's expense. Vareck came to my side, wrapping his large hand around my waist and pulling me closer to him.

"Are you sure it was a good idea to send Lou with him?" I asked, angling my neck back to look up at him. "Given their history?"

"Drayden won't harm him. Probably. Scare him? That's another story. He holds a grudge, but he is loyal."

"Not that I want the piece of shit to walk away from this, but I'm curious; what about that amulet makes him so hellbent on torturing Lou for it?" Atlas asked.

It was a question that had come to mind for me as well. I stared off into the distance and frowned, somehow worried for the leprechaun even though he could use a good punch in the face. There was something about the way he came to me when Sadie was missing. A tone in his voice. Concern? Guilt? I couldn't place it, but it wasn't like Lou to put on a show of caring.

"The amulet was my sister's," he began, and I snapped my attention back to him, catching the way the creases at the corner of his eyes twitched. "And Drayden's heart belongs to my sister, even in death. It was the last piece of her he had."

My lips parted on a gasp. "They were mates?"

"Not fully bonded, no, but fated all the same. When Maeve died, he did too, in a sense. Drayden blames himself. He's never loved another since."

"That is a long time not getting laid," Darroch mumbled. "I can see why he was so pleasant."

I glowered and shushed him, looking at my mom for reinforcement, but she didn't even look in his direction. Instead, she was focused on us, her eyes shifting to Vareck and back to me. Her gaze had narrowed as she thought silently. "Are you really mates?" she asked finally, changing the subject entirely and catching me off guard. "We don't need to see the bond mark. It's just not like you to jump into things."

"I-I . . . we're um, it's..." My attempt to speak came out in spluttering nonsense. I could feel the heaviness of Vareck's stare once again, waiting for how I would respond. Poorly, was apparently the answer.

"Complicated?" my mother finished for me.

"You know we love you, Meera, but you barely know each other," my dad added, sounding just like every father in the history of fae kind when their daughter was dating. Mating? It felt weird to refer to it that way, even if that's what it was. Call it my Earth upbringing, but mating is what animals did. While I could appreciate an animal in bed, I wanted a grown man for a life partner.

I cleared my throat, resisting the urge to look at Vareck. My skin felt heated, and a flush crawled up my neck. "Um, yes. It's complicated." The inside of my cheek throbbed from how much I had chewed on one spot. "It's not like we've accepted the mate bond—"

"Wait," my dad said quickly, holding up a hand. He looked back and forth between Vareck and me. "What do you mean 'accept' it? I thought you meant you chose each other as mates. That's what the cat said, didn't he?" When his question was met with an awkward silence, I finally shook my head. "You're *true* mates? Fated mates?"

My mother inhaled harshly. "That's not possible."

"Apparently it is," Vareck and I said in unison. The way our voices melded together made me smile, but it soon faded when my parents spoke again.

"How can you tell?" my dad pressed, coming toward us.

"I . . . I don't know. I can't explain it."

My parents exchanged a deep look of concern before speaking again. "No one has found a true mate since the curse."

I didn't know what to tell them. I didn't have an explanation either.

"Can I speak with you for a moment?" Vareck asked, though he didn't wait for me to answer. He pressed his palm into my back, guiding me away from my family and near a table by the window. Glancing over my shoulder, my parents watched with a strange look of concern mixed with awe, and maybe a touch of disapproval.

"Slow down," I hissed at him, pulling away slightly. He towered in front of me, causing my neck to bend back more than I cared for when we spoke. Vareck was huge. As a tall, plus-size woman, it wasn't often that someone made me feel little. Usually, I liked it with him, but not in this case.

"You're avoiding calling me your mate," he said in a dark tone. "Is there a reason?"

"You want to talk about this *now*?" I crossed my arms, feeling goosebumps rise on my skin.

He lowered his voice in an attempt to keep our conversation quiet, though we both knew we had an audience. "You're the one trying to pretend it didn't happen, as if there could be some sort of mistake when we both know what we feel."

"No. I am not *pretending* anything," I whispered harshly,

"I haven't had time to process what happened last night and newsflash, Vareck, it's kind of a big deal."

"Then talk about it. Stop avoiding the subject." The way he said it was so matter-of-fact, like we were talking about what to have for dinner.

"Now isn't the right time."

"Really? When is a good time? Maybe you can pencil me into your busy schedule. Somewhere in between working for the leprechaun and trying to run off when I'm not looking?"

I narrowed my eyes. "That's not fair."

"Neither is ignoring this. You said you were 'seeing me,' and that we were 'complicated.' I'd like to think if I said that about you, you'd be pissed off too."

"This—" I gestured between the two of us—"*just* happened. I *am* seeing you, but this *is* complicated, and I *don't* want to talk about it with my *family* in the room, Vareck."

"Then we'll be addressing this later?"

I sighed; the annoyance I felt was difficult to hide. "Yes. Happy?"

"Can you focus on your love life later?" Atlas said, interrupting us. I don't know if my brother intended to save me from the painful awkwardness of the conversation, but I was thankful for the reprieve, regardless. "Lou's portal was temporary, and we don't know how long we have."

I thought Vareck would snap at him. Or me. His body language screamed that he was ready for a fight. Rigid shoulders. Flared nostrils. Anger flashing in his eyes. Tense moments passed, then his features softened, and he nodded.

"Atlas is right," Vareck said on a tight exhale, walking away from me in a hurry. He reached for his coin purse and set it down on the table for Farris. The innkeeper stood behind his bar top, arms crossed, impatiently waiting for us to leave. He acknowledged the payment with a single dip of his chin. "Unless we want to extend our travel time, we should move quickly."

I got what I wanted. The conversation ended. But the way it ended didn't feel good.

My family led the way, and we followed them silently through the town, twisting and turning through different alleyways. Every time I heard a noise or muffled voice, I half expected the gang of misfits to emerge again, poorly crafted knives in hand, demanding payment. For their sake's, I hoped they didn't. My brothers wouldn't be nice about teaching them a lesson.

My mom used the end of Babe to push a creaky door open, peeking around the corner to make sure no one had entered the room. She ushered us in, and we followed. In the center of an abandoned home, a purple vortex swirled. Specks of silver magic crackled on the outer circle.

"Where does it lead exactly?" I asked.

Atlas twisted his lips, his nostrils flaring as he exhaled. "Your safe house outside Seattle."

"What?" I snapped harshly. My heart started pounding. "That fucking leprechaun. How did he know about it, let alone where it's at?"

"Unsettling, isn't it?" Darroch said quietly.

"Your guess is as good as mine," Atlas said, ignoring our brother. "Maybe he followed Sadie there when she was looking for you. Hard to say. I'm sure Cadoc is pressing him for that information as we speak."

Without another word, he walked through the portal. My parents and brothers followed, and Vareck placed his hand on the small of my back, gently nudging me forward.

Even though I was mad at him, his touch still felt soothing. I groaned internally. Even this part of us was complicated.

When we stepped into my safe house, the air was stale, and a thin layer of dust had settled over the simple furnishings. It was a small studio apartment that Sadie and I had set up on the outskirts of the Arcane District in case either of us got into trouble. As a bounty hunter, I dealt with some unsavory types. As an MMA fighter with an attitude and penchant for attracting the authorities when the intrusive thoughts won, Sadie needed a place to lay low on occasion. This was our solution. Registered with a fake identity and some forged documents, it kept the Wylde name unattached from its existence.

Everything looked the same as the last time I'd seen it. The only indication that Sadie had been here to meet me was a smudge in the dust on the counter where she'd tossed her keys.

"Anything?" my mom asked, setting her bat down against the wall as she looked at me with hope.

I reached for my power just as I had back at Farris's inn and came up short. When I told her as much, the worry lines on her face deepened.

My dad rubbed her back reassuringly. "It's okay, Molly. Meera will find her."

She twisted her nose as she sniffed, doing her best to hold back tears. "I know." She took a moment and cleared her throat, addressing my brothers. "Boys, get to the gym —" Darroch opened his mouth to protest, and my mom cut him off. "Not another word. The gym. There's a fight tonight. Darroch, run the betting. Fearghal, call in the Aron family to run security while Cadoc and Atlas are gone. And for fuck's sake, stop pouting. You're grown men. It's not a good look."

"Sorry, Ma," Darroch said, bending down to give her a kiss on the cheek. "We just want to find Sadie too."

Fearghal kissed her on the cheek as well, his apology silently written on his scarred face. "We'll call if she shows up at the gym." He walked by, glaring at Vareck, then squeezing my shoulder before leaving with Darroch.

For all the grief we gave each other as siblings, the boys loved deeply. They would forever and always protect their sisters, even when protection wasn't necessary. I imagined they felt helpless with Sadie missing. I understood the feeling. Not seeing a line to her was scaring me too. She wasn't on Earth or in Faerie. That left seven other potential realms, which felt like seven too many.

The small closet held some emergency clothes and two supply backpacks. I grabbed one, tossing it over my shoulder and handing the second one to my mom. I didn't know where our search would lead, and I wasn't sure if we would even need the items in the bag, but I'd been a bounty hunter long enough to expect the unexpected . . . and sometimes the unexpected was just needing a tampon.

The five of us entered the Witching Hour, and several heads turned our way. It was busy enough and there was a crowd, but it was not yet peak hours. Atlas wasn't small by any means, and four Wyldes walking in the door usually resulted in a fight by the end of the night, so naturally, those that knew us were wary. My brothers had been kicked out on more than one occasion. To my surprise, several patrons looked past us and straight at Vareck. Whether or not they knew he was the king was unknown. Men tried to keep their features schooled as they assessed him. Quite a few women eyed him up and down, a coy smile curling their painted lips. An overwhelming surge of jealousy spiked through me, and I bristled, looping my arm through his so they knew he was taken. The corner of Vareck's mouth twitched in amusement.

As usual, Amelia was at the bar, working flawlessly while she flirted with customers. She saw us, and her brows pinched instantly. Even though I waved in a friendly gesture, her lips pursed as she looked at Atlas. She pointed to the side of her bar while she stared at us. I'm not sure she blinked as she followed our every step.

Amelia tossed a bar towel over her shoulder and crossed her arms, shifting her weight onto one leg. "You're not allowed in here, Atlas. No Wylde brothers." She looked toward the front door. "Where's the rest of them, hmm?"

My brother remained stoic. "They're all busy. It's just me here." He held his hands up in surrender. "I'm not going to cause trouble."

My mother squeezed between Atlas and my dad, bumping them out of the way with her hips. "He won't do anything, Amelia. I swear it. We're just looking for Sadie. Have you seen her? Jared said he saw her here with Lou almost a week ago."

Amelia listened to my mom carefully, finally sighing and loosening the tension in her shoulders. "She pulled a gun in here, Molly. I kicked her out. Haven't seen her since."

"Can we just look around? Talk to people and see if they know where she is?" My mother was pleading, and that was something Molly Wylde *never* did. My dad rubbed his palm over her upper back.

"Please, Amelia. We just need to look and see if anyone saw anything. This was the last place she was seen," Atlas said, and after a brief pause, Amelia agreed.

"If you break anything, punch anyone, or so much as piss someone off, the hex I'll put on you will wreak havoc for years to come, you hear?" She waited until my brother agreed, and my mom breathed a "thank you" while squeezing her shoulder. Amelia waved a hand, revealing the hidden door to The Black Lounge.

My family rushed through, but something held me firmly in place. I held my arm in front of Vareck, shaking my head slightly.

Amelia turned to me. "Not going with them?" The corner of her mouth twitched.

I ignored Amelia as a whisper of Sadie pulled at my power. Even without tapping into my magic, I felt her. She wasn't close, but it was like a faint memory. She hadn't been here in almost a week, allegedly, yet there was an inkling of her presence.

"Meera?" Vareck asked, breaking my thoughts. "Are we following them?"

"No," I said, swallowing and feeling my mouth dry. An uneasiness settled over me.

Amelia shrugged, turning back to her bar.

"Wait," I said quickly, and she turned. "Can I look around the rest of the bar . . . check in the back room, maybe the portal room? I won't touch inventory or anything like that."

Amelia looked at me confused, tilting her head as she considered me. A smile curled up her lips, and I couldn't place why she felt the need to grin. What about this was amusing?

"Knock yourself out," she said, pulling the towel down from her shoulder and wiping the counter with it. She didn't bother looking at us before adding, "Grab me a bottle of gin on your way back. Room number six."

As we walked away, Vareck spoke softly. "What's happening?"

"I can feel Sadie."

"She's here?"

"No, she's not here. Her essence is."

"What does that mean?"

"I can't explain it. I don't think I've ever felt something like this before. If she was here, I would have known when we were at the safe house. But there was no thread leading to her."

"Is there now?"

Facing away from the stage, I reached for my power. The tiniest flickering thread pulsed like it was almost out of energy. "I have something. It's faint. She was back here," I whispered, mostly speaking to myself as I began to question what was happening. "This doesn't make sense."

I followed the thread, using as much power as I could, hoping it would brighten the golden string as I snaked through chairs, passing doors without even bothering to open them.

When I came to a stop in front of a door, a small plastic plaque etched with the number six made me pause, but the feeling of Sadie was stronger. "Six . . ." I muttered under my breath.

"Stop," Vareck said, putting his hand on my shoulder. "Something is wrong."

I grabbed the handle despite his protests. "The thread leads this way. My powers aren't wrong, Vareck."

I pushed the door open without another thought and the room was pitch black, more so than any room should be. That should have been my second warning, but it didn't stop me from walking in.

"Meera, wait—"

The tug of him grabbing my backpack wasn't enough to save me. The floor dropped from under me, my arms slipping through the straps with ease. I fell through darkness, my sense of direction lost as I plunged through a void. Vareck's panicked voice reached me as he shouted my name, but it was the cold, brittle laugh that followed that truly terrified me.

Amelia.

That bitch.

CHAPTER 5

VARECK

A split second. That's all it was. A single moment of time where I gripped her bag, the next, she was falling through a portal. I jumped after her without hesitation, tumbling through the threshold in a jarring twist as gravity played tricks with my sense of direction. The cackle that followed made my blood boil, but there was no time to dwell on anything but the present situation.

We landed with a thud, the air rushing from my lungs before it suddenly stalled, holding my body hostage as the wind knocked out of me. The metal of my swords clanged against the ground, and her backpack plopped beside it unceremoniously. Meera and I coughed as our bodies resettled into steady breathing. Heat saturated the air, baking me from the inside out. My head swam. I blinked a couple times, trying to clear the black spots in my vision. I slowly gained a clearer focus, taking in the uneven clay ceiling above us. Meera groaned, long and loud.

"Are you okay?" I asked through another cough as it racked my chest.

"Everything hurts," she mumbled, wincing as she spoke.

"Anything broken?"

"I don't think so." She paused, moving her legs and placing a hand on her stomach. "You?"

"I'll live."

I swallowed hard, throat dry, as I heaved myself up into a sitting position. We were in a small cave. One that had been recently inhabited, by the looks of it. The remains of a makeshift fire sat near the mouth. In the distance, rust-colored sand whipped around, twisting midair. My chest tightened at the sight of the wide-open, peach-colored sky.

Please, for the love of Faerie . . .

I got to my feet, untying my cloak. It dropped to the ground, sending a plume of dust everywhere. My swords were secured in their sheaths at my side. I adjusted them, repositioning the halter so they sat crossed over my back.

Meera sat up and frowned, taking off her outer layers before pulling her hair back in an attempt to tame it with the elastic band around her wrist. When she finished, I held my hand out to help her stand. Despite the dire situation we'd found ourselves in, sparks still lit up my skin when we touched.

"Thanks," she murmured, reluctantly pulling her attention from me to the entrance. My footsteps were leaden as I went to confirm what I already knew.

Twin suns sat high in the sky, one yellow, the other red.

There was only one realm with two suns.

We were fucked.

"Where are we?" Meera asked, shielding her eyes as she came to stand beside me.

"Eversus."

"As in the hell realm? *That* Eversus?" She motioned around us.

"That's the one."

Her head whipped around, copper strands tangling in the wind, slapping at her skin with every gust. "How do you know?"

"The two suns are a dead giveaway." I sighed and cursed under my breath. "Are you familiar with it at all?"

"Well, considering a hell realm isn't exactly a vacation destination, I'm going to have to go with no. From the looks of it, I can see why."

I hadn't expected her to know much. Eversus and its twin realm, Evorsus, were nigh impossible to get to. Few had the poor luck to visit it, and even fewer survived the journey.

I hummed in acknowledgment. "I've been here once. Never thought I'd come back." I adjusted the swords on my back, squinting as the wind billowed the gritty substance around. Everything about this place reeked of scorched air and death.

"You've been here?" she asked incredulously.

"Why does that seem so surprising?"

"It's a hell realm and you're the king of Faerie. Not exactly the safest move, especially when Damon is your only heir." Her tone indicated that it should be obvious.

I snorted. "Point made. But royalty aside, I'm also a fury."

Meera tilted her head, teeth sinking into her bottom lip in thought. "I thought it was just a rumor that furies originated from a hell realm, you know, because your father . . ." She trailed off. "So they came from this one? Is that why you came here? To learn more about your fury side?"

I hesitated, thinking about the best way to answer her

question. I didn't want to lie, but I wasn't keen on talking about it either. "Not here, no. They technically came from Evorsus, its sister realm." Her eyes narrowed a fraction, very much aware that I didn't answer her question as to why I had been here. She thankfully didn't push it. I cleared my throat, though it did nothing for the dryness that was beginning to coat it. "You should see if your powers work here. Some fae lose abilities in different realms."

"Do you?"

I shook my head. "Certain magics are less effective in some realms, though. You said you felt a tug leading you toward here when we were at the Witching Hour. Do you still?"

Her eyes brightened a second later, changing from hazel to a sparkling and vibrant green. The green faded almost as fast as it came and a small smile tugged at her lips. "Even better, I see the thread. Sadie's here." She took a step outside the cave, and I caught her arm, pulling her to a halt.

"Can you tell how far away she is?"

"Nope," she said. "I mean I *could*, but using my tracking that way drains my power really fast and leaves me disoriented. I lose my senses the more I use it. Following the thread is safer and won't take much out of me."

My jaw worked as I considered what she was saying. On one hand, her sister was here. Great. Given she was who we were looking for, that was a good thing. On the other hand, we were in one of the most dangerous of the nine realms with no way home.

The portal had dropped us in a cave somewhere then disappeared, which meant it wasn't an exit route, and I hadn't filled her in on the worst of it.

"Vareck?" Meera said, looking from my hand to my face. "We're here to find my sister."

"I'm aware."

She gestured to the expansive landscape before us. "Then let me go so we can find her."

"It's not that simple. She may not be in Eversus."

"I literally just told you I see the thread. Of course she's here."

I shook my head. "Eversus and Evorsus; twin realms. They are the two sides of the same coin." Meera started to speak, but I held my hand up, urging her to wait. "The land shifts at random. One moment you are in Eversus, the next, you are in Evorsus. There is no rhyme or reason. No geographic location that determines where. It's a hell realm that does what it wants."

"Well . . . that is a minor inconvenience, but it doesn't change what we have to do."

I sighed, pinching the bridge of my nose between my forefinger and thumb. "You said your power can work over any distance as long as what or who you're looking for is in the same realm. For all we know, she's weeks, maybe even months away from here on foot. There's also a very real possibility that Sadie could be in the other realm, and no matter where she is at this exact moment, there's no guarantee she will be in the same realm five minutes from now."

"And?" She cocked an eyebrow in challenge.

"You really need more of an explanation?" I pointed at her bag. "We have only what you have packed. And even if that includes the best survival kit in the nine realms, it won't change the fact that we don't have enough water. We don't have enough food. We aren't dressed for these conditions. The land can shift at any time. None of these things are good."

"All true, but it doesn't matter. You said the land does what it wants for any reason. That means we could stay in this exact spot, and the shift could still occur. Whether we sit here and twiddle our thumbs or start walking to find Sadie, those facts remain. It's not like the portal is still here to take us back so we can go get changed and grab more supplies."

"We have shelter at least," I countered.

"But we're not the only ones that know about it," She jutted her chin toward the sad firepit. "What if they—" She broke off abruptly, scanning the ground. Meera pulled her arm out of my grip to walk several feet and kneel down beside the fire. I came up behind her, watching as she crouched low and blew across the floor.

Sand scattered, revealing stones reshaped into a letter. W.

Wylde.

"Sadie was here," she breathed.

"How do you know?" I questioned. "Anyone could have done that."

"Really?" Meera stared at me deadpanned. "I don't think there are many people hanging around Eversus writing letters in caves. She knew I'd come looking for her. I feel her thread. She was here."

"And if she comes back?" I asked when she pivoted for the exit once more.

"Then she's close enough we should find her soon," Meera called over her shoulder, walking away from me.

Tension rose through my upper body. I worked my jaw, twisting my neck so it cracked. There was no way in hell that I'd let her wander off alone through Eversus. That was not an option. And there was apparently no way to stop her. Not one I was willing to risk, anyway. So like it or not, I followed.

The terrain was uneven leading away from the cave.

The ground was mostly sand and silt, making it twice as hard to wade through. Dark brown and black shrubs broke up the otherwise desolate expanse before us.

The moment I left the shade of the cave, the twin suns tried to roast me like a pig on a spit. I soldiered through without a complaint as I caught up to Meera. I would have to measure my steps carefully to not end up too far ahead of her. While she wasn't short by human standards, she was small compared to my six and a half feet in height.

"So," I said, attempting to cut through the heat and tension. "We're mates . . ." Internally, I cringed. Was that really the best I could do to segue into the conversation? Much as he was an asshole, Corvo might have a point about my lack of social skills.

Meera winced, shaking her head. "Do we have to do this?"

"This?" I cocked a brow.

She motioned between us, seemingly irritated. "*This.* Just . . . not now. I'm focused on finding Sadie."

"We are. Follow the yellow brick road." I motioned in front of us. "I'm just suggesting we talk while we walk."

She shot me a confused look. "How do you even know that reference?"

"Corvo is a bit of a cinephile. Guilty pleasure for him, I think. He made me visit your realm so we could watch it. Said it was a classic. Personally, I think the flying monkeys were more realistic than the humans."

She shook her head. "Stop changing the subject."

"Me? You're the one changing it. Addressing that we're mates clearly isn't what—"

She spun on me, heat flaring in her gaze. "I'm worried about my sister and not in the right headspace to deal with"—her hands gestured wildly between us—"this."

I didn't respond. I wasn't sure how. We just kept walking, letting the tension stretch. Mentally sifting through topics of conversation that she might consider benign, I thought about some of the books she read. There had been one with a zodiac, and I knew enough about it to speak. "Okay, what's your sign?"

She blinked. "My what?"

"Your star sign," I repeated in feigned nonchalance. "I'm a Scorpio. You?"

Meera stopped short, cocking her head at an angle. "Are you fucking with me?"

With a slow, coquettish smile, I loudly whispered, "I would think after last night, you'd know if I was fucking you."

My attempts at flirting with her failed miserably. Her expression turned from incredulous to murderous in an instant. "You know what I meant."

"Do I?" I stepped up, leaving only inches between us. Sweat gathered at Meera's hairline. Her fair skin was flushed pink, almost like she was blushing—if she were able to blush from chest to forehead. I worried about her skin in these conditions. We were fae and could heal better and faster than humans, but we weren't immune to sun damage.

"I'm a Pisces." She stepped around me and resumed walking.

Even though I felt like I was drowning, I nodded with faux smugness. "I can see that."

Her neck cracked from how hard she whipped her head to the side to stare at me. "What is that supposed to mean?"

I shrugged, letting the silence thicken. I counted to forty-three before Meera finally broke.

"So now I'm getting the silent treatment?"

"Did I say that?"

"You didn't say anything!" She snapped.

"They're highly compatible," I finally answered. "Scorpio and Pisces. Also Pisces are prone to avoiding confrontation. So . . ."

I wouldn't have seen it, were I not watching out of the corner of my eye. Meera stiffened.

Instead of taking the bait, she asked, "How do you know? I mean, I know the fae zodiac is like a big deal to some people, but the human one?"

"My human anthropology tutor was just this side of obsessed," I said, holding my thumb and forefinger apart with little space between them. "She and my etiquette tutor liked playing matchmaker in my teen years. The number of times I heard that I should look for a Cancer or Pisces are too many to count." I shook my head. Meera snorted.

"Did you?"

"Did I what?"

"Look for a Cancer or Pisces?" Her lips twitched with barely concealed amusement.

"No, I can't say I did, though it seems I ended up with one anyway."

And just like that, the humor faded from her expression.

"You're not going to let this go, are you?"

"This?" I asked, biting back a laugh when her left eye practically started twitching. "The answer is no. The fact that you are is both unsurprising and disappointing."

Her lips parted. A hint of guilt crossed her expression, but it was fleeting, and in its place came another rush of anger. "I told you I'm not in a good headspace. I woke up to find my sister is missing, and then I fell into a hell portal made by someone I thought was my friend. Why are you pushing this?"

My eyebrows inched towards my hairline. "You're serious?" I stopped and crossed my arms over my chest. "Let's start with the obvious. The fact is we are mates. Your sister is missing, yes, and we're walking to gods know where for who knows how long because we were double-crossed by a witch, the one you thought was a friend. All of that means something. If you'd rather fuck around with small talk like signs or how fucking hot it is here, I can do that, but I thought we had moved past that phase." Meera spluttered, opening and closing her mouth, but I held up a hand to stop her from speaking. She didn't want to talk earlier. Now it was my turn. "We found out we're mates with possibly the worst timing imaginable, Meera. I know that. Is it so hard to believe that I want to check on you and how you're processing this? Hear what you have to say about it? Given your avoidance on the topic with your family, I'm not exactly feeling confident about where you stand with things right now." Some of the anger started to seep out of her. She bit her bottom lip, tugging it between two teeth as uncertainty played through her expression.

"I assumed you were going to push on the subject of where we go from here," she said quietly. She wasn't wrong that I wanted to talk about that, but I knew she wasn't ready. While I was all in, it was painstakingly obvious Meera needed more time to adjust.

However, avoiding the subject entirely wasn't doing us any favors.

"You know what they say about assumptions."

She grimaced. "I suppose I deserve that." She started to pick at her nails while we spoke; a nervous habit I'd noticed during our time at the castle.

"You're going to hurt yourself," I said softly. She paused, and I motioned to her hands. "Picking. You'll go too deep. Last thing you need is for it to get infected here." Her cheeks darkened as her hands fell to her sides.

She sighed, dropping her gaze and taking a moment to gather herself. "I get really grouchy when I'm hot."

I couldn't help but chuckle. "I'm guessing that's the precursor to an apology?"

"Something like that." Pressing her lips together in a small smile, she looked away in thought and I measured the time by counting seconds in my head. "I don't know how to feel about the whole mate thing," she finally admitted, returning her attention to me. Meera kicked a small black rock with her boot and started walking again. "I thought fated mates weren't even possible anymore. Everyone said the curse took that bond away."

I nodded slowly, keeping pace beside her. "It was generally believed to be that way, yes. The fated bond wasn't common to begin with, but after the curse took effect..."

"Does this mean the curse is breaking down?"

"I don't know," I answered honestly. "No one would love that more than me, but after nearly forty years, it's hard to believe that it would suddenly start to unravel."

She inclined her head toward me. "You're scared to hope."

"Can you blame me?"

Her hazel eyes were soft when she glanced at me. "No, but stranger things have happened. I mean, we dreamed of each other for years . . ." Her voice trailed off, and I suspected where her train of thought went. "I guess it makes sense now."

"I'm not so sure about that," I said. "I haven't known or

heard of fated mates who dreamed of each other before they met."

Meera kicked another rock, strolling at a slow speed. Between the taxing suns and the topic of conversation, every bit of energy we had was being drained, but it was still better than walking with all of this hanging between us. "You said they weren't common though, yeah? How many fated pairings did you know?"

"A few," I said softly, picturing my sister's face in my mind and feeling a pang of sadness. "I swear, no one was as strongly bound as Drayden and Maeve. The elements rejoiced at their pairing. You could feel it in the air when they were together."

Meera frowned. "I'm surprised he even survived . . ." She swallowed hard, then winced like it was painful.

"Physically, he did. I imagine that had something to do with the fact that they hadn't completed the bond yet. Emotionally, he didn't. Whatever light once existed in him died along with her."

"Why . . . why did they wait?" she asked.

"They wanted her to go through the transition first." I remembered the fights they had over that. The halls of the palace shook when Maeve fought with him. "In truth, it was really Drayden who wanted her to. He had it in his head that if they completed the bond before she came into her full powers that it might hurt her."

"Would it have?"

I shrugged. "Honestly? I have no idea. Our father believed it would."

She squinted. "Your father was insane, though."

"He was," I agreed. "But he was also a genius and incredibly charismatic. He had a way of selling his ideas so they didn't seem as bad. He favored Maeve, too. She was the heir to the throne, and his firstborn. Before he killed her, you never would have guessed at his plans. It wasn't so crazy at the time for Drayden to think that he was right about Maeve and how it would affect her." I shook my head. Out of everyone, Drayden was the person who had been blindsided the most that day, and he paid the price. It was no wonder he didn't trust anymore. I fully believed the only reason I had his loyalty was because of my relationship with my sister.

"You said Drayden wanted to wait. Did that mean she didn't?"

I nodded. "Patience wasn't my sister's strong suit. I also think she was more affected by the strain it put on the bond."

"Strain?" she asked, and the odd note in her tone didn't escape me. Her toe caught the edge of another rock and Meera stumbled. I grabbed her arm to steady her.

"There are theories about the fated mate bond. Where it comes from. Why it exists. The general consensus is that if a bond is left incomplete for too long, degeneration begins. They were together for over a year when she was killed. Most couples don't wait more than a few weeks to complete it when they find their true mate. Sometimes just days."

Her eyebrows flew up. Meera stopped in her tracks to give me her full, undivided attention. "Days? Weeks?" Though her face was red from heat and exertion, some of the color drained away. "How could someone possibly know they want to spend the rest of their life with someone so fast?"

I had to work to keep from tensing at the implication. The admission that she didn't know. That she didn't feel it the way I did. That it wouldn't simply be days or weeks for us. That at the end of it, she might reject the bond entirely. It took everything I had to continue feigning nonchalance, like we were still talking about my sister when that was no longer the case.

"Most fated mates have a hard time being physically apart after they meet each other. The bond wants to be completed. Beyond the discomfort distance creates, it's believed that mates themselves can sometimes start to regress the longer it's not complete."

"Regress? What does that mean?" she asked, voice rising before she caught herself and cleared her throat. It was becoming harder to act indifferent when she sounded more panicked each time she spoke.

"Given fated pairs didn't usually delay long, there's not a definitive answer." I scratched my beard. "In those that did wait, there were multiple observations that didn't make sense otherwise. So the regression looked more like feral behavior. Increased agitation. Aggression. Sexual appetite. Men can become overprotective and overbearing in their drive to provide for their mate. Women experienced similar symptoms as they do when they are with child, in the sense that sometimes they got sick or experienced rapid mood swings. Maeve became territorial over Drayden and started nesting. It drove everyone crazy at the time because she was incredibly particular about how things were managed in the castle, especially in their wing."

She had been so close to the transition when she died. I remembered how we were all holding our breath, waiting for it to finally happen so they could complete the damn bond. What I would give to have even that version of my sister back. I closed my eyes, pushing away the thought.

"Is . . . is that going to happen to us?" she asked quietly. "To me?"

I sighed deeply. "I don't know," I said, wishing I had a better answer to give. "Do you intend to wait more than a few weeks before making up your mind?" I must not have done a good enough job hiding my frustration, because her expression soured.

"It's not like this is just dating now, Vareck. I wanted—*want*—to give it a shot between us, but mates are permanent. There's no undoing it if things go south. What if we end up not liking each other the longer we are together?"

How could she say that? How could she feel the bond, know it was there, and still think fate chose poorly? My lips pressed into a thin line, my anger simmering close to the surface. "Well, I guess we'll find out now, won't we?"

Meera reeled back like I'd slapped her. "You're upset with me. Over this." She shook her head, looking at the sky in disbelief. She was too busy being infuriated to notice yet another rock that she caught with her boot. Meera pitched forward, and I grabbed her once more.

"Careful."

"Goddamn rocks," she growled. She pulled her leg back to kick the black stone as hard as she could. "It's a damn desert. Why are there so many . . ." Her voice trailed as she scanned our surroundings. "There aren't."

"Aren't what?"

"There aren't rocks here. Not naturally. Look." She motioned all around us. I worked my jaw, biting my tongue despite the way she once again was changing the subject. I was only half paying attention when my eyebrows drew together.

She was right. There weren't rocks anywhere. Shrubs, tumbleweeds, sand, yes. But none of the shiny, onyx stones.

I glanced back where we'd been walking.

Every twelve paces or so, a black rock sat in the sand.

Some were no more than twice the size of a pebble while others were just large enough for Meera to keep tripping over them.

"It's a trail," I said, tilting my head, considering the direction it came from and where it was going.

"She left me breadcrumbs," Meera muttered.

"Breadcrumbs?" I squinted in confusion

"Hansel and Gretel. It's a fairytale by the Brothers Grimm. The two kids left breadcrumbs to find their way home." I frowned, and she squinted up at me. "It's so I can find her. Obviously."

I shook my head. "That doesn't make any sense. Sadie is your sister. She knows about your power. There would be no need for her to use rocks as a way of leading you to her. These aren't for you."

Meera twisted her lips while she thought. "If she was planning to go back, she might have been using them to help guide her." She waved her hand over her shoulder. "The cave blends in with the landscape remarkably well. I could see someone losing their way."

"Possibly, especially if she was looking for a food source. There's nothing out here. It's desert as far as the eye can see. Otherwise, what was her reason for leaving the cave?"

"Maybe she didn't know I would come looking but thought someone might and that's why she did this." She pointed at the path of rocks.

"You said leaving that 'W' in the cave was for you."

"Well, I don't know what to tell you." Meera threw her hands up. "We'll have to ask her when we find her."

"You can still see the thread, right?"

"Are you thinking she's in Evorsus?" The panic in her voice was undeniable, but it quickly dissipated as her eyes glowed bright green, then simmered down to their hazel hue. "If the realm isn't messing with my magic, she's still here."

I forced a tight smile. The twin realms weren't like others. I had no idea if the thread would feel different if her sister had somehow crossed into the other realm. Eversus and Evorsus were the same, and yet not, but both were filled with tricks and illusions.

I gestured for Meera to lead the way, but I couldn't shake the feeling that it wasn't just Sadie we were following. That someone, or something, was either tracking her too or . . . I glanced at Meera and reminded myself that she wouldn't be able to find Sadie if she were dead. It was the singular thing that kept me quiet despite wanting to voice my concerns. Meera wasn't listening to reason right now, her concern for her sister outweighing anything else.

We continued in uncomfortable silence. The only sound to be heard was our heavy breathing as the atmosphere took its toll on us. In the far-off distance, the ground was glassy, and the air seemed to ripple.

I prayed to the gods it was nothing more than a mirage . . .

The gods weren't listening.

CHAPTER 6

MEERA

Heat shimmered in the distance, turning the jagged ridgelines into illusions that danced just out of reach. My boots crunched on sand and something else—black pebbles? No. Another of Sadie's stones, strategically placed as makeshift markers . Each one settled deeper in my gut, a silent warning wrapped in a breadcrumb trail.

Something was wrong. Not just with the terrain or the oppressive dual suns that beat down on us like punishment. No, this wrongness clung to the magic in the air. It hummed, but not in the familiar way Faerie did. There was dissonance here. A tear. I wondered if this was the feeling of the twin realms that Vareck had described, but he never said he could sense the magic, just that its ability to split existed.

I swallowed past the dryness in my throat, pretending the tension in my chest was just dehydration. Vareck looked just as uncomfortable as I felt, which made me think we were both bad actors and couldn't hide it from each other.

"You said earlier you don't think these rocks are for me," I began quietly. "But you do think it's Sadie, right?"

Vareck didn't answer at first. His eyes swept the horizon, every inch the Dark King—tactical, restrained, simmering just beneath the surface. "I don't know. There's a discernible pattern and it doesn't feel like a coincidence. They're too deliberate and evenly spaced. That doesn't sound like a creature from this realm. That sounds distinctly human or fae. Someone wanted them seen, but I don't know for what purpose."

I shivered despite the heat. "Let's hope it was her. Otherwise I'm following these stupid rocks right into a trap and we're gonna die." Gods, wouldn't that just be my luck? Some hell-bound demons, giggling right as a dumb fae walks right into their bubbling cauldron of potatoes and carrots. Fucking Amelia.

"I won't let that happen."

"Well, we may not have a choice. If whatever wants to eat us decides to boil us first, please kill me. I'm hot enough already. Just end it."

He stiffened, clearly not liking my casual comments about impending death. Most of it was a joke. I was walking through hell. If I didn't laugh, I'd cry, and I was so dehydrated, I probably couldn't even cry if I wanted to.

We kept moving in silence, but a few paces later, I heard him sigh, and the sound of it put me on edge.

"Meera, we need to talk."

I groaned. "I'm not talking about the mate thing right now."

He growled softly. "This isn't about that."

I turned to face him, squinting as the bright light bearing down on us skewed my vision. "Unless you're about to magic up a canteen of water and air conditioning, I'm really not in the mood to have a serious conversation about anything."

His eyes flicked over me and I felt the weight of them. "You're burning. Your skin; it's going to blister if we don't find shade soon."

"I'm not a porcelain doll, Vareck."

"No, you're a fair-skinned ginger resembling a lobster," he said evenly.

"Hey—"

"And you're about to collapse from heat exhaustion. Something I can't treat here. So maybe take it easy?"

The worry in his tone caught me off guard. I blinked, and for a moment I didn't see the fury who took me to bed or the king who'd collared me. I saw the man who'd watched me sleep like it meant something. Who laughed at my sarcasm and held me like I was something worth holding on to.

I tore my gaze away. "We keep moving. If Sadie left a trail, she had a reason. That means she's close."

"Or something else is," he said, low and serious.

Before I could snap back, the ground beneath us shifted. Literally. A vibration rolled through the sand, subtle but distinct.

"What was that?"

We crouched, scanning the cracked terrain. Off to the left, the air shimmered differently. It bent in a way that wasn't heat-induced. More like a ripple.

He grabbed my arm, pulling me closer instinctively. "Evorsus."

A second later, the ripple flexed—and the world cracked.

The change sent me falling, or would have if Vareck hadn't caught me. I squeezed my eyes shut, palms pressing into them as a pressure built. A headache was building at the base of my skull thanks to dehydration and whatever other bullshittery was going on. He quickly wrapped both arms around me, holding me tight.

Another wave rolled through the atmosphere, sinking into my skin as the temperature noticeably changed. The world rattled and shook, and I felt as though I were spinning in a cyclone. Wind and shaking earth roared in my ears before it all fell silent and everything stilled.

"Open your eyes."

Slowly, I dropped my hands and let my eyelids flutter open.

The first thing I realized was the trail had vanished, and a deep panic burrowed into my gut. The black markers that had been so perfectly spaced, guiding in the same direction my magic was leading me, had vanished. Just—poof. Gone. Like they'd never been there.

I stopped cold and spun in place. The sand that had surrounded us had disappeared. Not blown away. Just no longer there. Just like the rocks.

"What in the nine realms . . ." I whispered.

Vareck stopped beside me. "Are you okay?"

I shook my head, throat dry. "They were just here. You saw them."

"I did," he said softly. "They are still there, in Eversus. We aren't. Welcome to Evorsus."

You would think twin realms would be similar, but this was the complete opposite. No wind. No heat. The air was cool, hushed, almost reverent.

And the sky—gods, the sky was spectacular.

Gone were the dual suns that had tried to roast us alive. In their place, embedded in a deep violet canopy studded with stars, two moons glowed with a silver-blue, casting strange shadows over the terrain. One intact, and the other one broken.

Where the desert had stretched endlessly, dense forest now surrounded us. Lush trees arched high above, their leaves glowing faintly in shades of emerald, sapphire, and amethyst. The ground beneath my boots was soft and mossy. The air smelled like petrichor, violets, and something sweet I couldn't place.

"This is incredible," I whispered, my voice too small for the magnitude of what I was seeing. "How did we move to the other side? I know the realms touch, but I thought you had to cross between them."

"We didn't move; the realms did." He gestured to the terrain. "They shifted around us. Eversus and Evorsus are two sides to the same coin, and the borders are unstable."

Magic hummed through the trees. Not menacing, exactly, but aware. Watching. Sentient.

I swallowed hard. "So we're just . . . in Evorsus now. With no way back to Eversus?"

He nodded. "Not unless the realms move again. Eversus is the land of the twin suns. It's a desert hellscape." That was putting it mildly. It looked and felt like a post-apocalyptic wasteland. "Evorsus is darker, and not just in the literal sense. Here, things are . . . beautiful. Alluring. Because that's what it's trying to do. Lure you in."

A chill skated down my spine, despite the temperate air. "Why did the portal drop us in Eversus and not here?"

"I don't know. These realms bleed into each other. Sometimes you walk far enough in one and find yourself in the other. Sometimes," he added with a glance upward, "they come to you."

I pressed a fist against my chest, feeling for the thread.

Still there.

Still tugging.

"She's here," I said, feeling a combination of relief and

despair. "Somewhere in this realm, or Eversus. I can see the thread still, but now that I've been to both, I have no idea which realm she's actually in. It looks exactly the same. My magic can't seem to distinguish between the two."

"That answers our earlier question then." His shoulders tightened slightly. "We should keep going. Follow the thread until something happens."

"Something happens?" I repeated.

"Until we find Sadie, or until the land shifts again."

"Awesome," I muttered, adjusting the straps on my backpack before I followed the thread once more.

We walked in silence for a while, the glow of the forest lighting our way in shades of cerulean. It should've been beautiful. But unease scratched at my psyche, like an itch beneath my skin.

I broke the silence. "You said Evorsus tries to lure you in. What did you mean?"

He glanced sideways. "Eversus will kill you directly with heatstroke or dehydration. Evorsus makes you comfortable. Complacent. It plays with your mind, because it doesn't want to kill you. It wants to keep you."

"Lovely. A hell realm with aesthetic."

Despite the tension, his mouth twitched. "You're not wrong."

We kept moving, the forest thickening. Somewhere in the distance, a howl echoed, low and mournful. I stiffened.

Vareck placed a hand on my lower back. "We're not alone in these woods. Don't engage with anything. Some creatures here look harmless but aren't. Others are worse."

"Worse than not being harmless? That's vague," I said, and he sighed. "Worse *how*?"

Vareck worked his jaw, considering my question. His hesitation made me worried, but what he settled on surprised me. "Among other things, furies originated from Evorsus."

"I thought you said—" I broke off, trying to recall his words.

"They're not from Eversus," he said.

"Who named this stupid place? Eversus. Evorsus. Fricken twin hells. It might as well be the same place. One has two suns, the other two moons. It's literally day and night."

He caught me by the elbow, his expression solemn. "They are very much not the same, day and night aside. Don't make the mistake of confusing them just because of their unfortunate naming being so similar. One is designed to kill the body. The other is designed to kill the mind."

"Okay, but if this one screws with people's heads, I'm kind of surprised furies come from here and not Eversus." I ran a hand through my sweat-soaked hair, scratching my scalp.

"Some would think that."

I cocked my head. "It's obviously wrong, so fill me in."

His lips twisted, like he was debating on what to say. "The way furies are thought of it doesn't surprise me that you'd make that connection. What truly makes them dangerous—makes *me* dangerous—is not the black eyes or the claws or the jagged wings. It's our ability to curse with our blood."

I reeled back. "You can do that?"

Vareck stilled, his gaze piercing me. "I can, but you have no reason to fear me. I would never do that to you."

I was somewhat taken aback that he assumed that was where my thoughts went. "I didn't think you would." Vareck could have hurt me a number of times since we met, but apart from putting that cursed necklace on me, he never did. Even then, that wasn't a physical or permanent sort of pain. It made my heart hurt because it felt like betrayal.

"Good." He dipped his chin. "Because there is nothing you could do to me that would make me use that power on you, including letting the mate bond die. You understand that, right?"

"I believe you, Vareck." And by the gods, I did. He sounded pained, like it hurt to even consider a universe where I chose that. My heart tightened in my chest, and I nodded. A question came to me, but I almost didn't want to ask. "Have you ever used it?"

He paused, and that answered my question before he even spoke. "Twice."

I could tell he was uncomfortable talking about it, so despite my curiosity I thought it best to let it go.

"So furies come from Evorsus," I mused, not really sure where I was going with my pivot in the conversation. I wanted to keep him talking. Learning about furies and fae and all things Vareck was quickly becoming a favorite pastime of mine. That thought was more than a little scary. I buried it, masking the vulnerability with an easy smile.

Vareck nodded. "It's why this place feels familiar to me."

"Familiar how?"

He took a deep breath, like he was drinking in the atmosphere and letting it revitalize him. "Like it's under my skin. As though I feel its history and remember it in lifetimes that are not my own. As if the essence of my soul is buried in the roots and traveling through the ley lines."

Something in his voice sent a shiver down my spine. A resonance, like the realm was tugging at some invisible thread inside him.

"That's not concerning," I muttered sarcastically.

"It should be," he replied. "Evorsus doesn't just call to furies. It *recognizes* them."

I swallowed hard. "But you're the last one."

He dipped his chin again. "As far as I know, yes."

"What did it want from them, err, you?"

He met my gaze. "To bring us home."

I didn't know what to say. I wanted to tell him the very notion scared the hell out of me, no pun intended, but before I could form a cogent response, a thought occurred to me. If the realm recognized him, would it recognize me through our bond?

We walked in silence, both of us lost in thought. The path shifted beneath us, bioluminescent vines lighting the way like we were being led somewhere.

The realization only added to the somber vibes that had befallen us.

We weren't just walking *through* Evorsus.

Based on what he told me, we were being guided.

"Is it just me or does it seem like we're being led somewhere?"

Vareck seemed unsurprised. Maybe he already knew that, or maybe he also came to that conclusion. "Evorsus isn't omniscient, but it is sentient. Is it leading us the same way as your thread?"

I paused, only now realizing that yes, it was. The pull from the land was the same direction as the thread that was attached to my sister.

He must have sensed my hesitance at answering, but I nodded. Vareck worked his jaw. "We follow the thread. Evorsus is full of illusions. Nothing is what it seems. Don't eat anything. Don't let anything touch you."

"Don't eat any poisoned apples. Got it."

"I'm serious, Meera," he said sternly. It was clear this place scared him more than he wanted to admit. "I'm voicing it out loud so we're on the same page."

The forest glowed faintly as we moved, lighting the narrow path between protruding roots. Strange birds cooed somewhere above, and the breeze carried whispers I couldn't quite make out, like the trees were speaking to each other. Gossiping about us.

My boots squelched against the damp earth. Despite everything, the realm was stunning. Wild. Alive in a way that Faerie hadn't been in years. I couldn't shake the sense that we were being watched, and despite searching for the telltale shine of hidden eyes in the bushes and treetops, I found nothing.

"You said something earlier," I murmured.

"About what?"

"This place. You said it wants to keep people. Trap them. Has it ever tried to keep you?"

He hesitated. "Yes."

I glanced at him. "And?"

"I didn't let it."

That was it. No elaboration. No story. Just those four loaded words and an uncertain glance at the still leaves and the silent trees.

I wanted to ask more, but it was clear he didn't want to discuss it further. Not because he didn't trust me, but because he didn't trust the forest not to listen.

CHAPTER 7

VARECK

The clearing looked safe. That was the first red flag.

Evorsus didn't do safe. It did alluring. Inviting. It seduced the senses with a welcoming whisper, *rest here*, even as every survival instinct I had screamed not to let our guard down.

Thick, lush grass blanketed the ground like velvet, soft and dry enough to sleep on. Trees rose around us like stained-glass walls, their jewel-toned leaves shimmering beneath the moon. Everything glowed faintly green, violet, and sapphire. It should've been peaceful. The perfect place to rest after many hours of walking.

It was anything but.

Meera walked around the clearing, near the tree line. Too close to the shadows. Too far from me. The tension that had coiled between us all day snapped taut again.

She hadn't said much since the shift into Evorsus. Not about the realm. Not about the thread. Not about *us*.

Which was fine.

Mostly.

Except it wasn't, and I was full of shit.

Every move she made—every glance, every breath—felt like a decision not to close the chasm between us. I tracked her from the corner of my eye, both hating the distance and embracing it myself.

Meera wasn't sure how she felt about the mate bond. It was my job to convince her to accept it. To *stay*. That was easier said than done when we were traversing the most dangerous hell realm.

With every step, it became apparent that Evorsus had taken an interest in her. The roots themselves had moved out of the way after Meera tripped and rolled her ankle. The branches lifted just so, making it easier for her to cross underneath them. She'd fallen twice during our trek before I found a suitable walking stick for her—yet another thing that appeared right when she needed it. The realm itself was accommodating her body while simultaneously wearing her down.

I wasn't sure if she noticed it. If she did, she didn't say anything. The last thing I wanted to do was make her panic when there was literally nothing we could do about our current situation. So I watched. I listened. I guarded.

She dropped her backpack with an unceremonious thud, exhaling as she stretched and rolled her shoulders. Crouching, she rummaged through the sack and pulled out a thin blanket and a package of dried beef. With mechanical precision, she laid out the cloth, her movements sharp and deliberate despite the exhaustion I knew was weighing her down.

"You're brooding," she said, sitting down and leaning back on her palms.

"Brooding?"

She gave a vague shrug and brushed a sweaty lock of

ginger hair away from her face. "Ya know, sulking but manly-er?"

The corner of my mouth twitched. "Manly-*er*?"

Meera pursed her lips. "Are you just going to repeat everything I say? If so, this conversation is going to get old real fast." Her voice edged toward sarcasm, but she sounded more annoyed than anything else.

I sighed. "I'm not brooding. I'm *thinking*. Namely about how to get us out of here once we find Sadie." It wasn't a lie. I was thinking about that. Maybe not at this exact moment, but Meera made it clear she didn't want to talk about *us* and while it frustrated me, I knew I'd get nowhere if I pushed it. I was coming to learn that my fiery mate had to do things in her own time.

"Oh," she said, straightening her posture. "I suppose that's fair. I've mostly been focusing on finding Sadie but once we do, we need a way back—to Earth or Faerie. At this point, I'm not picky."

I inclined my head, listening to the forest around us. "How much water do we have?"

She reached for the canteen hanging loosely from her shoulder and gave it a little shake. "About half. Do you think there's water nearby?"

I nodded. "I don't feel comfortable leaving you here while I go searching for it though. Not when these realms have a nasty habit of changing."

Meera cocked her head, considering my words. After a second, she reached for her walking stick and used it to climb to her feet once more. "All right. Let's find it. I'll leave the blanket here, so we have a way back to the clearing." She noticed my frown and added, "I can track it. It's a convenient skill to have here when I can't tell right from left and everything looks the same."

"Will you let me carry the backpack this time?"

"I already told you I'm capable of wearing it," she said, jutting her hip out and using the walking stick to lean on.

I walked toward her and picked it up off the ground, putting the dried beef back inside before closing the pocket. "And I don't think there is anything wrong with sharing the burden. We can trade on and off."

She hummed sarcastically as I wrapped my hands around both straps for a better hold. With two swords at my back, carrying it as she had done wouldn't be as easy. I was fine holding it. "Are you actually going to trade with me, or are you just going to take over?"

I repeated the tone of her hum and gave her a wink as we headed toward the water source.

"Can you track it and Sadie at the same time?" I wondered aloud as we walked.

Meera nodded. "It's just another thread."

"And you know which is which?"

She tilted her head one way then the other. "Mostly. When I search for something or someone I feel a pull. More strings means more pulls, but all I'd have to do is stop tracking one thing to know which is which."

"Hmm. Your ability to find things is fascinating. Especially when you don't have a witch mark. Could you lead us to water?"

Meera shook her head. "I mean, technically, yes. But I'd get a pull in too many directions if I just searched for water. It's different if I'm looking for a specific body of water, like Lake Michigan—that's a place. Whereas water in general is vague. Plants have water in them. People too. Not to mention all the many bodies of water that exist in a realm." She shook her head again. "I also have to have a connection to the object or person."

The further we went from the clearing, the louder the slight rustling of water became. "You have to know them? How were you able to track Damon then?"

"Photo," she answered. "If it's not a person I know or an object I've encountered before, I need a picture of it to anchor the connection."

"And everyone you work for knows this?"

She scoffed. "Of course not. I'm not giving away that secret to just anyone. But even a regular bounty hunter without my ability would be hard up to do the job if the client didn't provide that. You have to know what you're looking for."

Between the trees in the not-so-far-off distance, something was glowing. It wasn't until we were only ten or so feet from it that I was able to identify it as a series of pools. Each one was several feet higher than the last. Bioluminescent water spilled from one into the other, ending in a tiny lagoon at our feet.

Meera whistled. "This is cozy."

She hobbled over to me, but instead of reaching for me, she went for the bag I wore on one shoulder.

Now she sifted through it, muttering to herself. Wrappers crinkled as she pushed some granola bars aside, looking for what, I didn't know.

"Aha!" she said excitedly after a minute. "Found it."

I lifted a brow as she held up a vial of clear liquid with an eyedropper.

"And that is?"

"A potion. One that cost me a pretty penny to have made. After I nearly died from dehydration in another realm a few years back, I had Amelia make me a ton of this stuff. Every survival pack I make has it."

Immediate distrust filled me, and it was no doubt

written on my face. "The same Amelia that has a portal to Eversus in the backroom of her bar?"

The excitement she felt waned a bit. She lifted a shoulder and looked at the ground. "She made this when she was still my friend. I've used it before. I know it works."

"What exactly does it do?"

Meera smiled, and even with a leaf stuck in her hair and dirt smudged across the bridge of her nose, she still looked beautiful. Everything about her was pure. "This little guy is going to tell us if the water is safe to drink and not, ya know, poison or something."

She unscrewed the dropper and extended her arm over the pool, careful not to spill. A single crystalline teardrop fell into the pool and dispersed. Nothing happened.

"That's it?"

"That's it. If the water isn't safe, it turns black when the potion touches it. Clear means we're good to drink."

We refilled the canteens in silence, the quiet hum of the surrounding forest oddly soothing. Meera sat crisscrossed at the edge of the lowest pool and dipped her fingers into the glowing water. "You know," she said, not looking at me, "this reminds me of hiking trips with Sadie."

I turned my head. "You hiked?"

She snorted. "Tried to. My equilibrium isn't designed to keep me balanced for most physical activities, but I liked it all the same. Sadie and I used to go with our boyfriends back in the day." The mention of her with someone else made my muscles tense, but I hid the reaction. I didn't want her to stop sharing with me. "One trip ended with me twisting my ankle and falling off a ledge. Sadie laughed so hard she nearly peed herself."

"You fell off a ledge and she laughed?"

"It wasn't a big ledge. It was just enough to bruise my

ass and my ego." She smiled to herself, reliving the memory I wish I could have shared with her. "You better believe I acted like it was nothing, but internally, I felt every step of the way home."

"Sounds like you." I chuckled, the sound only slightly less strained than I felt. I could recognize what she was doing; telling me about herself and her past as a way of getting to know her and distracting us from our bleak reality.

"I may have two left feet, but I like being outside. And exploring nature. It's quiet. Peaceful. Away from everyone." Her fingers traced circles on the surface of the pool. "I didn't realize how much I missed it until now."

She didn't have to say it, but I heard the longing in her voice. For Sadie. For normalcy. For a time before hell realms and complicated feelings.

Uncrossing her left foot, she peeled off her boots and socks, hissing softly as she dipped her sore feet into the water. "That feels divine," she said, her eyes meeting mine. "I'm getting in."

"Are you . . ." My words died off as Meera reached for her sweat-soaked shirt and lifted it over her head. My mouth went dry.

Meera raised a brow. "We're in a glowing magic lagoon, that looks like a picture from a fairytale I might add, in the middle of a cursed forest. One, if we don't take the opportunity to soak in the magical spring, I feel like the universe will be personally offended." She pointed to herself. "It's me. I'm the universe." My tension from earlier lessened, watching her so at ease. "Two, we don't know when the next bath will be, or if it will be warm."

She pulled her feet out of the water and laid back on the forest ground. Meera ran a hand down her abdomen gently.

I tracked the movement in slow motion as she reached for the button on her pants.

"Vareck?" She unclasped them and drew down her zipper.

I swallowed, moving my gaze back to her face. She lifted her hips and pushed the fabric down. "Yes?"

"Get in the water with me."

I unfastened the straps on my boots, not able to tear my eyes away from the vixen in front of me. Meera removed her jeans without issue, then moved to her bra. This one had a front clasp. With a twist of her fingers the cups fell sideways, revealing my mate's rosy nipples, pebbled despite the warm air.

She sat up, letting the rest of the garment slide from her arms. Light from the twin moons caught her skin and turned every pale inch of her silver. Freckles dotted her shoulders and collarbone, and I felt every last ounce of resolve burn away as she slid into the pool.

She didn't look back. Didn't tease or flirt or ask me to join her again.

She simply sank into the glowing warmth with a soft sigh and rested her arms along the edge. Her breasts were wet and wanting. She tilted her head back to expose the long curve of her neck.

And fuck me, I followed.

The harness on my chest took but a second to undo. The dual swords at my back hit the ground with a light thud. Next came my shift, then the rest. The damp air clung to my skin as I entered the water, the warmth wrapping around me with a familiarity that should be unsettling.

I forced the thought from my mind to focus on the woman in front of me.

Meera opened one eye, her lips curling into the barest smirk. "Took you long enough."

I stopped just shy of reaching her. "You've been pulling away all day. I didn't want to cross a line."

Her expression softened, the smirk fading into something quieter. "If I didn't want you here, I wouldn't have asked."

I moved closer, slow and careful, until our legs brushed beneath the water. "You don't have to pretend with me, Meera. Not here. Not now."

She looked away, her throat working as she swallowed. "It's not pretending," she said, voice quieter now. "It's protecting. I've spent most of my life building walls. It's not easy to let someone past them. Even you."

I reached out, letting my fingers skim her shoulder. She didn't flinch, just breathed in a little deeper.

"That's not going to work for me," I said, and her eyes snapped back to mine.

"What?"

"I won't be just another person who gets the watered-down version of you. The edited one. I want all of you, Meera. The sharp edges, the stubborn pride, the fear, the fire. I won't take pieces."

"That's a lot to ask."

"It's everything," I said simply. "But I won't settle for anything less. You shouldn't either. No one should."

She didn't speak for a long moment. Her gaze drifted down to the space between us, then back up. Something fragile and fierce flickered in her eyes.

"And if I can't give you that?" she whispered.

"Then I'll wait," I said, stepping even closer, "but I won't settle. Not for scraps. Not for silence. And definitely not for just tonight."

Silence stretched between us, heavy and sacred.

Finally, she reached for me.

"Then don't settle," she said softly, placing my hand over her heart. "Because I'm trying. And if you're patient with me, I think I can get there."

My thumb brushed against her collarbone, feeling the quickening of her pulse beneath her skin. "That's all I need to hear."

She exhaled slowly, then leaned in, pressing her forehead to mine.

"I'm scared," she admitted.

"So am I," I whispered back, anchoring her to me with both hands now. "But I'm not going anywhere."

Then she kissed me, not with hesitation, but with trembling truth.

And for the first time, I felt her *choose* me.

Her mouth found mine with a hunger that didn't surprise me so much as it consumed me. This wasn't about slow discovery or tentative touches. It was about connection. Raw and real. A reclaiming of something fragile and new before it could be buried again beneath fear.

The water lapped around us as I pressed her gently against the smooth stone wall of the pool, my hand trailing from her hip to the small of her back. Her fingers dug into my shoulders, her legs parting to pull me closer.

She whispered my name against my lips, and the ardency in her voice made something in me snap.

My control.

My restraint.

All of it.

I lifted her easily, her legs wrapping around my waist, our bodies aligning as if molded for this. And maybe they were.

True mates weren't supposed to exist anymore.

But gods help me, this didn't feel like fiction.

It felt like fate.

Meera's breath hitched as I lifted her higher, her back pressing against the slick stone. Water cascaded in soft rivulets down her skin, pooling where our bodies met. Her thighs tightened around my waist, grounding me in the present moment—one where there was nothing but her. No forest. No thread. No cursed realm with too many eyes.

Just Meera.

My mate.

I kissed her again, this time with no restraint. Her mouth opened under mine, hungry, hot, tasting of want and something dangerously close to surrender. My hands roamed her body like I was memorizing it by touch; over her ribcage, up her sides, cupping the generous curve of her breasts. She gasped into my mouth when my thumbs brushed her nipples, already sensitive from exposure and desire.

"Vareck…" she whispered, arching into my touch.

The sound of her voice—needy, breathless—tore a groan from my throat. I kissed my way down her neck, nipping just beneath her ear where her pulse fluttered like wings. "Say it again," I murmured against her skin.

"Vareck."

I slid a hand between us, cupping the heat between her thighs. Her hips bucked into my hand, a soft moan spilling from her lips as I slid a finger inside her. She was hot, tight, and so damn ready.

"Gods, Meera," I breathed, watching her grind against my palm. "You feel so damn good."

"More," she gasped, fingers digging into my shoulders. "I want more, and I don't want it slow."

I pulled my hand away and lined myself up in one fluid motion. "I can give you more," I growled, voice thick. I angled my hips, grasping my cock in hand to notch it at her entrance. In one hard thrust I pushed inside her, burying myself to the hilt.

Her head fell back, a sound that was half gasp, half curse escaping her lips. She clenched around me, tight and perfect and fucking mine. I hissed, holding still. For a second, I couldn't move. I was too far gone just from the feel of her wrapped around me.

"Fuck me, Vareck," she said, voice ragged.

I set a punishing rhythm, driving into her with a force that sent water splashing around us. Meera met me thrust for thrust, her legs locked around my waist, her nails scoring down my back in open challenge. Her moans turned desperate, wrecked, as I pounded into her, the slap of skin on skin making the water start to wave.

"Harder," she begged, breathless. "Don't hold back."

So I didn't.

I gripped her ass with both hands as I angled my hips just right. She cried out, her whole body trembling as I hit the spot that made her legs quake. "Right there," she choked. "Gods—right there. Please . . ."

"I've got you," I growled, thrusting harder as the telltale flutters of her inner walls began to quicken. "Come for me, Meera."

Within moments, her orgasm ripped through her like a storm, her body clenching tight around me, drawing a snarl from deep in my chest. I followed her over the edge seconds later, burying myself one final time as I spilled inside her, stars bursting behind my eyes.

And everything in me screamed to mark her.

My fangs lengthened, a flash of pain behind my

gums as the beast in me surged forward. My mouth found the spot where her neck met her shoulder—the space where instinct said *here*. My body begged. My soul howled.

She tilted her head back, exposing her throat to me, trusting and wrecked and glowing with the aftermath of pleasure. Her lips were parted, her breath shaky.

I hovered there, teeth grazing skin. Her pulse thundered beneath my tongue.

"Vareck," she whispered, dazed but steady. "Are you going to...?"

My voice was hoarse when I answered, teeth trembling with restraint. "I want to. Every part of me is screaming for it."

She hesitated—just a breath. Barely a shift in her heartbeat.

But I felt it.

And I pulled back.

Not away—never that. But I dragged my lips down her neck instead, slow and deliberate, letting my fangs retract. With a growl of frustration I bit down, not hard enough to break skin, but hard enough to bruise. Hard enough to claim without crossing her line.

Her body jolted, a strangled moan ripping from her throat as I sucked. Her thighs clamped tighter around my waist, her hands fisting in my hair as I slowly pumped into her again.

"Vareck—fuck," she gasped, eyes flying open, pupils blown wide. Her whole body trembled as her second orgasm overtook her, unexpected and raw.

I held her through it, teeth still latched to the new bruise blooming across her neck. Her nails raked my back, her hips twitching with aftershocks.

When I finally pulled back, breathless, I looked down at the mark I'd left; red, angry, and shaped by my need.

Not a bite.

But it was a promise.

"I'll wait," I murmured against her skin, voice low and reverent. "But make no mistake, Meera. That spot is mine."

She turned her head, eyes heavy-lidded and shining with something deeper than lust. "I know," she whispered. "And when I'm ready, you'll be the only one I give it to."

CHAPTER 8

VARECK

My eyes snapped open. The forest was still. Too still.

And in Evorsus, silence was deadly. The usual chitter of animals or brush of the wind was notably absent from where I lay with Meera. After the pool, we'd returned to the clearing and decided to get some rest. Meera fell asleep almost instantly, dragged under by exhaustion, secure in the feeling of my chest pressed against her back. My arm was draped over her waist, and our legs were tangled together.

In another time, another place, it would have been a luxury for me to be able to lay with Meera like this. Since the moment we met, nothing went as planned and it seemed the universe was equally conspiring against us as it was rooting for us.

But this wasn't a vacation. We weren't camping in some tropical forest. We were in the twin hells, and currently the only sound I could pick up was her deep, even breathing and the slow pounding of my own heart.

I listened closely, my fingers fisting in Meera's t-shirt as I pulled her close.

From behind me, a single step made the faintest of sound. Then a second.

They knew we were here.

I inched my face forward, letting my lips ghost over my mate's ear. Meera was curled into me, her brow furrowed in sleep, oblivious to the danger surrounding us.

"Wake up." I spoke as quietly as I could manage, so as not to alert our visitors that I was aware of them.

"Mmmph. Five more minutes," she grumbled.

"Meera," I said, placing firmness in my tone. "Time to wake up."

She groused, moving to sit up. I kept my arm around her waist, pinning her to my side. Meera blinked, the sleep clearing from her features in a second flat. "What are you …"

The words died in her throat as the shadows shifted around us.

They emerged from the trees without a sound.

Dozens of them.

Not the usual forest predators one might imagine, like lions, bears, other apex predators often found on Earth and in Faerie. No, these creatures were tall, spindly things with shifting layers of skin. Dressed in rags and other makeshift materials, they stepped closer. At first, one might think they were faceless. While indentations marked where eyes, a nose, and mouth were present, the features themselves were missing.

The one nearest me stopped and cocked its head, as if regarding me. I slowly sat up, pulling Meera along. That's when it happened.

The molding of a face stretched unnaturally across its surface like melted wax. It shifted to something human. Familiar.

My stomach twisted.

My own face stared back at me, impassive in a way that was unnerving. I shifted to my feet, years of combat training engrained in me. With one hand, I kept Meera glued to the front of my body, and with the other, I reached for one of the swords strapped to my back; Hex Cleaver.

A grin slowly stretched across the creature's face.

"What the freaking fuck is that?" Meera stood instantly. "You know what? Never mind. I don't want to know until they're gone." Her voice was steady, but I could feel the tension radiating off her.

Magic hummed in the air around us as her eyes changed from hazel to an ethereal, glowing green. "Go back to where you came from," she said, pouring persuasion into the order. Enough so that my own legs locked under her magic's pull.

The Nameless paused.

For a beat, I thought it worked.

That for once, I'd make it out of an encounter with them unscathed.

Unfortunately, that was hope talking.

The one in front of us did something I'd never seen before.

It spoke.

"Stand down, cursed king."

"Shit," she whispered, swallowing hard enough I felt it.

"Meera, they're immune," I said. Despite the fear that rattled my psyche, my voice was strong and sure.

"But they're human-ish," she said. "They speak fae. Clearly they can understand.

"Like calls to like, my Queen."

The Nameless were revenants. Fae that had died on Evorsus and the land had chosen to bring them back to a semi-living state in this form. They were single-minded in their desire to hunt and kill, but this one did something so wholly unexpected when he spoke. I didn't have time to think about what it meant, only what I had to do. "I need you to run and hide. The Nameless are flesh-eating parasites. They travel in groups and will devour anything they come across."

"No," she said, fierce as ever. "I'm not leaving you to deal with these things."

"You need to."

"*No*," she argued. I loved that fire about her, even if it drove me fucking insane. At that moment, I didn't have time for the pushback.

"Your persuasion doesn't work. You don't have an elemental power."

"I was raised by redcaps—"

"You're fae. They *eat* fae."

"You're fae too! If it's not safe for me, it's not safe for you," she insisted, pulling herself into a fighting stance.

"I'm not . . ." I said, voice dropping as I struggled to speak. My fury started to rise like smoke from beneath my skin and there was nothing I could do to stop it. My instincts knew the odds were against me. The fury inside me knew we had to protect our mate. Suppression wasn't an option.

She opened her mouth—probably to argue—but two things happened in quick succession.

The uninvited guests stepped forward. The one that spoke reached for Meera. Grime-covered fingers brushed her skin, but before it could do anything more than touch her, I lost it.

My eyes darkened until they were nothing but endless black. My fingers cracked as they elongated, turning into curved, obsidian talons. From my back, twin wings erupted with a sound of tearing fabric, huge, wraith-like and leathery. They ripped clean through the shirt I wore, shredding the material with ease.

My teeth lengthened, my fangs sharp and prominent as the fury surged forward, no longer leashed. My voice dropped, laced with something deeper. Otherworldly.

"Hide."

The word wasn't a request. It was law.

Meera's body jerked as the persuasion took hold. She twisted in my arms, searching for an opening through the horde, then darted for the trees.

My mate bolted to the left toward a small gap in their ranks. Two of the Nameless advanced toward her.

I moved faster.

No hesitation. No mercy.

One swipe of my talons and the first creature dropped, its stolen face peeling away like wet parchment. The second shrieked when I decapitated it with Hex Cleaver, its voice pitched high and broken before giving way to silence.

My chest heaved. In the span of several seconds, I'd taken down two of the assailants, but over a dozen more still remained.

Keeping one eye on the direction Meera fled, I blocked them from following her and descended into bloodlust. The Nameless came at me faster in desperation, too many wearing faces that didn't belong. An innocent child with doe-like eyes. An old man with a curved back, wrinkled and worn. A woman who, if you squinted through the madness, looked eerily similar to Meera.

I didn't. I couldn't.

Instead, I fought like I had been bred for it. Fury wasn't

just an emotion for me. It was a whole other being that was rage incarnate and lived beneath my skin.

My wings slashed through the air, the serrated edges cutting them limb from limb. My talons ripped flesh from bone, and the black shadow of my fury rising cloaked the clearing in shadow. I felt their minds—cold, curious, hungry—and I gave them a single truth to carry back to whatever pit they crawled out from: *She is not yours.*

Not now. Not ever.

I didn't know how long had passed. It could have been seconds. It might have been hours. Time warped and collapsed in on itself as I fell into the battle. And then it was over.

When the last one stood among the bodies of its brethren, it didn't lunge. A sickening feeling twisted in my gut.

The Nameless sidled closer. Slower. More deliberate in its actions than others. They'd attacked blindly when I guarded the path that led to Meera. This one didn't, and that worried me.

Its skin shimmered, face shifting beneath the translucent veil like water struggling to freeze. The dread in my gut expanded as green eyes formed. Ginger locks sprouted from its bald, peeling scalp.

My stomach dropped.

It was her.

I stepped closer without realizing it. That's when I saw the illusion wasn't perfect, only close enough that my mind hesitated, and my fury stayed its wrath.

I focused on the differences.

The hair wasn't quite right. It curled too much in the front. Her eyes were the glowing emerald shade she wore when using magic, but the beauty mark beside her nose was missing. A myriad of freckles stayed camouflaged beneath the dark skies of Evorsus, but if I had to guess, they wouldn't line up with my siren's either.

"Help me."

Everything in me went still.

The beauty mark appeared.

The hair framing her face lost some of its curl.

Those differences dropped away one by one until it was Meera. *My* Meera.

I couldn't strike her. Even when my brain screamed that it wasn't real. That it wasn't her. My body refused to move.

The illusion crept closer.

Its eyes—*her* eyes—held mine, pleading and hollow.

"Help us."

I cocked my head, but the calculation was brief. The small, distant part of me that wondered if something more sinister was at play was instantly silenced when it struck.

Long, jagged fingers plunged into my side, sharp and sudden, knocking me off balance. I staggered, blood seeping out from between my ribs.

"VARECK!"

Her cry cut through everything. The fog. The confusion. The lie.

I looked up.

Meera stood just beyond the trees, her face a mirror of rage and fear.

I saw her. The real her.

"She's ours," the creature said, its voice losing all traces of the ruse it had created, and instead reverting to the cold, lifeless tone of Evorsus.

"She's *mine*," I hissed in response, voice dropping dangerously low as my fury let go of its bloodlust and descended into the ice-cold wrath it wielded so well.

My wings snapped out, catching the Nameless mid-lunge. My talons tore through its illusion, shredding the false skin until the creature shrieked and crumpled into a pile of dismembered limbs at my feet.

Amidst the blood and gore, it still wore her eyes as it died. And the sight of them lifeless sent me reeling.

I stumbled back, fighting the bile rising up my throat.

Silence dropped like a curtain.

"Vareck?" she murmured softly, and I tensed. Was I certain this body was truly hers and not another creature that learned her mannerisms while I was fighting? How sure was I that the real Meera stood before me?

I turned toward her.

She didn't speak. Neither did I.

We just stared at each other; her eyes locked on the blood at my side, mine on the way her hands shook. My fury receded in slow increments, enough for my claws and wings to shrink and vanish into flesh, but the edge of it remained, like heat clinging to the last embers in the hearth.

"You okay?" she asked.

I nodded once, chest still heaving. "Yeah."

"You hesitated."

"I know."

And she didn't say anything else.

She didn't need to.

I took a step forward, the distance between us charged with silent tension.

"How do I know it's really you?" she asked, her voice barely above a whisper.

"Ask me something only I would know," I replied.

Her lips parted, and her breath stuttered.

"How many years did you dream of me?"

"Four. Why did it take you so long to find me?"

A flash of something sparked across her features before she buried it. "I didn't think you were real."

Then she was running, stumbling forward with an urgency that couldn't be denied.

Crack.

Her palm connected with my face.

My head turned with the blow, not from the force—though she'd put some oomph behind it—but from sheer shock.

"What the fuck was that for?"

"You *compelled* me," she seethed. "You stole my will and made me run away like some helpless damsel!"

"I had to." My voice was low. Firm. "You weren't leaving, and—"

"How *dare* you. It was my choice."

"You chose wrong," I snapped back, my own anger rising. "I'm sorry my decision hurt you, but I'm not sorry I did it." Her mouth opened, red cheeks flushing a deeper color that concerned me.

"Why?"

"You were in danger."

"That's not a good enough reason, Vareck."

"It's the only reason I need!" The anger in my voice echoed through the trees.

Meera narrowed her eyes. "This isn't the first time we've been in danger together. And guess what?" She threw her arms out wide, gesturing to our surroundings. "We're in the middle of *hell*. It won't be the last! You didn't compel me to run when we were facing off Irene and her band of thugs. Why now?"

Her eyes roamed over me, stopping on the wound at my side. When she reached for it, I stepped back. "Don't," I growled defensively. Hurt flashed over her features. When Meera backed up a step, then two, I knew I'd fucked up.

"Please don't run," I said softly. "I didn't mean to hurt your feelings."

"You didn't," she replied stiffly, and we both knew she was lying. When I lifted a hand to reach for her, she moved away and held her hands up, palms out. "You don't want to be touched. I won't touch you."

My chest squeezed, but I refrained from lashing out. Enough was enough.

"Do you remember what I told you?"

Meera scoffed. "You've told me a lot of things. You're going to have to be more specific than that."

"About furies. How our blood can curse someone?"

She sniffed once and hummed. "Yes."

"When my fury takes over, if I bleed on you while it's at the surface and it mixes with your blood . . ." I struggled to form the words. To force them from my lips. To think that it could ever happen to her. "The curse takes hold, and you descend into madness."

"Just from blood touching blood? Even if you didn't mean to?" she asked warily, eyeing my wound with tight concern.

"Even then. There is no intent needed for the outcome."

"I feel like I should have known about this before we attempted a blood oath."

"I had my fury locked down tight and knew there was no danger to you."

Meera pursed her lips. "Your eyes are blue right now, so your fury isn't in control."

I nodded. "But it's not far from the surface right now either. Sensing my mate is in danger has it on edge. I don't want to risk you touching it and something happening."

Meera rolled her bottom lip between her teeth before biting into the soft pink flesh. "That's why you didn't want me here during the fight?"

I inclined my head again. "There isn't a single part of me that would ever purposely injure you, but if we slipped just once and our blood came into contact with yours . . ." I shook my head. "I couldn't risk it. I couldn't risk *you*."

Meera softened a fraction. "I understand you don't want to hurt me, but compulsion isn't the answer. Taking my free will away—taking my *choice* away—is not acceptable. What I do in my life is not your call to make, and that includes when we're in danger."

"If something happened to you because of me, I wouldn't be able to live with myself. Not after watching . . ." I broke off as my voice began to crack, unable to finish.

Meera quirked her brow. "There's more to this than you're admitting. Something you aren't telling me. Have you accidentally hurt someone before?" Her voice was soft. Empathetic now.

I shook my head and ran a hand through the rough strands to pull them away from my face. "No, but my mother did."

She squinted at me for a suspended second. Then another. Too quickly understanding washed over her features and her lips parted as she breathed in harshly. "Your . . . father?"

I dipped my chin. "They were caught in a situation not so dissimilar to this one. They were traveling between realms and were caught off guard by assailants. There was a fight, and they both ended up bloodied by the end of it. My father startled my mother by putting his hand on her shoulder when it was over. She stabbed him before she realized who it was." I tapped the center of my chest. "Right here. Her claws went straight through him. Missed his heart by a millimeter."

Meera covered her mouth with her fingers. "Oh my god."

"No one knows this. While my father physically recovered, that was the day he was cursed. The downward spiral into madness followed soon after."

"How old were you?"

I smiled bitterly. "A year old." Young enough that I didn't remember the man he was before the incident. It was both a blessing and a curse on its own.

"You were just a baby," Meera murmured. Her eyes watered with sympathy for me, and my chest tightened uncomfortably.

"You don't need to feel bad for me," I said, clearing my throat to push down emotion. "I knew my father as the mad king, nothing more, nothing less. It was my mother, brother, and sister that held out hope for him. For a cure. They loved him, even when he killed them."

Her lips parted. The watery sheen in her eyes overflowed. Silent tears fell down her cheeks. "That's heartbreaking. I don't know what to say."

I shrugged. "He might have been good once. I wouldn't know. What I do know is that they protected him when they shouldn't have. When he was too far gone. I was angry with all of them for a long time after they died because of it. I couldn't understand why they wouldn't act against him when he was so obviously insane." I stared at nothing, my vision drifting to a blurred background, seeing a time that came and went decades ago. "I think I understand their mindset now, for what it's worth. Not that it saved any of them in the end."

Meera wiped at her tears with the back of her hand and palm.

"I get it, Vareck. I really, truly do. What you saw—*gods*—what you experienced would be enough to create an immense fear and an immeasurable void in anyone, no matter who they are. I'm sorry you had to go through that, and I'm happy you told me because it helps me understand, but we need to set one thing straight right now." Meera crossed her arms and lifted her chin. "You can't compel me, even to 'save' me. What if you had died and I couldn't break through your persuasion? What if I couldn't help you? Did you think about that?"

My throat closed in on itself. *Yes,* I wanted to tell her. *I think about it every fucking second we're in this godsforsaken realm. That something will happen to me and I won't be there to protect you.*

But that's not what she wanted to hear, and I wasn't going to lie to her.

"Yes, I have thought about it," I said finally, the words heavy with my quiet truth. "But when faced with two impossible choices, I asked myself which one I could live with. Your anger at being compelled and my possible death, or you losing your mind? It's not even a question. I would pick your sanity every single time."

Meera looked away, her jaw clenched. "It's not your choice to make. That's the point I'm getting at."

"I know," I admitted, voice low. "But you didn't understand the consequences yet. I should have told you sooner. I'm sorry I didn't, and that I took your will from you because of it."

"You already said you're not sorry you did it. Which one is it?"

"Both. I'm not trying to own your decisions, Meera. But

I *am* trying to keep you alive long enough to be mad at me for them."

"That's not fair," she whispered, finally meeting my gaze. "You think it's noble, what you're doing. Sacrificing yourself to protect me. But it's selfish."

I blinked, taken aback. "Selfish?"

"You don't get to shoulder the world and then die on that hill without considering what it would do to the people left behind," she snapped. Her voice cracked at the end, revealing the rawness beneath the anger. "To me."

I exhaled slowly. "You're right."

She tilted her head. "What?"

"You're right," I repeated, a bit louder. "What was that phrase you told me about? I've spent so long having to carry my own fridge, I forgot how to let someone carry it with me."

Meera blinked rapidly, emotions flashing across her face too fast to catch. She almost smiled.

"I hate that you compelled me," she whispered.

"I know."

"I understand your reasoning, but it's not enough for me to tell you it was okay. Don't do it again."

I lowered my head in a partial agreement. "Only if you promise not to throw yourself in front of the next pack of flesh-eating revenants we meet."

She glanced at my side, seeing it had healed. "I make no promises."

I groaned, starting to take the remains of the shredded shirt off my body. "Gods help me."

"I'm pretty sure we're beyond their help." She jerked her chin toward the forest edge. "We should go. That fight probably drew attention. You can get cleaned up at the pool before we head out."

I nodded. "You want to lead, or should I?"

She glanced at the trees, then back at me with a smirk. "You're the one who shredded your shirt mid-rampage. Pretty sure if anyone sees us coming, they'll assume you're the monster and I'm your hostage."

I chuckled, the sound dry but real. "Fine. I'll lead."

With blood on my hands and her fire at my back, we walked into the dark like it was ours to claim.

CHAPTER 9

MEERA

The deeper we went into Evorsus, the less creepy it became.

Suspiciously so.

We stopped at the tree line, where the thread dipped into a hollow carved out within the forest. An entire village nestled in a natural landscape, like some hidden grove untouched by time or horror.

It was adorable. That was the problem.

Pastel domes rose like confections, their glassy surfaces veined with gold. Glowing vines curled over them like ribbons on a gift. Lanterns bobbed above cobbled paths, casting soft, pulsing light that hummed at the edge of hearing.

It was so out of place in this realm, and I didn't trust it for a second.

"This feels like a trap," I muttered, crouching behind a twisted tree trunk.

"It is," Vareck said, eyes sweeping the scene. "They just want you to think it isn't."

Then there were the creatures.

Round and soft, maybe three feet tall, with oversized

eyes that shimmered like sapphires, and fur in pastel hues. Their ears were huge, perky like a desert fox, and they chirped as they moved with the frantic glee of toddlers after birthday cake.

"Have you ever come across them before?" He shook his head. "Compared to the Nameless, this entire place is like a bedtime story."

Vareck's voice dropped to a harsh whisper. "Which means we're in the kind of nightmare that waits until the lights go out."

"Probably," I agreed, "but it's Evorsus. When do the lights go out?"

"We shouldn't stick around to find out."

Except the golden thread led into that village. Sadie's thread.

One of the creatures toddled past us, dragging a basket of glittering fruit. Another floated overhead on a petal-shaped glider, waving at a neighbor carving a flute from a mushroom stalk.

Everything about the village screamed too cute, too perfect. My nerves were shot just being close to it.

I looked at the thread. It shimmered like it knew I was stalling, pulsing in time with my heartbeat. "That's Sadie's thread," I said quietly. "I don't care how cute they are. I'm going in."

"You're not going alone," Vareck said without hesitation.

"I wasn't asking permission."

His jaw flexed. "We do this together, or not at all."

I stared at him. This wasn't ego. It was armor. His way of protecting me.

"Fine," I said. "Together."

He nodded once, and we moved, quietly and carefully,

toward the village that looked like a dream, but there was no hiding the sinister undertones that permeated the air.

The moment we crossed the invisible threshold, the atmosphere changed. It turned warm and sugary, almost intoxicating. Faint hints of fruit and flowers, spun sugar and summer wind danced at the edge of my memories. The pastel creatures didn't spare us a glance. Either they didn't care, or we'd just stepped into the softest trap ever laid.

We stayed in the shadows, weaving between curved walls and glittering plants. I ducked behind a citrusy bush that smelled like pineapple and oranges fused together and waited, holding my breath, as another fuzzy local bounced past.

"This is insane," Vareck hissed behind me, his voice barely audible.

"Not the first time you've said that," I whispered back.

"Also not the first time I've been right."

I shot him a look over my shoulder. "You didn't have to come."

"I did, actually. Because if I let you go alone into a glowing goblin village full of suspiciously helpful miniature teddy bears, and something happens to you, I'd have to level the whole realm. And I'm really trying not to do that today."

A smirk I couldn't suppress made its way to my lips. "So this is you being restrained?"

"Terrifying, isn't it?"

Gods help me, I almost laughed. We were in danger, undoubtedly, and yet Vareck was flirting with me. I found my temperature rising at the easy banter between us despite everything.

A tiny creature padded by us on feet shaped like puff-balls, humming a tune that sounded suspiciously like a lullaby. It pulled me back to the situation at hand. It paused, turned its massive eyes toward us, blinked slowly . . . and kept going.

I held my breath until it was out of sight, then muttered, "Okay, I'm officially freaked out."

"You should be. That thing looked at you like it's already seen your obituary."

"Well, it better know I bite."

"I have a feeling they do too."

I shook my head and crept around the edge of what looked like a bakery. Sweet spice drifted from inside. "Apparently, Evorsus has a sense of humor."

"I think it's got a god complex and no off-switch."

"That's an apt description too."

We ducked low, slipping behind a string of glowing mushroom lanterns. My hand brushed his as I steadied myself, and for a second, he didn't pull away.

"You really think she's here?" he asked, glancing at the surrounding structures while looking for any hostile movement. "It's not just her thread going through this place? We could go around the village."

"I know she's here. I can feel it."

He nodded once, and I caught the flicker of something beneath his expression. Not doubt, exactly. *Worry.*

"She might be your sister," he said after a beat. "Just don't forget I have a claim on you too."

That made me pause. Not because I was going to argue it, but because I was his mate. There was no denying it.

"I won't forget," I said. "But I can't choose you over her."

"I'm not asking you to," he replied. "Just . . . don't forget what I'm willing to do for you."

I swallowed the tightness in my throat. "Vareck, I don't need a savior."

"No," he said, scanning the path ahead, "you need someone who'll follow you straight into the trap anyway."

Despite everything, I smiled. "Then I guess I picked the right guy."

"That you did."

My chest tightened at the sentiment, but I didn't voice it.

We moved forward again, quieter now, watching as more creatures gathered around what looked like a garden party. A few were playing what resembled musical chairs, and another one was spinning in slow, dreamy circles as flower petals fell from the sky like confetti.

"They really are kind of cute," I mused.

"Need I remind you this realm excels at illusions. Those petals are likely venomous. Keep going."

It was a worthy reminder, and it was easy to see how quickly this place could make you feel safe. Cute was a disarming aesthetic. I crouched again near a softly glowing bush, one hand on the thread that vibrated softly in my grip.

"We're close," I murmured.

"Good," he said, eyes narrowing. "Let's get her and get out of this candy-coated nightmare."

Not much further. Past a fountain that burbled liquid gold. Past a building shaped like a teapot. Past a patch of glowing cabbages tended by a trio of creatures humming in harmony. Every corner looked like a cartoon dream. Every moment felt like a trap.

And then I saw her.

My heart stopped.

She was sitting on a throne-like chair made of twisted

vines and silk pillows, a drink in one hand and an oversized sunhat perched on her head. Around her, the creatures bustled and preened—fanning her with big heart-shaped leaves, painting her nails, offering trays of sparkling fruit.

"Sadie?" I breathed in disbelief.

She didn't hear me. Not yet.

But someone else did.

"Vareck?"

"Damon?" Vareck said, his voice laced with equal parts confusion and dread.

A man stepped out from behind Sadie's chair. One that I recognized. Beside my sister he appeared taller, more intimidating. Still beautiful in that terrifying, immortal sort of way that suggested he'd already gone through the transition. He had a glass in hand filled with something that looked like wine. His glass was half full, his frown half-formed.

The Crown Prince of Faerie gave us a slow, wicked smile. "Well, this just got interesting."

CHAPTER 10

MEERA

"What in the actual . . .?" I said mostly to myself, stumbling toward her makeshift throne. "Sadie! Why are they fanning you? Why is the prince here?"

My sister snapped to attention, her warm brown eyes lighting up, and without a word, she dropped the glass in hand and ran toward me, knocking Damon aside. We collided in a bone-crunching hug that felt more like a lifeline than a greeting.

"Oh my god, Meera!" Her voice shook against my shoulder. "I tried to find you. I thought you were kidnapped."

"I was," I said into her hair. "You, on the other hand, look like you were tossed into a resort for Care Bears and have been getting the royal treatment."

She pulled back, eyes bright and fierce. "After you vanished the night you apparently nabbed this one"—she angled her head toward Damon, who stood quietly—"I tried finding you. When I couldn't, I tracked down Lou. Cornered him at the Witching Hour. He told me the fae king took you."

"I heard, and he did. Kind of. It's a long story. And after

you disappeared, Mom and Dad hired Lou, and he tracked me down and tried to hire me to find you."

Red flashed through Sadie's eyes. "The fuck?"

"I think we should start from the beginning," Vareck interjected, reminding us both that we were not alone. His tone was calm, collected—everything Sadie and I were not. He looked at his nephew, dipping his chin once. "Good to see you both in one piece."

My sister pulled back, narrowing her gaze on Vareck. "Wait, who are you?"

I stepped between them before he could say something that would make her want to punch him. "He's, um . . . my fated mate."

Sadie blinked. "Excuse me?"

"Yeah, so apparently the curse is weakening or something because you remember that guy I was dreaming about . . ." I lowered my voice and widened my eyes to give Sadie the hint.

"Yeah, and?"

"Well," I jutted my chin toward Vareck. "He's real. This is him."

Sadie blanched. "No way."

"Yes way."

She slapped a hand over her mouth. "Okay, but you were kidnapped by the fae king. So where does this guy play into—" She stopped short, the pieces coming together in her expression. "Ooooh shit. *You're* King Vareck?"

He inclined his head once, calm and unapologetic. "I am."

Her eyes snapped back to me, and she muttered not so quietly, "And he's your fated mate?"

"Erm. Sort of. Yes." I cleared my throat and winced. Yeah, it was a tad painful to hear even to my own ears.

Vareck's jaw tightened. He said nothing, but the air around him shifted; quieter, colder. Not angry. Just . . . distant. Like he was pulling the pieces of himself back. Away from me. I sighed. I needed to do better at this.

Sadie didn't seem to notice. She stared between us, frowning. "So let me get this straight. You've been off playing royal mate with the freaking king of Faerie while I've been stuck in a nightmare dimension with knockoff Ewoks?"

Damon sighed and rolled his eyes. "This keeps getting better."

"It wasn't a vacation," I muttered defensively, glancing at Damon with an apologetic look. "We've been attacked multiple times. After I was taken from my apartment, I fell out of a castle window. I got kidnapped by some asshole brownies at the castle and hauled off in a freezing wagon. Well, one asshole. The brother was mostly going along with what his bitchy sister wanted. Then Lou's cousin tried to force me into prostitution, then his familiar knocked over a bottle of pixie dust, and let me tell you, Atlas was right. That stuff's no joke."

"You got kidnapped by brownies? Why didn't you use persuasion?" She raised a brow.

"There were . . . circumstances preventing me from being able to. That changed later. I have my powers back now."

"You have them *back*?" she repeated slowly, then narrowed her eyes and pursed her lips, assessing Vareck. "So this is all your fault."

Vareck sighed. "I don't have to explain myself to you."

"That's not really helping your case," Sadie snapped.

"Wasn't trying to make one," he said, voice steady.

"Okay," I cut in, rubbing the bridge of my nose. "Let's

not do this. There's a lot to unpack, and none of it's going to get better if we turn on each other."

Sadie crossed her arms. "Fine. But I'm still mad."

"Welcome to the club," I said, then waved a hand. "Now go on. Tell me about Lou. Portal. These weird bears."

She nodded. "Right. I tracked down Lou at the Witching Hour, cornered him. He told me you were with the fae king, and I was about to knock his teeth out when Amelia dragged me away. She asked me to grab something from the back of the bar before I left to chase more leads. Next thing I know there's a portal in front of me and she's gabbing some bullshit about playing the long game."

"Guessing we went through the same portal, then," I mumbled.

Sadie cocked an eyebrow. "One minute I'm reaching for a light switch, the next—poof. I'm landing flat on my ass in the middle of a cave."

"That's where I found her," Damon said, stepping into the circle with a dry look. "Or she found me, I suppose."

"Wait, how are you here?" I asked, and Sadie groaned.

"I would very much like to know that answer as well," Vareck chimed in.

"I figured you already knew, seeing as you are the reason I am here," Damon answered coldly, ignoring his uncle altogether.

"I deserve that," I said softly, nodding. "For what it's worth, after I handed you over to Lou, my intent was to track you back down. People aren't property. I wasn't okay with what happened."

He scoffed but decided to answer my initial question, and maybe not for my benefit, but to inform Vareck. I had a feeling my sister had heard the story more than once considering she mumbled in a familiar tone she had when she was annoyed. "Not long after you left, your man Lou knocked me out. The witch made a speech about the fact I was bait and that I shouldn't take it personally, though I can't imagine how anyone wouldn't take it personally when they were kidnapped and then shoved through a portal into Eversus."

"I'm really sorry, Damon. There's nothing I can say that justifies it, but I really am sorry." He inhaled sharply, then nodded. It wasn't forgiveness, but it was something. I turned to my sister. "And you; are you okay?"

"I'm in a fucked up Wonderland. Why wouldn't I be okay?" She laughed lightly, barely hiding the strain in her voice. "I landed in a cave with this one," she jerked her thumb toward Damon, "who scared the shit out of me, and it's been a fucking treat ever since."

"Here we go again." Damon leaned casually against the wall and crossed his arms. "You burst out of a portal through the ceiling without warning and I'm the one that scared you?"

"You were shirtless and standing in the shadows *like a creeper*," she shot back at him, wrinkling her nose. "What did you expect?"

"For the last time, I was shirtless because that hell realm is *hot*. As for the rest, I expected you not to throw a rock at my head when I offered to help you stand up."

"You startled me!"

"You asked where you were, and I answered, and politely offered my hand while you were laid out on the ground. Sorry for being a gentleman."

They glared at each other.

"Okay. . ." I drawled, feeling the tension between them. "What happened then?"

Damon raised his brows, glaring at Sadie. "Yeah, Sadie, what happened then?"

"Look, we would've sat in that cave for gods know how long if we did what you wanted—"

"'That cave' was shelter, and I was doing the smart thing and not wandering around Eversus like I was on a goddamn vacation."

"I wasn't wandering," she snapped. "I was looking for a way out. We weren't going to find one playing cave trolls."

"If you would have listened to a word I said, you'd know there was no way out of Eversus, but instead, you spent a solid hour shouting at the ceiling before declaring it a dead end, scribbling in the sand, and then storming off into the desert."

"I was yelling at Amelia!"

"Right. Because obviously she can hear you from *another realm*. My mistake! Who knew interdimensional communication was possible simply by yelling through a portal. Bravo! What a discovery." He clapped mockingly, his voice dripping with sarcasm.

"All right, gods." I held my hands up to stop the arguing. "You left the cave. Obviously. Did you go back?"

Damon jabbed a thumb at Sadie. "She wandered too far. We couldn't get back. I warned her—"

"In my defense," Sadie interrupted, "the terrain started to shift. Damon said something about the landscape changing, but he explained it like an idiot."

Damon's hands flew into the air. "How else do I explain it? In the *twin* hells"—he held up two fingers—" that means two; okay? The *twin* landscapes"—he gestured grandly to the village around us—"change and flip at random. With magic." He flailed his hands. "Poof."

"In my continued defense," Sadie said, folding her arms

in classic sibling fashion, "I thought you were dehydrated and hallucinating."

Damon's eye twitched, and I almost smirked. "And now we're here. We lost the cave and the consistent shelter. Lost the stream of food that damn witch had the decency to toss down. Was punched and kicked when I grabbed her during the shift so she wouldn't get hurt. Got prodded and pushed by the baby bear army. I said Evorsus was dangerous, and maybe we should be calm and observe what they wanted from us. She decided to start a revolution."

"I didn't start a revolution," Sadie argued. "They just stopped shoving me when I shoved back. Then they started fanning me. I wasn't gonna tell them 'no, don't be nice to me.'"

"You conquered them?" I said slowly. Because of course my sister would shove back and prove herself to be the strongest. There was no world in which Sadie took that kind of crap from anyone. Not even in hell.

"I wouldn't say conquered."

Damon snorted. "She made them braid her hair and bring her drinks."

Sadie shrugged. "They offered. I said yes. You're just mad they don't like you."

Vareck, who'd been silent through most of this exchange, finally spoke. "How long have you been playing queen?"

"Hard to tell," Sadie replied, then looked at Damon. "We've had bedtime tea, what, maybe three or four times?"

Damon nodded. "Three."

"Bedtime tea?" Vareck repeated.

"There's no sun here, just a moon and a half, so I'm guessing three days. They bring us bedtime tea and tuck me in."

"They bring her tea. I won't drink it," Damon corrected.

"You rearranged the seating. Bold move," came a familiar voice, dry and unmistakably feline.

I turned, and my stomach dipped.

"Corvo?" I breathed. "How are you here?"

Vareck's shoulders tensed beside me. "Of course it's you."

Sadie blinked, glancing between us and the sleek, smoky-black and silver feline who appeared on the 'throne' Sadie had vacated. The pastel creatures began fanning him without hesitation, one going so far as to attempt hand-feeding him some sort of sparkly fruit.

Sadie eyed him warily. "Who are you?"

Damon straightened. "Oh great. The talking cat is here. We're saved." There was no mistaking the equally dry quality in his voice.

Corvo's tail flicked in annoyance, presumably at Damon's tone.

"That's Corvo," I murmured. "He's . . . it's complicated."

"I'm right here, Meera," Corvo said, sniffing the offered fruit in disgust and turning away to show his asshole to the dejected pastel teddy bear. "Vareck's right, you know. 'Complicated' doesn't sound like a compliment."

I rubbed my temples. "Corvo, seriously. What are you doing here?"

"Checking in." Corvo sighed like we were all disturbing him. "This was my realm. Back when I was a demon. God. Demongod. You get me? Before the cat thing."

"Wait, wait . . ." I stared at him, holding my hands out in a pause gesture. "So all that weird stuff you said before about being a god was actually true?"

"Yes, Meera," he said dryly. "I occasionally tell the truth. Usually when it's inconvenient."

Sadie looked from me to the cat. "Okay, you're going to need to explain that."

"I'd love to," Corvo said, watching the little bear creatures toddle up to Sadie with a platter and goblet. They chittered and made a motion of tapping their mouths with their paws. "But you've got a more pressing issue."

"Which is?" Sadie asked, taking the wine and a piece of sweet bread before patting the bear on its head in thanks. They gestured the same to Damon and he took a piece of shiny fruit.

"They're fattening you up so they can eat you."

The words dropped like a stone in water.

"Come again?" Sadie spluttered. As her drink slipped from her fingers, Damon caught it, then smiled big at the tiny hell bears.

"They're not worshiping you," Corvo clarified, curling his tail around his paws. "They're seasoning you."

Vareck swore. "You want to maybe lead with that next time?"

"Can you command them to like, *not* eat us maybe?" I asked, scrubbing my hands down my face.

"They don't listen to me anymore. I'm a cat, remember?"

"You said this was your realm," Damon growled. "Can't you control them?"

"I used to," Corvo replied. "Then the whole getting-cursed-into-an-adorable-form thing happened, and my loyal minions turned me into their house pet."

"Lovely," I muttered. "What now?"

Corvo stretched. "Well, if you don't want to be dinner, I suppose I could go fetch some help."

"Drayden," Vareck said instantly. "Find him or Kaia. Anyone who can get a witch to open a portal."

"Wait," I said. "What if they try to eat us while you're gone?"

"Don't let them eat you." Corvo paused, cocking his head. "I mean, I thought that went without saying. Kinda shocking you made it this far to be honest."

Damon frowned. "I think what we all want to know is when they consider us 'ready.'"

Corvo tapped his chin. "Could be an hour. Could be a few days. Could be now. Time is weird here." Corvo licked his paw and pointed it at Sadie. "That one's kinda scrawny, meaty for sure, but you know meat is better with marbling, so I imagine it'll be longer for her."

"Then hurry," Vareck growled.

Corvo looked over his shoulder and purred. "What's the magic word?"

Vareck gritted his teeth. "Please."

Corvo smirked. "And?"

Vareck looked like he'd rather stab himself than say it. "Thank you."

Sadie snorted. I pressed a hand over my mouth to stifle my laugh. Damon just shook his head, muttering something about never trusting cats.

Corvo smiled, infuriatingly smug. "There it is. Back soon."

And with that, he vanished into the shadows, leaving us behind in the pastel village of doom, surrounded by smiling creatures who were starting to look far too interested in our nutritional value.

Sadie stared at the now-empty throne. "We need a plan in the meantime."

"Agreed," I muttered. "Let's just hope Corvo brings back someone who doesn't want to turn us into a stew."

CHAPTER 11

CORVO

I popped into Faerie mid-argument. The faint scent of blood greeted me like an old friend. Drayden stood near the dungeon wall, arms folded and scowling. Cadoc, Meera's serial killer brother, loomed nearby, calm as ever despite the blood on his knuckles. *Or maybe it was because of?* Who knew? Kaia stood off to the side with her arms crossed, the picture of judgment. As usual.

The only one who looked as done with their talking as me was the bound leprechaun who'd seen better days.

"Finally," Drayden muttered. "The damn cat's here."

"Language," I said, tail flicking irritably.

Cadoc frowned. "You give a shit about the word damn?"

Kaia rolled her eyes. "It's the word *cat* that he takes issue with."

I pointed at her with a paw. "That one. I'm a god. Act like it, peasants."

Both Drayden and Kaia groaned. Cadoc simply appeared confused.

I could see the relation to Meera. Over and over I said I was a god, and still the confusion. Alaska in the winter was brighter than the two of them, but perhaps he also gave good pets.

Kaia shook her head, refocusing on the surly asshole and his mini-me. "Pretty sure Vareck said *not* to torture him."

Drayden arched a brow. "I didn't."

~~Cadoc~~ Drayden Jr. shrugged. "No one said anything to me."

Lou groaned softly, head lolling against the cold stone. His lip was split, and he looked a sickly shade of white. Despite his haggard, and frankly, repulsive appearance, he stared at me with surprising clarity. Had to give it to the guy; he was a survivor. Few walked away from a visit with Drayden. And even if Junior was the one delivering the blow, we all knew who was in charge in the dungeons.

Sadly, it was not me. There would be more tuna and orgies if it was.

"Gotta say," I added dryly, "for someone who looks like a meat sack that lost a bar fight, he's still got better posture than most of the fae court." Namely because his head wasn't bowed in reverence at the sight of Vareck or Kaia, let alone Drayden. Brown nosing wasn't good for the spine.

Drayden ignored me.

Kaia didn't. "Where have you been? Vareck and Meera went missing at the Witching Hour."

"Solving your problems, apparently." I licked my paw then nibbled at my toe beans, trying to scratch the itch that never went away. "I need a portal. Preferably one that leads directly to Evorsus."

"Why would you need a portal to the twin hells?" Kaia blinked. "You can go there whenever—" She broke off, catching on faster than the other two did. Apart from that leprechaun.

"I take it," Lucian paused to catch his breath, "the king and his lass found themselves in a *situation?*" He grunted while he sat up, wrists tied behind his back and leaned against the wall. A cough rattled through him and the green of his eyes glowed faintly with power despite the dungeon's natural affinity for neutralizing magic. I sensed something in him. Something different, like Meera, but not the same.

. . . something *old.*

"Yes," I said flatly, not relaying my observations for the peasants present. If they couldn't sense a predator in their midst, it wasn't my job to protect them. It's not like any of these assholes fed me second-dinner when I asked. "And if I wanted to yeet them into the void, I'd do it myself, but I'd prefer not to traumatize the entire court by returning them in pieces. So they need a portal. A real one. Anchored by a witch."

"Wait." Drayden turned, frowning. "Vareck and his dream girl are in Evorsus?"

"And Damon," I added. "And the redcap woman. Her sister. Family get together." That I wasn't invited to, rudely. As a matter of fact, I showed up and they pretty much asked me to leave. I questioned why I should help them, but my life was tied to V's, therefore it was non-negotiable. And his was now tied to the reckless ginger. Alas, I liked her, so I supposed it could be worse.

Kaia's face blanched. "You left our king and the crown prince in Evorsus? *Alone?*" Her voice was a whisper, but it might as well have been a shout. My ears flattened on instinct. "What the actual fuck, Corvo?"

"I didn't *leave* them," I snapped. "I came to get them help, obviously. They're the ones that went through a portal to begin with and now my realm is in feeding mode. Which means if you three don't figure out the portal situation, I'll be attending a banquet I very much don't want to host."

"They're going to be eaten. Great," Kaia said with a flat affect and purple fire burning in her eyes.

"Can't he just pyroport there?" Lucian said with a nod toward Drayden. "That's what he did from Warwick."

Drayden's jaw tensed. "I can't go between realms."

Kaia pinched the bridge of her nose between her forefinger and thumb and began to pace. "Fuck. Fuck. Fuckity. Fuck."

Cadoc turned to Lucian, kneeling down and grabbing a fistful of his shirt. "You know everyone. Who can open a portal to Evorsus?"

He coughed, wincing. "You need someone who knows how to tap into the ley lines. Someone who's touched them before and isn't afraid to bleed for it."

Kaia narrowed her eyes. "Who?"

Lucian looked past her, locking eyes with me. "You know who."

My tail lashed once as though it were a whip, punctuating the gravity of my response. "No."

"Yes."

Kaia turned slowly to me. "Who is he talking about?"

I didn't answer.

Drayden's voice dropped. "Corvo."

"She's the last person we should be calling on," I muttered.

"My sisters are stuck in a hell realm," ~~Cadoc~~ Drayden Jr. ground out. "Who. Is. It?"

I sighed, dramatic and long-suffering. "Amelia."

Drayden's brow furrowed. "Who?"

"She didn't seem *that* powerful when I met her," Kaia said, ignoring him.

Lucian rasped, spitting a glob of blood onto the dungeon floor. "She's a chameleon. Looks are deceiving. You want a portal to a hell realm? She's the one I'd ask, just be prepared to pay the price—and I'm not talking coin."

I closed my eyes, tail flicking back and forth as I played out options in my mind, but I was coming up short. Of course it had to be her.

It always was.

Kaia stepped forward. "Corvo, you should return to Vareck. Help them stay alive. Amelia runs the Witching Hour. She's easy enough to find."

"Careful, Beauty," Lucian said, his green eyes glowing faintly as he looked at Kaia, but she scowled. "She cares for no one in this realm or the next, you understand? She isn't your friend, she doesn't care about the kingdom, and if you're coming to her for something this big, she knows you have no other options. She likes it that way."

Kaia pressed her lips together. "Noted. Drayden and I will go and see what her price is. Corvo? Go help them."

"Well, this is going to go to shit," I grumbled, already turning. "Tweedledee and Tweedledum are being sent to bargain with a devil while I try to stop my subjects from eating my familiar. Fucking great."

I vanished before Kaia could utter another word.

Next stop: the witch I loathed most.

CHAPTER 12

VARECK

The food was excellent.

Spiced fruit skewers, honeyed bread, roasted nuts with sweet glaze, and drinks that left a faint aftertaste of vanilla and citrus. These creatures, whatever they were, had gone all out.

But it wasn't hospitality.

Now that we knew the truth—that this wasn't generosity but preparation—it tasted like poison.

Sadie poked at a pastel dumpling with the edge of a dagger she'd acquired somewhere between hugging Meera and threatening to gut one of the fuzzballs who got too close. "They're really committing to the whole pre-sacrifice pampering thing, huh?"

"Nothing says 'tenderize the meat' like a foot massage and fresh fruit," Meera muttered.

I kept my voice low. "We can't wait around for Corvo to bring us a portal. We need to come up with an escape plan. "

"He'll be back, and we'll be okay," Meera said, ever the

optimist. I loved that about her, but I'd seen too much to believe it myself.

"Corvo will find Drayden, or Kaia, or both of them. You're the king of Faerie. They won't just leave you here to die," my nephew muttered.

I exhaled slowly. "And what if they're too late?" I asked, turning to Damon, who had planted himself furthest from the group, arms crossed and mouth drawn tight. "Corvo admitted he has no idea when these things will decide we're ready to be dinner. You think they'll give us a second round of appetizers before turning us into the entrée?"

He didn't flinch. "I think running off into the magical murder realm with no portal and no exit point is a great way to end up dead. We should wait. If they try anything, *then* we run."

"Wait until their teeth are already sinking in for a taste?" Sadie arched her brow, flicking the end of her dagger toward Damon. "Solid plan, princeling."

"You've got a better one?" he shot back. "Because last I checked, you leaving the cave is the reason we're about to become dinner for the baby murder bears. If we hadn't left the cave, then we would all be there right now and safer than we currently are."

"No one made you follow me," Sadie snapped back, which inevitably devolved into bickering, as was the norm between Meera's sister and my nephew, I was coming to realize.

If Sadie was fire, Damon was the oxygen that fed her.

"I know there was no notice in Eversus when the shift occurred, but is there any way to tell when the landscape is going to start shifting while in Evorsus?" Meera asked quietly, ignoring them.

"Not until right before it happens," I replied. "There's

also no telling what will be on the other side of this if it shifts back to Eversus. The carnivorous bear creatures might be the least of our problems."

Her lips twisted. "Evorsus is eternal night. Eversus is eternal day. Do these things ever sleep?"

"I haven't seen a single one close their eyes," Damon answered, mid-argument with Sadie.

"Maybe not sleep, per se, but they do rest," the redcap countered. "There are times they get kinda slow, and their glowy little lanterns dim down. Then they curl up on us like cats. It's one big cuddle pile."

Meera frowned. "It'll be hard to make an escape with them literally on top of us, assuming we have that long."

"There's also the fact that I'm pretty sure they don't sleep, they just watch us," Damon pointed out.

"How do you know that?" Sadie asked.

"Unlike you, I can't fall asleep just anywhere surrounded by anything. They might be cute, but I never trusted them."

"So you pretended to sleep?" Sadie said. "No wonder you're such a dick. This is exactly why I sleep when I get a chance. You never know when the next one will be."

And once again, the bickering continued.

We let them argue. It seemed to soothe them somehow. Or maybe it just helped them ignore the threat slowly encircling us like a morning fog. Inescapable.

"They're not going to stop," I muttered to Meera.

"I give it ten more minutes till it turns violent," she whispered back, not looking up from her half-eaten food. "Five if Sadie remembers she still has that second dagger in her boot."

"We need to get moving before then."

"Agreed."

Sadie and Damon were now arguing about which of them would be a more appealing entrée. Sadie claimed she was too stringy to be worth the trouble, citing Corvo as her source; Damon insisted she had *main course energy*. I tuned them out.

"We go when they go into rest mode," Meera said quietly, her eyes scanning the perimeter. "When the lanterns dim."

I nodded. "How long do you think we have?"

"Hard to tell," Meera murmured as she looked past me. "But the ones in that corner are already starting to flicker."

I followed her gaze. Sure enough, the glow from a cluster of lanterns near the far huts pulsed slower than the rest.

"We'll need supplies," I said. "More of them. We're almost out of water and rations are low. We should grab whatever we can carry without drawing attention. Is everyone armed?"

Meera gave a slight nod. "Sadie's got a couple daggers and her bracers that summon axes, if that still works here. My magic still works, so hopefully hers does too. I don't know about Damon. I have what I grabbed from the safe house. What about you?" Her eyes flicked to the swords I'd been wearing since we left Warwick. "Anything else besides those?"

I tapped the hilt of a blade still strapped to my back. "I only have Wyrd Reaper and Hex Cleaver."

Meera arched her brow. "You named your swords?"

I shook my head. "They were named well before my time. I simply use their names in respect to the blades."

Meera nodded. "Hex Cleaver. I take it that one cuts

through magic?" I tipped my chin in answer. "What about Wyrd Reaper? I haven't heard of that one before. I'm guessing it doesn't cut you down with some harsh words." Her lips curled in a half-smile at the joke, but I couldn't bring myself to share it. Not with the pressure we were under.

I glanced toward the tree line, watching as the shadows deepened and the air around the village started to hum with a muted and faint frequency. A change was coming, but was it simply the down time Sadie and Damon spoke of? Or was it a land shift?

"It cuts fate," I said quietly.

Meera blinked. "Excuse me?"

"Wyrd Reaper. It's a god-blade. Created by Amoret herself. It's said to sever destinies."

"Does it?" she asked.

I lifted my shoulder. "No idea. I use it to remove heads from bodies, so I suppose that is severing one's destiny. Can't have one if you're dead."

Meera snorted. "You sound like my brothers right now."

"I imagine they are right every now and then."

She chuckled. "So do you always carry around . . . god-blades?"

I cocked my head. "Just these two. Hex Cleaver, because it's useful. Wyrd Reaper . . ." How did I explain the complicated history that belonged to this blade? "The last person to carry it was my father. I like to think that in using it, I'm righting the wrongs."

"That's very . . . noble," she paused. "I'm surprised you didn't have it melted down instead, given your relationship with your father."

"I hated him," I said bluntly. "But I can't change who he

was or what he did. All I can do is be better, do better, and hope that it wipes some of the red out of my family ledger."

Her lips pressed together in a sympathetic smile. "It's not your job to wipe it out."

I shrugged. "If I don't, no one will. My family fucked over an entire realm and a half. Reparations must be paid. Besides, you can't simply unmake a god-blade."

"What do you mean?"

"They're sentient, in a way. It comes from the power that gods used to create them. Trying to unmake one is a great way to end up on the sharp end of its curse."

Sadie's voice interrupted before Meera could ask more. "If you two are done comparing magical cutlery, some of us are still prepping to avoid becoming the next course."

"You two were literally just arguing about everything while we made plans to leave," Meera said, "so sue me if we were talking about weapons."

"We were still listening to you." Sadie scoffed and held up a pouch. "Food for maybe two days between the four of us. Fruit won't travel well, so we need to eat that first. The cheese will be okay for a day, and the bread will be stale, but we'll have something. I have some flint. A few herbs. And this," she said, patting her boot, "for motivational stabbing."

"We should fill up our canteens too," Meera added, taking ours and handing them over to Damon. He took them and casually went to a table, filling them from a pastel pink pitcher. After capping them off, he slipped the straps over his head crossbody style and refilled a wine goblet to avert any suspicions.

"We should learn each other's abilities," I said when he returned, taking the sack from Meera and tucking it into her backpack. "Assuming your magic still works in this realm. It will help to know what each of us can do in a life-or-death situation."

"Mine are simple," Sadie offered, twirling a dagger between her fingers before sheathing it in one fluid motion. "I'm all redcap. You probably already figured that out."

"Yeah," Damon muttered. "The homicidal edge gave it away."

She grinned without apology. "What can I say? It's part of the package. We don't have flashy magic, but battlelust is a real thing. If my eyes turn red, you should run and leave the fighting to me. I won't be able to differentiate between friend and foe."

"Good to know," I said. "Do you have any minor abilities? I know some redcaps do and some don't."

Sadie picked at crud beneath her nails with the sharp end of the blade. "My bracers summon axes, and so far, that has worked here. I've got a *slight* healing power, and I do mean slight. It's not strong enough to actually heal most injuries, but I can take away pain for a short amount of time and sense where people are injured." Her eyes glowed for a brief second and she flicked her gaze to my side where the Nameless had stabbed. Point made.

I lifted a brow. "I'm assuming that's a useful skill to have as a professional fighter."

The grin she flashed was nothing short of diabolical. "It is."

I nodded, then looked at my nephew. "Damon?" While I knew the broad strokes of what he could do, I wasn't sure on the specifics. Except now those specifics might make all the difference in the world. He was my heir to the throne, and I realized how little I actually knew about him. As a king, it wasn't a proud moment.

He sighed, brushing hair off his forehead. "I'm pretty standard high fae. My element is air. Mom is light fae and Dad was dark fae, so I've got both aspects to my power."

"That's cool," Meera said. "Do you also have the same . . . peculiarities as Vareck?"

Damon's eyebrows shot up and he looked at me. "You told her about that?"

"She's my mate," I answered. Never mind that I told her *before* I knew that. "But to answer your question, Damon can't lie. Amoret's affinity passes to those who are spirit elementals."

"Wait," Sadie held up her hand. "You can lie?"

"I can. I'm a dark fae spirit elemental and a fury. The Einer bloodline descends directly from the goddess Amoret."

"I thought all the furies were extinct," Sadie said.

"That has been the general consensus," I agreed. "I believe I'm the last one. I have to ask that you don't repeat that if we make it out of here alive."

"When," Meera corrected. I hoped she was right. Sadie made a zipping motion over her mouth to convey that she understood.

"Your secret is safe with me, but don't spirit elementals always have a familiar? Or are you different because of the whole fury thing?"

I sighed. "Unfortunately for me, Corvo is my familiar."

Meera snorted. "Don't let him hear you talking about him like that. He'll leave us here to become dinner."

"How does one end up with a god bound in a cat's body as a familiar?" Sadie mused, wiping her blade on a makeshift leaf napkin.

"I suspect it has something to do with him being bound in animal form," I replied. "I don't know for certain, but he was already stuck as a feline when my father summoned him. His line of thinking was that he was going to have a demon under his thumb. Easy to control and manipulate. Instead, he ended up with Corvo, and since I was there, the familiar bond snapped into place instantly. Whatever power my father thought he'd have disappeared the moment that connection was made."

Sadie opened and closed her mouth. "Damn. Your dad really was crazy if he thought he could control a demon in any form."

"Indeed."

"Your turn, sis," Sadie said with a thrust of her pointed chin toward Meera. Where my mate was soft, her sister was hard angles and sharp edges. She reminded me of Maeve, in a way. Louder, though. While Maeve had had a big personality, she often kept it for those closest to her and opted to be standoffish around outsiders. Sadie did not seem to care about what anyone thought.

"I think everyone here knows what I can do, but just to make sure our bases are covered, I can track people and objects. I don't exactly know my lineage, but we think I'm part high fae because I have pretty strong compulsion powers."

"You don't say," Damon muttered dryly.

Meera cringed. "I really am sorry about the whole kidnapping business. If it makes you feel better, Vareck kidnapped me later that night and took me back to Faerie for questioning."

Damon snorted. "Right, because I'm sure everyone has been so concerned about finding the 'party boy prince.'" He rolled his eyes. "I don't know what my uncle told you, but if he kidnapped you, I can assure you it had very little, if anything, to do with me."

"Hey," Meera said sharply. "Vareck has been looking for you. So has Kaia and half of Faerie. I couldn't tell anyone a damn thing because of the contract so they were tracking any leads they could find. And I was planning on leaving the castle and tracking you myself as soon as I had my powers back. I don't know what kind of relationship you two have, but he wasn't going to stop until they found you."

I placed a hand on her knee beneath the table. "It's fine."

"It's not," she argued back quietly. "I went missing and Sadie wouldn't rest until she found me. The same was true for me when she disappeared. If that's how he really feels, it's sad and I feel bad for him. He needs to know the truth."

"It's fine," Damon repeated after me. His cobalt eyes, several shades darker than my own, were fixed on Meera like he was seeing her in a new light. "Point is, we know about the persuasion. It's also pretty obvious you can lie, given the entire charade you put on while luring me away from everyone at the castle."

A fault blush stained Meera's cheeks and she looked down. "Yes, I can lie. Again, sorry."

"Stop apologizing," I said, shooting my nephew a narrowed glance as I continued to speak. "You've said your piece. He will forgive or he won't."

Damon ignored me entirely. "Has the realm affected your powers?"

She shook her head, then paused. "Well, I don't know. I can still track. That's how I found Sadie. I don't know if my compulsion works. We were attacked once, but my compulsion didn't work on them, so I don't know if it will be useful at all."

He leaned back and ran a hand through his hair. "Could you find a portal out of here?"

"I already tried but came up with nothing. I didn't think it would work, but I figured it couldn't hurt to try."

"Why do you say that?" Damon asked.

"Because looking for a portal can be too vague," she said with a frown. "They're not a person or a specific object, and if I haven't been to that portal before, it's like searching to find the concept of a door. Also, there may not be a portal here at all. When I tried, threads appeared, but they intertwined and looped around, some coming back to me, some reaching for the sky. I don't know. It wasn't anything I had ever seen before, and none of them could really be followed."

"You followed the thread that mattered," Sadie said, pointing to her own chest. "You grabbed your emergency bag. What all do you have in your magic backpack?"

Meera smiled faintly. "Random tricks. Illusions, short-term shields, maybe a charm or two. I have the water potion, which has come in handy. But as far as tracking, we might be out of luck there. My magic's always been weird. Unreliable until it's not. Like it's waiting for the right moment."

I thought back to the night we'd shared when her fingers blackened. Whatever magic that was, it didn't come from Faerie. I would know.

It took a moment for me to consider whether or not I should say anything but now seemed as good a time as any. "That night when the bond snapped into place, your fingers turned black. Like something had burned through you from the inside out."

Meera blinked. "What?"

Sadie's head snapped toward her, then to me. "You've seen that too?"

Meera turned slowly. "What do you mean, 'too?'"

Sadie looked guilty. "Yeah, so funny story there. I thought it was a trick of the light or maybe some weird magical backlash the first time it happened. It didn't last more than a few seconds, and you didn't say anything so I figured it was harmless."

"I don't even know what you're talking about," Meera said, brows drawing together while she looked at her hands. "Why'd you never tell me about it?"

Sadie shrugged. "Like I said, it went away quickly and didn't seem to hurt you. I wasn't sure if you knew and were keeping it a secret for whatever reason. I didn't want to push if you weren't ready to tell me."

"I tell you everything," Meera murmured, flexing her fingers as if expecting to see the black again. "I've never seen it. I don't feel anything different happening in my body so I don't know how many times this could have even happened in general."

"It didn't feel like a magical backlash when I saw it," I said. "It felt . . . old. Like something buried deep woke up for a second."

Meera frowned. "Woke up? You're not seriously saying I'm possessed by some ancient entity, are you? Because I feel like I would know if something was living inside me."

"No," I said carefully. "I'm saying there's something in your bloodline that doesn't come from Faerie."

Damon chimed in, more curious than cautious. "Could be Hellkin blood, or a forgotten godline. There's a lot of lost magic out there."

I lifted a brow at my nephew. "Hellkin, huh? How do you even know about that *extinct* breed of hell fae?" Fae was a very loose term. Hellkin weren't fae. Not even remotely. They came from a different realm but evolved so similarly to fae that you wouldn't know it. Convergent evolution was the theory.

Damon met my stare with a bold one of his own. "Surprising as it might be, I read, Uncle."

When I turned back to Meera, she was still staring at her fingers. "I'm not opposed to being something weird. I just wish I'd known about it sooner. It's another clue about where I came from."

I watched a second longer, something tight settling in my chest. She wasn't afraid of what she was or where the magic came from. Like everything else so far, she approached it with a quiet curiosity that felt innocent somehow. My mate was collecting pieces of herself and fitting them into the whole of who she was.

The glow in the air shifted, barely perceptible, but enough. We all froze.

Whatever further questions she might have had would need to wait.

Meera turned her head slowly and whispered, "Lanterns are dimming."

The soft flicker of light near the huts had begun to fade, and the pastel creatures grew sluggish, their movements dulled.

"Prep time is almost over," I said. "We move when the lights go down."

Damon grumbled, "I still think this is dumb."

"Dumb keeps us alive," Meera said, already on her feet. "Let's hope that trend continues."

"No, dumb kills people," Damon argued, wiping his palms. "You live in the Earth realm. You should know that."

"Well, good thing we're not in that realm, then." Meera slung her bag over her shoulder, tension tightening her jaw. We all felt the edge creeping closer.

"We need to be mindful that land can shift at any time," I whispered, reaching for Meera's hand and squeezing. "We stay together. All of us. Understood?"

The three of them nodded in agreement and we waited until the last lantern dimmed to a soft glow.

And then we ran.

CHAPTER 13

CORVO

I materialized in Amelia's apartment. For a witch, she was freakishly clean. There were no half-melted candles, open spell books, or pungent herbs. Only the faint scent of lemon and a black-on-black color scheme that would put the Addams family to shame. That was a great show decades ago. Black and white, of course. All my favorites were.

Saving these stupid fae was becoming a full-time job, and in case no one noticed, I was a god cat. I wanted to eat and sleep and sneak over to other realms to indulge in my guilty pleasures. Working was not part of the plan, yet here I was.

The witch was hunched over a stove, stirring a pot with a liquid mixture that resembled tar while belting out "The Smallest Man Who Ever Lived". I cleared my throat.

"Amelia, baby," I began, tail flicking. "I didn't take you for a Swiftie."

She froze, spoon in hand. "What do you want, Corvo?"

I shifted side-to-side in discomfort. It was always the eyes; glowing red as hot coals. It was a good deterrent if you didn't want someone looking at you for too long. "I need a portal. And I also need you to cooperate when a certain someone arrives about said portal."

A single black brow arched as she looked in my direction. "Cooperate? With whom?"

"Oh, just Kaia . . . and possibly Drayden," I said nonchalantly. She cursed under her breath, dropping the spoon. The tar-like mixture bubbled noxiously. "They're going to request a portal. I need you to be the lovely person I know you are *deep, deep* down and make one for them. Don't demand their firstborn or something equally . . . unsavory."

"You're fucking with me." Glowing red eyes focused on me with an unnerving intensity. Every creature belonged to one of two categories. Peasants, such as Vareck, or equals, like Amelia.

I gave her my best godly shrug. "Unfortunately, I'm not. I give it less than fifteen minutes before they find you. They'll look at the bar first, naturally."

She pinched the bridge of her nose between her forefinger and thumb, then breathed deeply. I'd seen her do it a number of times over the years. Typically someone died shortly thereafter. I was hoping to avoid that little show. "Where do you need a portal to?"

"My realm."

Her eyes cracked open, narrowed in my direction. "Why? You can literally pop in whenever."

I crouched, hoping I came across as detached, but also serious. It was a complicated balance. "Yeah, but my dumbass familiar and his saucy redhead—who I actually like—ended up in Evorsus. I need to pull them back before the fuzzy inhabitants turn 'em into hors d'oeuvres. Damon's there too for some reason, and while V thinks he's a twat, I kinda like the guy. He feeds me under the table even when Eleanor tells him not to. He's been doing that since he was a tot. He may act tough, but we bonded. What can I say?" Amelia reached around to flip the burner off.

"Sounds like a *them* problem." Her stance was casual. Too casual. My inner detective smelled something, and it wasn't whatever concoction she had in that pot of hers.

"You wouldn't happen to know anything about *them* being there, would you?"

Amelia didn't answer. She just reached for her wine—because naturally she was drinking red in a murder-glam kitchen—and took a long sip for the dramatic pause. I would have done the same thing if I had thumbs. Instead I was cursed with adorable toe beans.

"I might," she said finally, lips curling. "But if I did, it would be purely hypothetical and involve circumstances that were . . . fluid."

"Fluid," I echoed, taking a deep breath. My whiskers twitched in annoyance. "You launched a fury-descended king and his chaos grenade of a mate into Evorsus. That's not fluid, that's a war crime."

She twirled the wine in her glass while watching the burgundy liquid with disinterest. "I'm not the one who let two ticking time bombs wander through the Witching Hour unsupervised. Maybe next time, keep a leash on your bonded."

"First of all," I hissed, tail swishing like a blade, "you've got a real flair for theatrics, and it's not as cute as you think it is. Plausible deniability won't work for someone who's not denying *nearly enough*. Second, I'm about to make this a *you* problem if you don't help get them out of there. "

Amelia gave a slow shrug, the kind that meant she was proud of herself and also deeply unconcerned about consequences. "They weren't exactly *not* meant to go there."

I blinked. "You really just put the fun in funeral, don't you?"

"Sometimes you need the right kind of pressure to learn what someone's made of," she said, lifting her brows. "Evorsus tests people. I'm just . . . accelerating the lesson plan."

"I swear to the gods, if he dies in there and takes me with him, I'm haunting your overpriced sofa for eternity."

She smirked. "Then I'll finally have a pet."

I growled. "This isn't a game, Amelia."

"No," she agreed. "It's a strategy. You just don't like that it's mine."

"This isn't a pissing contest over powers." I jumped up onto the counter, eyes narrowing to slits. "Drayden's coming. So is Kaia. When they demand a portal, you'll be ready. You'll smile that creepy wine-mom smile of yours and open the damn door to hell like the helpful hostess I know you can pretend to be."

She studied me over the rim of her glass. "And if I don't?"

I stepped closer. "Do it. Or I tell them all what I know."

She clenched her jaw. "Mighty balls you've got there, cat."

"How big are yours, witch? Tossing the prince, the fae king, and his mate into a hell realm to be eaten," I growled. "What were you thinking? I thought you were trying to stay under the radar?"

Her eyes flashed. "As I said, it's strategic."

I leaned in. "I'm his familiar, Amelia. He dies, I die. And as I said, I like the redhead. Make the portal, or explain to Kaia and Drayden why you won't."

She turned away, shoulders rigid. "I knew you before any of those fools, Corvo. I thought you were my friend."

"I am, and that's why I'm warning you," I said quietly. "Drayden and Kaia are on their way, and they're not in the mood for riddles."

Her grip tightened on the stem of her wine glass until a tiny fissure appeared, traveling up until it curved over the goblet. Red liquid seeped out slowly, spilling over her fingers like blood. "Let them come," she said, voice low and vicious. "Let all of Faerie's army come for all I care."

I tilted my head. "Still holding that grudge?"

Her laugh was sharp and filled with bitterness. "Some debts age well. Like wine. Or poison."

"Just don't let yours kill the king."

She set the glass down with a click. "I'll make the portal."

I swished my tail, wrapping it around myself. "Knew you had it in you."

"I didn't say I'd be nice about it," she muttered, already moving to gather her tools.

"In all the years I've known you, no one has ever accused you of being nice."

She waved sarcastically. "Bye, Corvo."

"Your secrets aren't doing you any favors, Amelia." As I faded into shadow, I whispered just loud enough for her to hear, "You really should tell them the truth."

Her only answer was the shatter of glass against the wall.

CHAPTER 14

MEERA

With silent steps, we weaved between squatty pastel huts, their thatched roofs shimmering faintly under the moonlight. The ground beneath us was spongy and warm, like the soft moss that grew in the shade by the river's edge, squishing slightly with every step we took. Shadows clung to the walls like ink stains—our best allies.

Until they weren't.

The chirping started softly, almost like music, but quickly turned sharp and loud, a grating noise that made my ear ring and my jaw clench. Then the pastel creatures rounded the corner, moving fast despite their short legs. They poured into the clearing ahead, blocking our path. Their big sapphire eyes bled black as they watched us with unsettling focus.

The murder bears went from looking harmless to demonic in about two seconds flat. I would've been impressed if not for the fact they wanted to eat me for dinner.

The expressions on their faces twisted. Grins widened into leers. Their fur bristled, lifting away from their skin to become something closer to bramble. The shapes of their mouths, once set in endearing smiles, split to reveal rows of pointed teeth, now more piranha than plush toy.

"Shit," I hissed, heart stuttering. The air was thick and sticky, clinging to my skin like syrup. "Did you see what just happened to their teeth?"

"And you wanted to stick around," Sadie muttered to Damon.

"You're the one that fell for the cute baby bear act," he shot back. "Have some bedtime tea, why don't you?"

"Shut up and keep moving," Vareck ground out and then he tensed beside me. I could see the lines of pain around his mouth, the sweat on his brow. The shallow gash in his side from the Nameless was giving him grief, even if he was loath to admit it. "Head for the tree line," he snapped, voice hoarse with strain.

More of them filtered from their little huts as we tried to make our way out, but too many had come. Our path was completely blocked, and there was no safe way to the trees.

Sadie crouched, knuckles cracking as she knocked her bracers together. With a hiss from metal splitting air, twin axes appeared, gleaming wickedly. The grin that spread across her face was borderline feral. "They wanna snarl like rabid beasts?" she muttered. "I'll show them beast mode."

Damon groaned, casting a glance over his shoulder. "That's not what they said. Right, Meera? No one actually said anything about beast mode—"

The words died in his throat.

Two of the fuzzballs darted straight for me, candy-colored blurs, knocking him down unexpectedly. I staggered back, heel catching on a vine half-buried in the ground. My arms pinwheeled for balance, but ultimately I failed at stopping my fall. I hit the dirt with a grunt, the air getting knocked from my lungs on impact. A yellow bear flew up, aiming for Vareck's chest as he swung out. Another one came out of nowhere and landed on his back while he cursed.

A pink murder bear lunged toward me with glee, its tiny mouth stretching into a nightmare smile as it latched onto my ankle. Its paw—once soft and chubby—now sported inch-long talons that dug into my skin.

I shouted, pain flaring up my leg, and kicked out wildly. My boot connected with its head in a hard thunk, and it loosened its hold on me while letting out a growl. "Nah uh, nope. Not today, Satan." I fumbled in my attempt to crab walk backward, but Sadie was there. My sister was little more than a flash of red hair and steel as she lunged for the creature.

"You wanna bite, little fucker?" she sang while sweet-talking them. "Let's see who's got bigger teeth." She swung an axe and its blade rang as it split the air, slicing through the bramble fur and meat of our attacker. Bright pink blood sprayed across my boots as the thing shrieked a high-pitched wail that rattled my bones.

It wasn't a death cry. It didn't sound angry or defeated.

It sounded like it was calling something.

Sadie and I looked at each other instantly. "That wasn't good, was it?"

I pointed toward the sea of pastel. "Decidedly not."

More shapes loomed behind them. Dozens of the creatures converging like a tide.

We didn't have time to ponder what else that sound might summon. It was time to move.

A burst of dark wind blew my hair back and sent dust spiraling into the air. Black, bat-like wings exploded from Vareck's back with a crack. He stepped in front of me, his icy gaze burning bright, voice slicing through the chaos. "Run! I'll hold them off!"

I blinked, still sprawled, adrenaline roaring in my ears. Fear curled like smoke in my throat, but so did something else. Rage.

"You can't hold them all off by yourself!" I shouted, pushing myself to my feet. "You're still injured!"

His jaw clenched. Muscles bunched across his shoulders, as Vareck regarded the approaching horde in front of us. "Watch me."

"No." I stepped forward, glaring up at him, daring. "If you stay, I stay—and you CANNOT compel me."

I pushed the words with a pulse of my own persuasion magic, letting it crackle in the air between us. A warning. A line.

He stared at me like I'd slapped him. Like the world had tilted sideways.

"Stop being difficult," he ground out, voice taut, low and furious. "You know what can happen—"

"I do," I snapped. "And it's my choice, right? You took it from me once, and you said you wouldn't again." I jabbed a finger toward his chest. "Or was that just lip service?"

"Of course not—"

"Then you need to trust that I know how to take care of myself. That I can be more than a liability here!"

"I never called you—"

"You didn't have to," I said. "Your actions spoke for you."

Before he could answer, Sadie cut in with a growl. "Like hell I'm walking away from a fight. This is *literally* what I live for."

"You three idiots are going to get us all killed while arguing over who gets to fight the army of murderous teddy bears!" Damon shouted. Then, before anyone could argue, he grabbed Sadie by the waist and slung her over his shoulder like a sack of potatoes.

"Put me down, you limp-dick bastard!" she shrieked, punching his back with both fists. "I swear to every twisted god—"

"I think the words you meant to say were 'thank you, Prince Damon, for saving my bloodthirsty arse,'" he replied with maddening calm as he took off toward the tree line.

I turned to Vareck. "Don't you dare."

"Then you better start running," he said, gaze locked on the horde moving in.

I cursed and grabbed his arm, yanking him with me as I sprinted after Damon.

My lungs ached. My legs screamed. My ankle pulsed painfully where I had been injured. The ground beneath our feet had shifted to something harder, rockier—no longer soft and squishy, but jagged stone veined with glowing cracks. Like Evorsus itself was angry that we'd escaped.

"I'm not made for this!" I huffed, each breath burning as it tore through my throat like sandpaper.

"I would have carried you!" Vareck shouted back, not even out of breath. Show-off. His wings flapped, stirring the air into chaotic eddies. A gust slapped my cheek, hot and dry like a furnace blast.

"Yeah? And then what?" I managed between gasps. "We get overrun because I'm basically dead weight? I'm not as small as my sister, in case you didn't notice."

"In case you haven't noticed, I don't care if you're not small, and I carried you just fine at Farris's place," he said with an easy confidence. "Could always fly."

"Away? And leave Sadie here? Are you out of your mind?"

He gave a strained grunt—almost a laugh—but didn't argue. His hand hovered near my back as we ran, just enough to catch me if I stumbled. Not touching. Just close. I hated how much that made me want to lean in.

We tore through the woods, but the woods weren't the same. At least they didn't look the same.

Behind us, the sounds of pursuit followed; frantic chirps, rustling bushes, the occasional unholy shriek. Black eyes flickered between trees, closing in. The lanterns the creatures had carried earlier bobbled in the dark like the torches of a mob.

On the way to the village, branches had lifted out of my way. Roots shifted underfoot so I didn't trip on them. The forest had been accommodating, but now it turned against me. It was like it wanted me to be caught.

"They're not chasing us," Vareck said suddenly, eyes scanning the canopy. "They're corralling us."

"Great," I panted. "Now we're cattle."

"They won't touch you," he growled, barely ducking a low-hanging branch. "I vow it."

My foot hit a rock, and I stumbled. Vareck caught me by the elbow, steadying me before I face-planted.

"Thanks," I muttered, heart punching wildly against my ribs.

"You're welcome," he said, too softly.

We kept running . . . until there was nowhere left to go.

The trees ended. The ground vanished. We skidded to a halt at the edge of a cliff, hearts hammering, breath ragged. Damon had put Sadie down as they assessed the edge.

Beneath us stretched a jagged canyon of endless dark, glowing faintly with unnatural light. The glow shifted as if aware of our presence. The wind screamed upward from the depths, and it carried voices. Not words. Just whispers.

No escape. No fallback. Just wind and eternity.

"We're trapped," Vareck said grimly.

"No, you smell that? It's water," I said, stomach twisting. It was subtle, but the unmistakable scent of fresh water was nearby. I swallowed thickly, then turned to him. "We jump."

He blinked. The world paused as our breath caught. "Absolutely not."

I swallowed hard. "They'll eat us. You said it yourself—they're herding us. This cliff is the pen."

Sadie glanced over her shoulder at the approaching mob.

Damon looked at Vareck. "We could each—"

"Fuck this," she said . . . and jumped. Sadie vaulted off the cliff, arms spread like wings. The wind claimed her in seconds, chanting a dark lullaby that rattled my bones.

"Sadie!" I didn't think. Didn't weigh the consequences. Didn't wait for someone to stop me.

"Meera, NO!" Vareck yelled, voice cracking.

Too late.

I launched off the edge without a second thought, the wind snatching the scream from my throat as I plunged after my sister into the abyss.

CHAPTER 15

DRAYDEN

"Are you sure this is the place?" Kaia asked, looking down the row of townhomes lining the street. Despite every other door having some sort of personalization—a custom knocker, a welcome mat, a wreath, a potted plant—this entry had nothing. In any other circumstance, I would have assumed this place to be uninhabited.

"Positive," I grunted, lifting my hand to the door. I knocked twice.

Lucian gave me the address, and considering I left him under Cadoc's care, I was fairly certain he wouldn't lie to me. Not when one word from my lips could mean the difference between remaining alive and experiencing a very slow death.

Inside, footsteps shuffled toward the door. Unhurried and yet agitated all the same.

Three different locks disengaged. Kaia and I shared a wary glance.

Most witches were reclusive, yes, but they were also arrogant in the belief that nothing could end them. After all, only one species carried the magic of gods and demons.

For this one to have so many safety measures in place was odd.

Especially if she was as powerful as both Lucian and Corvo alluded to.

The door slid back an inch.

It was that exact moment that something in me, long since buried, slowly cracked an eye open.

There were a handful of moments in my life I would never forget, even if I wished I could.

The very second in time the familiar bond snapped into place with Vyrexis.

The feeling of the wind above and below me as we flew into battle together.

The first day I saw my beloved . . . and the way my world stopped at the sound of her very last breath.

I never, and I truly mean *never*, expected that moment —standing at the doorstep of an unmarked home in the Arcane District of Seattle—to be another one that would be locked into my memory forever.

And yet, as a pair of blood-red eyes regarded me warily through the crack in the door, my entire world shifted.

"What do you want, Kingsguard?" Her voice was low. Not quite deep, but sultry. An unmistakable raspy quality that roused a part of me I'd long considered dead.

I gritted my teeth, fingers curling into a fist at my side.

"We need a portal."

"Find someone else," she muttered, moving to close the door.

Kaia moved faster than any being truly should and slipped her boot between the door and the frame, preventing it from closing.

"There's no time for us to find someone else. The fae king, his mate, and the prince have been taken into one of the hell realms. We need your assistance creating a portal and we need it *now*."

A pregnant pause filled the silence.

"Which realm?"

"The twin realms," Kaia answered. "Evorsus, specifically."

The crimson-eyed woman narrowed her gaze, opening the door a fraction further to reveal a shock of dark hair.

"What makes you think I have the power to open such a portal? I'm nothing more than a simple witch."

"We have a reliable source," Kaia said, twisting her words expertly. I might have been impressed with how Kaia was handling her had I not been rendered immobile.

"Hmm. The same reliable source that gave you my address?" Kaia didn't answer, but apparently her nonreaction was more than enough. "So, you have the leprechaun, then. Few know where I live, and few know the depths of my powers. Combined, the list is rather short."

Kaia exhaled stiffly. "Yes. Lucian is our source."

Amelia widened her eyes playfully, humming in amusement. "*Lucian*, is it? That was the name he gave you? That's simply . . . delightful. He so rarely gives out that name. Even *more* rare is the likelihood of him giving out his name, my abilities, *and* my address, all to the same person."

"He wasn't as forthcoming as you might believe. He had . . . incentive."

"Ah, I see. Still suffering in the dungeons now, I'm assuming?" When she didn't get a response from either of us, she tutted, but it was lacking sincerity. "Poor dear. Always hard to control, that one. But it would seem you could be his Achilles heel, Commander. Must be quite the crush he has on you for him to give away so much information, 'incentive' or not."

"So it would seem. And now you know that we know you can open the portal, Amelia, so let's get on with it."

The sound of her sigh brushed over my skin, and I tensed. It was new and familiar all at once.

She stepped back and opened the door, giving the first full view of her. At five foot nothing with long black hair, she was pretty, but not the most remarkable beauty I'd ever seen . . . and yet she was. The idea of it warred within me.

"Fine, I'll make your portal, but I expect payment first."

She didn't look at me. Not for a second.

My brows furrowed in confusion. Maybe I was wrong. Maybe this feeling was mistaken, but that isn't how it worked.

"There is more where this came from. Name your price," Kaia said, unloosing a pouch from her waist that was filled to the brim with gold coins.

The witch, a woman with rounded ears and sun-kissed skin, laughed quietly. The hairs on my nape stood straight. A chill crawled down my spine.

"I don't take coin," the witch said, seemingly annoyed. "And I suspect your leprechaun captive told you as much, but you think you can offer it still. You're asking for a portal into the Fold. No amount of gold is worth the magical back-lash of something like that if it were to go awry."

Kaia hid her frustration well, but I'd known her long enough to tell what the pucker between her brows meant. "We didn't ask for one into the Fold. We asked for—"

"You don't know what you are asking for," she said, cutting in sharply. "Eversus and Evorsus are overlapping realms that run on different timelines. If I were to open a portal into one of them, who's to say it would open now, or six months from now, on the other side?"

Kaia had no answer, and I couldn't speak.

"Have your attention, now, don't I? I can do what you ask, but I can't manipulate space and time in the twin hells. I don't know where the portal would appear. There is no map of either realm, and they could be stuck in one or the other for months, or even years. So yes, Commander, you're asking for a portal into the Fold. It's a convergence of the ley lines, and it's the only location that exists in both realms at the same place and time. Regardless of which realm they are in, they can access it . . . assuming they have a means to *find* the Fold, of course." She lifted a sharp, sculpted eyebrow and Kaia scowled.

"They have a guide that can lead them."

Amelia snorted. "Must be one hell of a guide." Her lips curled up on one side in a Cheshire smile. "So, as I said, you want a portal through the ley lines, which is going to cost *me,* therefore it's going to cost *you.* I won't make it without my payment upfront."

"If not coin, then what is it you want?"

Amelia's lips curled into a sinister smile. In the long silence, I heard the music playing in the background. Nothing I was familiar with, but the emotion was heard with every word sung. Love. Desire. I wanted nothing to do with either.

"A favor to be paid later, for a favor now."

Kaia stilled. "I—"

"Not from you," the witch said. For the first time since she'd opened the door, that crimson gaze slid over Kaia and onto me. There was a weight there that a lesser man would crumble under. "From *you.*"

Those were the first words my second-chance mate spoke to me.

And if I had my way, they'd be the last.

"No."

Her expression didn't change. If I didn't know better, I would've said she was unsurprised by my response. With a slight shrug, she adjusted her grip on the door and took a step.

"If that's the case, then good day to you—"

"Wait!" Kaia pushed her way forward, into the foyer, but there was no way I would cross that threshold. The witch's lips curled downward in displeasure. "There must be something else we can pay with? Anything. Please."

Silence spread, thick and uncomfortable. Amelia folded her arms over her small chest and cocked a hip. "I suppose I could ask for something else," she murmured. "But I'll expect payment from you both."

"It's just one portal," I started to argue. Crimson irises flicked to me, unreadable in their depths.

"And the price just went up." She raised her brows, challenging me, but I bit my tongue. "It's one portal I have to keep open for an undetermined length of time. Portal intra-realm are easy. I could get you there with a snap of my fingers. But realm to realm?" She shook her head. "It must be stable and have an energy source that won't burn out after a few moments. I refuse to use my own life force, which means I need you to get me something, along with my payment. You can view it as payment from you both or simply supplying the materials. I don't care, but I won't do the portal without it."

Fucking witches. I pressed my lips together. Kaia looked at me and sighed, then glanced back at Amelia.

"What is it you need?"

There was a sadistic gleam in her eye when she answered. "Dragon scales."

Kaia choked. "Dragon? How in the nine realms do you expect us to get—"

"I'll do it."

Kaia turned to me, her mouth slightly gaping. "*No, you won't.*"

"Then you won't have your portal." Amelia shrugged. "Makes no difference to me."

"I said, I'll do it," I repeated in a harsher tone. Amelia narrowed her eyes.

"Drayden." Kaia grabbed my bicep and dragged me away from the porch. "You can't be serious. Last time you saw Vyrexis, he nearly killed you."

"It's been over thirty years. Maybe he's cooled off."

She made another choking noise and sliced her hand through the air in the universal symbol of 'enough'. "Unlikely. What are you going to do if he hurts you again?"

"Try not to let him."

She slapped my arm. "This isn't funny."

"I wasn't laughing," I said in all seriousness. "I'd rather take my chances with Vyrexis than write her a blank check in the form of a favor. Right now, she's our only option. We have to get Vareck."

Kaia sighed, holding my gaze while she silently weighed everything happening. She knew I was right. Duty and loyalty were paramount in our positions. We had no other choice.

Amelia cleared her throat and said, "I don't have all day. Either you accept the price, or you don't. I won't offer a third alternative."

"I'll get your dragon scales," I said to her.

"Twelve of them," she replied, lifting her chin a fraction.

I nodded once and looked at Kaia.

She didn't like it, but she didn't have to. Nearly forty years ago my familiar abandoned me. We both felt the moment the bond was extinguished with her death, leaving a thread only attached to us. Forever severed. The loss of my beloved was more than either of us could bear. He blamed me, which was fine. We were in agreement in that regard. When I tracked Vyrexis years later, he made it clear I wasn't to return; not without her.

She was dead, and he wouldn't forgive me for it. There was nothing I could do. I hadn't forgiven myself either. Getting those fucking scales wasn't going to be easy, but something told me it was still the better choice.

I listened to my gut when it came to things like this.

"As for the other means of payment," Amelia continued, "I need you to find a compass, but not just any compass. The one I want doesn't point north. It leads you to what you most desire, but you mustn't use it. The magic it holds works only once."

Kaia cursed under her breath. "How am I supposed to find that?"

Amelia lifted a shoulder in a partial shrug. "No idea. That's not my problem. You want a portal to the Fold— that's my price. Take it or leave it."

"How do I know if it has been used or not?"

"If this glass has cracked, the magic has faded."

Kaia pressed her lips together, not liking this one bit. "Fine. We'll be back."

Amelia saluted her in a mocking goodbye. "I'll be here. Do send my love to Lucian when you see him."

I stopped on the bottom step of her porch.

Fire threatened to surface.

That thieving leprechaun was a thorn in my side for many reasons. Now this? They were familiar with each other. What I didn't know was *how* well he knew her, or in what capacity.

And for reasons I absolutely hated, jealousy began to surface.

If Vyrexis so much as suspected a bond had formed—against my will or not—he'd burn me alive in seconds.

It mattered not.

There were no second chances for me.

CHAPTER 16

MEERA

The river caught us like a fist.

Hard, fast, and mean.

It punched the breath from my lungs in a single brutal strike. Darkness swallowed me whole, cold and thick, curling around my limbs like a vice. I tumbled, spinning end over end in the churning current, disoriented and blind. I couldn't tell which way was up. Water roared in my ears, louder than my thoughts.

The river was a living thing; angry, wild, and intent on dragging me under.

My limbs flailed. I kicked out, reaching for anything—rock, root, a scrap of air—but all I caught were currents that twisted and spun me like a rag doll. Panic bloomed in my sternum, cold and sharp. My lungs screamed. My chest burned. Something brushed my arm—slick, soft, and moving upstream. Not a branch.

I twisted, clawing at the water. My fingers scraped stone, and I pushed, hard, muscles straining.

My head broke the surface. With a gasp, air filled my battered lungs like broken glass. Water streamed from my face, my ears ringing, vision blurred. "Sadie?" I choked, my voice rasping like someone took sandpaper to my throat.

"Best field trip ever!" Sadie whooped somewhere to my left, her voice echoing down the river.

I sputtered, vomiting a little bit of water and bile. "Are you *actually* insane?"

"Maybe?" she yelled, her laugh maniacal. Despite the significant danger we were still in, I found myself shaking my head and almost smiling at her absurdity. The moment was short-lived.

The current dragged us downstream. I twisted in the rapids, trying to orient myself, but the river had other plans. Foamy water whipped around me, frothing over submerged stones and half-drowned tree limbs. A thick, brackish scent filled my nose, a mixture of sulfur and crushed wildflowers, and the banks blurred past in streaks of dark green and violet. Trees leaned over the water, their branches skeletal, like arms reaching for the riverbed.

Behind us, faint but distinct, I heard Vareck's voice, rough and panicked.

"Meera!"

"Come on, boys, the water's just fine!" Sadie called, letting out a cackle even as she dipped under the water before popping back up.

"Nope," I muttered, coughing up more water, eyes stinging. "This is a terrible idea. This was never *not* a terrible idea."

The current surged faster, frothing and snapping at us like it had something to prove. Whitecaps foamed around partially submerged boulders, spinning debris in dizzying eddies. The river narrowed and the banks rose on either side; steep, jagged, closing in like a throat about to swallow us whole.

Something roared up ahead.

It wasn't the chatter of the baby bear murder cult, or even the wind.

This sound was deeper. Hungrier.

A low, guttural growl that rumbled through the water itself, shaking my body, reverberating through my ribs.

My heart stopped.

I turned, straining to see through the mist curling off the surface. The sound grew, swelling into something monstrous. I didn't need to see it to know what it was.

Waterfall.

"Oh, shit," I breathed.

And then the world dropped out from beneath me.

My stomach launched into my throat. For a heartbeat, I was weightless. Then we hit the plunge.

Twelve feet. Maybe, fifteen. Not high enough to kill us, but enough to make the world tilt sideways. Again.

With a massive splash, we crashed into the pool below, the impact jarring every bone as I went under. A deeper cold crawled into my muscles and clenched. I kicked hard, lungs screaming.

We surfaced in a deep, clear lagoon, the water glowing faintly with an eerie violet shimmer, like moonlight trapped beneath the surface. I swam to shore, limbs aching and heavy, then collapsed onto the hard sand, coughing and laughing all at once.

We were alive. Barely.

Sadie crawled up beside me, strings of red hair splayed across her cheeks, grinning like, well, a redcap high on adrenaline. "That was amazing."

"You're insane," I wheezed, tasting river water on my lips.

"You keep saying that like it's an insult."

A moment later, Damon splashed onto the shore, dragging himself up like a half-drowned cat. He glared at us, his wet hair plastered to his face. "I regret every life choice that led me here. Next time, I'm letting the woodland creatures win."

"You should be thanking us. That was character development."

And their arguing commenced.

Vareck landed last, wings folding neatly behind him. His boots barely disturbed the sand.

Silently, he offered me a hand.

I hesitated, then met his eyes and took it. His palm was dry, warm, and grounding. His grip lingered just a second longer than necessary as he pulled me up without speaking a word.

Far away, but not far enough, the chitters started up again. Too close for comfort.

We didn't talk about it.

We just moved.

The path beyond the lagoon, opposite the way we came, sloped upward. The air felt thicker here. Humid and somehow charged.

Vareck walked ahead, silent but tense, like he was holding back something sharp. His wings had vanished again, tucked away. Damon trailed behind, dripping and scowling, his soaked shirt clinging to his back. Sadie strolled beside me like this was just another day in Seattle and not a hell realm where we were continuously sidestepping our impending doom.

"You know, this place isn't so bad for the right kind of person. If there were a consistent portal in and out of here, I could see it becoming a popular vacation spot for adrenaline junkies."

Damon's voice broke the silence. "You are going to get us all killed."

Sadie didn't even look at him. "You're just mad your dramatic belly flop didn't earn you an applause."

Damon made a noise that was half growl, half exhausted sigh. "I've been stabbed. I've been kidnapped. I've been tied up and dragged around against my will. But this? Being here with you? This takes the cake."

"No one asked about your sex life," Sadie quipped.

"I didn't say—" he broke off, connecting the dots.

Sadie smirked. "Bit defensive there, princeling."

"Do you *ever* shut up?" Damon asked, dragging a hand down his drenched face.

"Nope," she said brightly. "It's part of my charm. If anything, I get louder when I'm tired."

I couldn't help the snort that escaped. Gods, she was being obnoxious right now. They both were. I wondered if they had hate-fucked already or if this was still the lead up.

Up ahead, Vareck's shoulders were bunched in a solid line of tension. He didn't look back, didn't say a word. Just kept walking like the ground had offended him personally.

I picked up my pace until I was beside him. "You going to talk to me and tell me what's up, or . . ."

A suspended moment passed before he ground out, "Or."

"All right," I drawled. "Just pretending I don't exist?"

His jaw flexed. "Not possible, even when I wish it was."

I blinked, reeling back. "What?"

"Nothing," he replied all too quickly. Too stiff. The lie sat between us.

I frowned. "That was a hell of a thing to say."

He didn't respond, just kept walking, fists clenched at his sides.

"Seriously? After everything, *that's* what you say to me?"

"I didn't mean it," he muttered. "This *is* why I was choosing silence."

"Oh good," I snapped. "You just said it, but you didn't mean it, apparently. That makes it all better."

He stopped again, turned toward me with stormy eyes. "I can't ignore you or pretend you don't exist. Like my fury, you're ingrained in me. Even when I'm not with you, I'm thinking about you. That's not helpful in times, like now for example, when I want to shake you for jumping off a fucking cliff. I should have just—" He broke off and exhaled harshly. "Never mind."

My breath hitched.

There it was. A tender wound ripped open, ugly and bleeding.

"You should've what, Vareck? Compelled me?"

"I said never mind, Meera. Drop it."

"So what, then? You're mad because I made a choice you didn't like? Because I didn't wait for your approval before I chose to act quickly over getting eaten?"

"You jumped *off a cliff*," he growled, voice full of barely controlled rage. "With no idea what was below. You had no plan. You can't fly. You just chose to throw yourself over the edge and say fuck it without considering the conse-quences."

I stared at him, heart thudding. "Oh, I'm sorry. Because compelling me to run and hide like a damsel in distress would have been a better alternative, then, would it?"

"You're putting words in my mouth now."

Maybe I was. Or maybe I was saying the things he thought but couldn't voice because he *knew* how it sounded. "Am I? Because for someone awfully obsessed with my safety, you are also the person that put a magic nullifying collar on me."

His expression crumpled for just a second. "That was different."

"Was it?" I demanded. "Because I was kidnapped by brownies, then robbed by a gang at knife point because of said necklace. That was *before* you found me at the brothel where I was going to be forced into prostitution, in case you forgot."

He opened his mouth—then closed it again, jaw tightening. "This isn't about the necklace. This is about you not thinking about your actions."

"That's rich, coming from the guy who tried to fight a small army while bleeding out."

"I knew what I was doing."

"So did I."

We stood there, breathing hard, neither of us moving.

Eventually Vareck's jaw eased the slightest fraction, just enough for him to ground out, "I'm not doing this." He walked ahead, moving faster than I could keep up with.

"What's that supposed to mean?" I shouted, throwing my hands out.

"Not now." He growled his final two words, shook his head, and picked up his speed, his hands balled into trembling fists.

Damon appeared at my elbow, wiping drops of water from his face. "It means you jumped off a fucking cliff and he needs a minute to figure out how to say you're stupid."

Sadie rolled her eyes. "It worked out fine."

"Only because I was there," Damon muttered, flicking water from his sleeves.

Sadie narrowed her eyes. "Oh yeah, because our savior,

the fuckboy prince, jumped in after us and magically saved the day."

Damon's nostrils flared. "Redcaps." He took a long, deliberate inhale and turned, stalking ahead without another word.

Sadie blinked. "What the hell does that mean?"

I shrugged. "I think it means he needs a minute before he calls you stupid? Guess it runs in the family."

She snorted and looped her arm through mine.

"They're so dramatic," she muttered.

"Yeah . . . are they?" A hint of guilt taunted my thoughts. If I was so sure they were in the wrong, why was it there?

"They are. Pretty sure the ladies in Faerie aren't the do-it-yourself types and they don't know how to handle that kind of female independence," Sadie said, firm in her assessment. After a moment of silence, she changed the subject without even pretending to segue into the topic. "So, you and the king?"

I lifted both eyebrows in her direction. "You and the prince?" I shot back.

"Oh, come on. I would never."

"Need I remind you that you were dating the witch who threw us both in here?"

"Incorrect," she said firmly. "Not dating. Just friends with benefits. You were friends with her too."

I sighed. "Yeah, well, look how well that's turned out for us."

"Hey." Sadie bumped my shoulder with hers in a caring manner. "Amelia fooled us both. We're not talking about her right now, though, we're talking about you and Vareck."

I inhaled a deep breath and let it out, blowing a raspberry. There was no escape from the conversation. "What about us?"

Sadie squinted at me, disbelieving. "Seriously? You're fated mates. That's *huge*."

"Yeah . . ." I trailed off. "Huge."

"You don't sound excited about it."

"I . . ." How could I explain it to her when I couldn't even explain it to myself? "It's not that, exactly."

"Then what is it? Because the guy is totally crazy about you and he's hot as hell. I love you, but like, you're living a fantasy right now and don't seem to see it. The man you've been dreaming of for years turns out to be real, *and* he's single, *and* he wants to commit?" Sadie let out a low whistle. "I'm not looking for anything serious right now, but if I was, I would jump at the chance you have."

I sighed. "I know I'm lucky, okay?" Frustration bled into my tone despite my attempt to keep it at bay. "It's just . . . look, Amelia was our friend, right? And our friend shoved us into a hell realm where the inhabitants want to eat us, and honestly, we have no idea why she did it. How good a judge of character am I? I trusted Amelia, and I have no idea how long she's been playing us. Hell, I even trusted Lou to an extent. Look where those choices got me."

Sadie's brown eyes softened. "Meera, you made a mistake. That doesn't mean everyone you meet is going to double-cross you."

I snorted. "This from the woman that only casually dates because the idea of settling down hurts too much after Klaid the Fuckwit broke your heart, what, six years ago? Seven?"

Sadie inhaled sharply. "That's not fair."

"All I'm saying is pot, meet kettle," I motioned from her to me. "Mating isn't like marriage. It's forever. Being fated on top of that?" I shook my head. "At least when chosen mates get together, they've usually spent enough time together that they feel confident that they know the other person. I've known Vareck for like two weeks."

"You dreamed of him for years."

I rolled my eyes. "We weren't exactly talking in those dreams."

"But you were getting to know each other," Sadie teased, a smirk curling her mouth.

I nudged her with my elbow. "Stop. You know what I mean."

"What? I'm just saying, the body does talking of its own."

"Sadie."

"What?"

"Shut up."

She threw her head back and laughed like she didn't have a care in the world. Like we were back home on one of our hiking trips and I'd just busted my ass walking on flat ground. Like we weren't in a hell realm we might never escape.

I swallowed hard, pushing that thought away.

"You're scared," she said after a short pause. "I'm no expert, but I am ninety-nine-point-nine percent sure that's normal. Mom was always talking about our emotions and being allowed to feel our feelings, right? Fear is normal." Although she paused, I could sense she wasn't done talking, so I didn't say anything. "So feel it, but if you let it control you, then you could lose out on something really special."

I pressed my lips together. "How do I know it's not a mistake? That what I feel for him now, I'll feel in a year? A decade? A century? We live over five-hundred years, Sadie. That's a long time to just make the decision on a whim."

"But it's not a whim," Sadie insisted. "Meera, you've been a romantic all your life. You read those smutty books where the girl gets kidnapped and forced into marriage all the time. How does it work out for them? Must be good or you wouldn't keep reading."

I scoffed. "Those are stories. That's different."

Sadie shrugged. "Maybe. Maybe not. Fated mates were just stories too and now you've got yourself one. All I'm saying is, if the universe picked one person out of the nine realms and slapped you upside the head with a bond saying, 'this person is the one,' maybe you should listen to it."

"You're awfully pro-mating for someone who has been against it her entire life."

Sadie snorted. "To be fair, it's easier to give advice than take it. For another, I don't have a similar experience to go off of. The boy I thought I'd mate and spend forever with turned out to be a serial cheater who couldn't pick up his dirty underwear off the ground. I've gone from one bad decision to another since then. Mating isn't in my cards. At least not anytime soon, if ever."

I bumped my shoulder against hers, chastising her negativity. "Don't say that. You never know what's waiting for you out there."

Sadie shrugged. "I'm not mad about it. Before Klaid, all I dreamed of was becoming a great fighter. He threw all my plans off. Once he was in the rearview mirror, I refocused on that goal. But you're not like me, Meera. Even as a kid you used to daydream about Mr. Perfect. While I was out there picking fights and throwing punches, you mated your dolls, choosing which other doll you thought was their best match. You had a list, remember? What you wanted in a mate. You were so excited to fall in love, even before you understood what it meant."

I shuddered. "Ugh, don't remind me. It's embarrassing

to think about. Even so, I grew up, and it turned out that men are"—I glanced toward Vareck, who was probably a hundred feet ahead of us—"complicated."

Sadie laughed. "It's not just men. Women can be a handful too, but they know how to find a clit."

I choked on a snort. Vareck paused, his shoulders going rigid. He looked back, scanning me from head to toe. I waved him off and after a suspended moment, he turned back to walking. "I can say with absolute certainty that Vareck doesn't have that problem."

Sadie grinned. "You've been dreaming of him for years. I'd damn well hope he knows where it's at after all this time." We both stifled our laughter, holding it in as much as possible, which just made it all the worse. My side cramped up and I grasped it.

"Fuck, you've given me a cramp."

"I've given you a cramp?" Sadie demanded, clutching her own stomach. "Way to place the blame."

"Least I'm blaming you for being funny."

"This is true. I am hilarious."

We both gave it a second to catch our breath, and I intentionally put a few more paces between our party. "So, have you and Damon hate-fucked yet, or—"

Smack.

"Okay, okay," I said, rubbing at the spot on my bicep she'd just backhanded playfully. "Still working toward the deed, then."

"I wouldn't touch that playboy with a ten-foot pole."

"Okay, Grinch." I rolled my eyes, glancing at the mark she left on my sunburned arm. It wouldn't sting as much if I hadn't been halfway cooked from our trek through Eversus the other day.

"I'm serious. After Klaid's fuckery, I learned my lesson. No more players for me."

"What did you say about making a mistake?"

"Oh, I made a mistake," she agreed wholeheartedly. "Dating. That's the mistake. Friends with benefits is the way to go."

"Oh yeah," I said sarcastically, waving my hand at the scenery. "That's worked out so much better for you."

Sadie frowned at me. "Amelia played us, but at least I wasn't trying to have a relationship with her. Could you imagine how much more this would suck if that was the case?"

"True . . ." Once again, my thoughts turned to Vareck. I wanted to say yes. To give in to this mate bond and whatever craziness came with it. But Sadie was right. I was scared. Mistakes like my friendship with Amelia made it hard to trust that anything but family would last forever.

"Do you remember what Mom and Dad said when we were growing up, about mating?"

I scrunched my face, immediately recalling the awkwardness of the sex talk when I was young. "I'm assuming you aren't talking about when they sat us down and fumbled through 'the talk', so you're going to have to be more specific."

Sadie laughed, shaking her head. "Oh gods, definitely not. Not that. Just the process of choosing a mate. They met at a gathering. Mom was there to compete against the other redcap females in the Fae Games. They weren't from the same town, but they decided to make a go of it anyway after the games. Dad followed her when she left Odenhal to move on to the next leg of the competition and six months later they mated."

"Right," I nodded. "Mom and Dad were lucky, though. They've said that time and again."

"You know what they also said?" she prompted, glancing between me and Vareck. "When you know, you know."

I swallowed hard on my now dry throat. "What if you're not sure?"

"Then take your time and make sure that's not the fear talking," Sadie said quietly. She hesitated before adding, "Otherwise a good thing might slip through your fingers."

CHAPTER 17

VARECK

The humidity and tension thickened the longer we walked.

While I knew I needed to talk with my mate, my frustration with her hadn't abated. I walked away for a good reason. The words I'd said in anger were bad enough, and I wasn't willing to risk making it worse. Sometimes saying you're sorry isn't good enough to repair the damage your words have caused, and I wouldn't make that mistake. Despite my good intentions, the silence between us made each second excruciating.

Night stretched on.

And on.

Quite literally since that was the nature of this realm. While Eversus was a land of two suns, Evorsus was eternal night with two moons to light the way. The smaller of which hung in the sky, illuminating the scattered fragments of the broken one that spun with it.

"I've never seen a moon like that before," Meera said softly, glancing up. She tripped over a rock, hopping on one foot as she tried to catch her balance. "Did something crash into it?"

"Not exactly," Damon answered, keeping his voice low.

"Are you going to explain or just leave us hanging?" Sadie cut in half a beat later. Damon sighed, and for once I felt like I understood my nephew.

"Uncle," he called lightly. "I believe you're more familiar with the twin hells." I wasn't sure if it was a slight or not, but I answered regardless.

"Noxathra," I said, pointing to the fractured moon overhead. Its pale shards hovered in uneven orbit, like shattered glass frozen mid-fall. "It was believed to have been a prison. A sentient spirit resided there. Something ancient, dangerous. When the moon shattered, that being was released. We think that's what plunged Evorsus into eternal night."

Meera, who walked slightly ahead, faltered. A shiver visibly ran through her. "Is that what's watching us? Some ancient evil?" She put two and two together quickly, but I expected nothing less of my intelligent mate.

"If you believe the stories," Damon murmured.

"Where do these 'stories' come from?" Sadie asked. "Last I checked, the teddy bear cult didn't talk."

"Not in a way we understand, but all life forms communicate," I said. "So while *they* don't talk, it's worth remembering there are worse things in this realm than Corvo's worshippers."

Sadie raised an eyebrow, craning her head to the side to stare at me over her shoulder. "Do tell."

I lifted a shoulder in a shrug. "Old blood stains these woods. The land holds onto those memories like a wound that never fully scabbed over. We've found ruins with warnings carved in languages long forgotten, half-burned journals from men and women who lost their minds trying to translate them after returning to Faerie. The land itself whispers . . ." I trailed off, not liking the unsettling way that they all looked to me. "And if you listen long enough, it speaks to you. It starts to make sense," I finished.

"Awesome," Meera muttered. "Haunted hell rocks. Totally fine."

Sadie smirked. "Does the land whisper sweet nothings, or is it more subtle suggestions, like the 'die screaming' variety?"

Damon grunted. "Depends on your definition of sweet."

Sadie rolled her eyes, throwing her head back with a snort of derision. "I think you're fucking with us."

Damon shrugged, like he hadn't a care in the world. "Think what you want, Sadie. But there are ruins scattered throughout this realm from Noxathra. There are ancient carvings, pre-dating anything we know of in the other realms. Evidence is everywhere if you just pay attention. I doubt all that work was put in so they could fuck with someone thousands of years later."

"I didn't say *they* were fucking with me. I meant you," she retorted.

"I wouldn't fuck with you in public. I'm not much of an exhibitionist," he said casually, and Sadie's steps stalled slightly. Meera didn't seem to notice, but Damon did. A small smirk appeared before he quickly schooled his features.

Before Sadie could start another argument, Meera turned around to face us, walking backward now. "So we're just marching through eternal night, under a broken moon that used to be a prison, surrounded by cute-but-murderous cultists, the Nameless, and probably other creatures too that we've yet to encounter. Now you're telling me something might be *watching* us that predates written history?"

"Checks out." Sadie shrugged, then looked down at her sister's feet. "Turn around before you fall over."

"I want to file a formal complaint with fate," Meera muttered, eyes flicking to the sky again as she turned back around. "Specifically about mine."

"Is that so?" Her comment made me bristle despite my best effort to brush it off. She seemed to realize the insinuation and then gave me an apologetic look over her shoulder.

"Sorry, I didn't mean . . ." She slowed down, watching her steps carefully.

Sadie seemed oblivious to the exchange. "Maybe the next creature we encounter will speak in a language we understand. I have some questions I want answered. Like where the exit is."

"Well, the Nameless spoke, but I don't think they were up for conversation, and honestly, I'd rather not run into them again," Meera said. Damon came to an abrupt stop.

"They spoke?" He looked at me for confirmation and I nodded. "What'd they say?"

"They said, 'stand down, cursed king' when Vareck was getting ready to fight, and when I said they were fae and understood us, they said, 'like calls to like, my queen.'" My entire body tensed at the memory. A revenant had no need for a leader. They knew who I was without question, and they wanted me dead. The Cursed King. Meera, however, was different. I felt it deep in my bones. They coveted her. She left out what the Nameless said afterward. *She's ours.* Whatever evil coursed through the veins of Evorsus had some perverted desire to claim her. I feared what that truly meant.

"They called you a queen, but then they attacked you?" Sadie said with a sigh. "This place, man. Teddy bears offer food and foot massages so they can eat you, and zombies, or whatever they are, call you a queen, but think you should be dead. What I'm hearing is that if it seems like a compliment, you're about to be killed. Got it."

"They aren't zombies," Damon said quietly. His gaze lost focus, and I watched curiously as a frown formed between his brows. His lips moved as he muttered to himself, repeating, 'like calls to like.'"

"Sure looked like a zombie," Meera said, brushing a hand over her face and pulling my attention to her as she swiped away a curl. "The way the skin was all weird and the missing eyes. Right up until they change and look just like you. Shapeshifting zombies."

Sadie stopped walking, so we all came to a halt, her voice rising as she spoke. "They shapeshift? Say what now?"

Meera shushed her and nodded, but I answered. "They trick you by changing their appearance. They can mimic voices. It's how they lure in their prey. In the middle of a battle, there's always confusion. You're turning one way or the other, fighting. One second you think you're standing beside your friend, the next, your 'friend' kills you. Don't allow them the opportunity."

She pointed at Damon while ranting, an edge of concern leaking into her voice. "You mean to tell me that before you guys showed up, his clone could have just appeared out of nowhere and tried to kill me? Some sort of monster version of him this hell realm created just switches places with him, and it even sounds like him? No wonder people don't make it out of here alive," she muttered.

"That wouldn't have happened. I know what the Nameless are," he said, but Sadie frowned, dubious at his confidence.

"Whatever they were, they were creepy." Meera shuddered, rubbing her arms.

"They're just parasites looking for their next meal. They use fae to regenerate, so at least we know what they want and there's no point trying to reason with them. You have to kill them all as quickly as possible. If we face them, follow my lead."

My nephew scoffed, shaking his head in a way that suggested he was strongly opposed.

"You disagree?"

"I do. You actually believe that? They use fae to regenerate? It's horseshit. Regenerate to what?"

"They're revenants, Damon. Fae-like creatures returned from the dead. Understand?" I said, pushing back. Annoyance flared deep in my chest. The mocking tone in his every word, the way he questioned me with authority when he had none just added fuel to the fire that already burned within me.

"That part is true. They are revenants. The rest is story time nonsense the elder fae use to scare children," he countered. "They're trapped here, understand? This isn't their domain." His matter-of-fact attitude sent flames through my veins. "They don't eat fae, and they don't 'regenerate' to their former selves. There's no evidence to support that. They're—"

"Evidence? First of all, I've been here. I've seen what they can do. I know firsthand, more than you could ever know. Building on that, the council of advisors know far more than you do in regard to the realms. The council, which you are not a part of, is a highly respected group of fae, men and women alike, who have dedicated their lives to knowledge. Knowledge they use to help me keep our kingdom safe. Make decisions that best serve our people. You claim they don't eat fae or use them to regenerate. I've seen otherwise, and I believe the burden of proof lies with you. What's your source, nephew?"

"Have you even read any of the books you have in that giant library of yours? Or do you really just rely on the council to educate you?" He boldly took a step forward, not quite a challenge, but close to it.

I narrowed my gaze, assessing his posture. "I suppose in all that spare time you have between fucking every maiden in Faerie that lifts her skirts and fucking off on accepting any type of royal duties or royal presence, you were intensely studying the vastly unknown history of Eversus and Evorsus? How could that be so when there is so little information documented? Enlighten me, Damon, please. Go on."

He crossed his arms and looked off into the distance. "You're right. What evidence could I possibly have, Uncle? Sounds like you have it all figured out."

"I didn't think hell could get worse," Sadie said, elbowing Meera in the side as she broke into our conversation. "But apparently, family tension does the trick. Who knew?"

"We should keep moving," Damon muttered, walking ahead without waiting for a response. He brushed past Sadie, and she didn't even take the opportunity to start giving him a hard time. Instead, she tilted her head and considered me, then turned and followed his path.

"Was that really necessary?" Meera asked softly as we followed several paces behind them. She gestured toward my nephew. The muscles in his shoulders and upper back were bunched together and tense. His footsteps were heavier; his speed quicker.

"To point out his lack of respect for his position? Absolutely."

"You're still moody with me, and don't want to deal with it, so you take it out on him. Got it. Good talk." Meera huffed, moving her feet a little faster to put space between us.

I scrubbed my hands down my face and growled in frustration, loud enough for all three of them to turn and glare at me over their shoulders. Sadie pressed her finger to her lips, shushing me. If I wasn't careful, she'd be the only of them still willing to talk to me by the end of this.

The silence was going to kill me. I spent too much time alone with my thoughts as we walked for hours. The broken moon shards cast an eerie light over us. The farther we went, the quieter the forest became, like even the monsters knew better than to linger in these parts.

Every now and then, one of us would stumble. Sadie the least, Meera the most, though she tried to hide it with a grimace. I started looking for another walking stick for her when I saw she was limping. Not badly, but it was still noticeable. She refused my offered hand. The stubborn fire in her eyes still burned but was gradually dimming like the mushroom lanterns from the pastel nightmare.

She was done. We all were.

We found shelter in a hollowed cliff side. A crooked mouth of rock opened into a shallow cave. It was deep enough to provide shelter, dry enough to sleep, and only smelled mildly of sulfur. Compared to the clearing, this was a generous space. We might actually be safe for the night.

Sadie dropped down near the mouth. "I've got first watch," she said, cracking her knuckles like she was settling into a fight. "I slept like a baby in the bear village. It only seems fair."

I didn't argue. I wanted Meera alone.

"You sure?" Damon asked. He stood next to her at the front as he scanned the forest.

Sadie grinned at him, then shot him a wink when he looked in her direction. "Are you volunteering to keep me company, princeling?"

"No, I was asking to be polite," Damon responded.

"He'll keep watch with you," I said, clapping my nephew on the back harder than necessary.

Damon's head whipped toward me. "Why exactly will I be doing that?"

"You're not injured, that's why." I took Meera's backpack and began to rummage through it, looking for something I could use as a light before muttering, "Is there a candle in here? Something?"

Damon grimaced. "I've got bruised ribs from cliff jumping and blisters the size of—"

"Your ego?" Sadie said under a cough.

Meera pointed to a side pocket. Inside were strangely shaped sticks, and I didn't know what to do with them. I handed one to her silently, and she bent it in half. A crack sounded before the stick filled with an unnaturally yellow glow. She shook it and gave it back to me as it started to glow a little brighter.

Returning my attention to Damon, I said, "We don't know what else is lurking out there. Best to have two pairs of eyes. You're still standing on your own two feet." With that, I shot a pointed look toward Meera, whose limp had worsened severely over the last hour or so. "You'll manage."

"C'mon. You can keep me awake with your whining," Sadie said with a smirk, patting the ground next to her.

Their bickering followed us into the cave as I led Meera toward the darker end, further from the mouth and whatever might still be listening outside. The space narrowed, the ceiling dipping lower, and the shadows grew thicker, our only source of light providing a sickly color as it illuminated her face. Meera sat on the cold stone, arms wrapped around her knees, eyes vacant and fixed on nothing.

I knelt. There was too much lingering between us. Too many unspoken words.

"Why?" I finally said.

She didn't move. "Why what, Vareck?" Her voice was quiet, not meek, but lacking emotion. If not for the faint trembling of her injured foot, I'd wonder if she were being obstinate. I was pretty sure that wasn't the case, given her physical symptoms had been worsening over time. We were all exhausted, but this realm seemed to be taking a toll on Meera more so than the rest of us.

I studied her face. She had dirt on her cheek. The river water had dried in her hair, leaving frizzy copper ringlets framing her flushed face. Hazel eyes flicked toward me, tired and guarded.

In an ideal world, I could wait to address it. We didn't live in the ideal, especially not now. Our reality was bleak. It was literally hell.

"Why did you jump?"

Her jaw tightened. Teeth bit down into her plump bottom lip. "I didn't want to be eaten."

"That's not what I meant, and you know it."

She released her bottom lip to purse them together instead. "You're still mad."

I think it went without saying I was furious, but I wanted an explanation for her actions, not to belabor my anger. "I'm trying here, Meera."

She sighed. "I jumped because Sadie did. Because the options were that or being eaten, and I'd rather take my chances with the unknown when the other option is certain death."

I sighed, taking a seat next to her. "I was trying to tell you to stop. I thought we were on the same page. I'm trying to keep you safe. I don't compel you; you don't do anything stupid. Then you went and jumped off a cliff."

"I'm not a toddler whose hand you need to hold so I don't walk into the street."

"Honestly, that's a great comparison." I rubbed at my temples to soothe the growing tension that knotted together.

Meera's brows furrowed and her nostrils flared. "The river caught us, Vareck. What is the big deal?"

Dropping my hands, I rested my forearm against my thigh for support, and I sighed. "Because of Damon. The river only caught you that way because of Damon."

She blinked, quietly trying to make sense of my response. "I don't know what that means."

"Had he not intervened," I said, my words sharper than I intended, "you'd have hit the water like stones dropped from the castle towers. That cliff was easily three hundred feet. You would have broken every bone in your body on impact. Do you understand that?"

"What? No—"

"You felt that gust right before you hit the water? That was him. He jumped after you two and redirected your momentum. He's an air elemental, remember?" I wiggled my fingers in a weak attempt to mimic his power. "Slowed you both enough that you didn't break when you hit the water."

Meera stared at me, color draining from her face. Her

mouth opened then closed. I'd stunned her. In a quiet voice she asked, "How'd you know it was that steep?"

"I scented the water too, but just looking at it was enough to know it was too high. It was an abyss. Then I flew down after you counting every second, but I was too slow. I know how fast I can fly, and I wasn't going to make it. If not for Damon, you both would have died. If you were lucky, it would have been on impact and not because your body was broken and you slipped beneath the water and drowned."

"That's why you're mad," she said eventually. "Because we could have died. *I* could have died."

I nodded. "I almost lost you. Again. You didn't listen when I told you not to jump, and this was right after we had the conversation about me being able to fly."

Meera's voice was small, ashamed. "I'm sorry."

"I'm not looking for an apology."

"Then what are you looking for?" she said, frustrated now.

"I just want you to listen. To understand. Do you think I wanted us to get attacked? Eaten? Of course not. Why would I tell you to stop if it puts you in more danger? What would be the point of that?"

She sighed. "Fair enough."

"We're partners, Meera. At least, I think we are. And partners listen to each other."

She seemed to accept what I'd said, but then she crossed her arms, and her body language said otherwise. "Do partners also walk away? Because you did."

"I had to." She raised her brows in annoyance, urging me to continue. "I've seen what happens when people don't." My voice dropped, weighted and heavy with the memories that flooded me. "Maeve and Drayden. Their fights were legendary. Explosive. No boundaries, no brakes. And the last thing they ever said to each other before she died—" I shook my head, not wanting to repeat it. "Those words couldn't be taken back. No apologies. No atonement. No forgiveness. Just unending grief. It tore a hole in Drayden's heart in which he has never recovered from, and never will."

Her body went still beside me, the tension she held in her shoulders loosening. In a barely audible whisper, she breathed, "Oh . . ."

"When I walked away," I continued, "it wasn't because I didn't care. It was because I care deeply. And I was angry. Too angry to say anything worth hearing."

Meera leaned her head back against the wall. "I don't know what I'm doing."

"Neither do I." Gods, that was the fucking truth. "But I'm trying. I don't always know what I should do, but I have seen firsthand what not to do."

"I'm trying too, Vareck."

I turned to face her. "Are you?"

She hesitated, then nodded once. "It may not seem like it, but I am."

In our moment of silence, Sadie's voice drifted through the cave mouth. "If anything crawls in here, I call dibs."

Damon groaned. "On what?"

"On its teeth," she said cheerfully.

Meera smiled softly, and I let out a breath that might've been a laugh.

It wasn't peace.

But it was something.

We sat there in the dark, the broken moon and its twin casting pale light into the mouth of the cave. The jagged shadows made her look ethereal. I held my hand out, palm up, and placed it on her thigh. Placing her hand in mine, our fingers laced together, and I brought our joined hands to my lips, placing a kiss gently on her skin.

"I don't want to lose you," I said, so quietly I wasn't sure I meant to say it out loud.

She squeezed my hand and turned slightly to meet my eyes.

"You won't."

CHAPTER 18

MEERA

The water shimmered, a luminous, almost electric blue. Perfectly still, as though the world itself had stopped to hold its breath.

Vareck stood in the center of the pool; shirtless, drenched, powerful. He didn't need to turn around. He knew I was there. I saw it in the way his body stilled, not from surprise, but anticipation.

My voice cut through the quiet. "Have room for another?"

His head turned slightly, enough for me to catch the glint in his icy eyes. "Get in," he commanded. No hesitation. No polite dismissals or feigned indifference. Just raw want in the form of two words.

That was all the invitation I needed.

I pulled my shirt over my head, slow and deliberate, watching the way his gaze raked over me. My skin prickled beneath its intensity.

"You know this is a dream, right?" I said, kicking off my boots.

His expression didn't change, but there was something

wicked in the curve of his mouth. "I'm aware, yes." I undid my pants slowly, letting him watch as I peeled them down my legs. Finally, I slid out of my panties and let them drop.

Standing completely bare, my pulse thundering, I looked down at my own body, then up at him. "We don't have to hold back here," I murmured, the implication of my words clear.

He didn't speak. Just stared at me, his eyes fixed on my face like it was the first time he'd ever seen me. It was almost enough for me to come undone.

Almost.

But when he said, "I don't plan on it," his voice thick with desire, it lit a fuse inside me.

I crouched at the pool's edge and slid into the warm water.

The warmth of the water spread across my skin, but it was nothing compared to the searing heat of his gaze. I waded in slowly. The silence between us was no longer weighted with distrust and tension. It was no longer marked by communication breakdowns and relationship flaws. Now it was charged; driven by need and longing.

Vareck didn't move as I approached. He let me come to him. Let me step into his space until I was close enough that the rise and fall of his chest brushed against my breasts.

"Then what are you waiting for?" I whispered, tilting my chin up to meet his gaze. "Claim me, Vareck."

His hands were on me; frenzied, calloused, and gripping my skin so tightly as though he'd reached his breaking point. Vareck hauled me forward, his mouth crashing into mine with a hunger that made my knees buckle. I clung to his shoulders, fisting my hands in his wet hair as he kissed me.

Our mouths warred. His tongue plunged past my lips, demanding, claiming. And I gave it to him—matched his hunger with my own. Because gods help me, I wanted this just as badly.

He backed me up until I felt the cool, slick stone wall of the pool against my skin. His hand cupped the side of my face, his thumb dragging across my cheekbone before tangling in my hair and yanking my head back, exposing my throat.

"You've haunted every dream I've had for years," he growled against my skin. "I wish I could be gentle and make love to you the way you deserve, but I'm too far gone for that."

I gasped, moaning as his lips moved down my neck. The pointed end of his fangs scraped against the sensitive skin where the curve of my neck met my shoulder. "I don't want gentle."

He growled, an animalistic, primal sound, and then his hands slid down my thighs, the water sloshing around us. He gripped the backs of my legs and picked me up before placing me on the ledge. Legs spread and vulnerable to him, I shivered.

His eyes met mine, a shade darker than they should have been. His fury was near the surface. "Keep your eyes on me," he ordered.

And then he buried his face between my thighs.

I cried out, my back arching, fingers scrambling for purchase against the slick ground beneath me. His tongue was relentless—slick, sinful strokes that had me shaking in seconds. He sucked my clit into his mouth, humming deep in his throat, and the vibration shot through me like lightning.

"Vareck—gods—fuck, don't stop," I begged, heels digging into his back as my hips rolled against his mouth.

He didn't. He pinned my thighs wide, his mouth devouring me. His tongue plunged inside me, curled and stroked, then he shifted—one hand sliding up to pinch and tease my nipple while he worked me toward the edge again.

I shattered for him, clenching and pulsing around nothing. My vision went white.

But he didn't let up.

Before I could come down, he rose from the water like some beautiful, wrathful god, the planes of his chest glistening as he stood to his full, imposing height. His cock jutted out from his body, thick, hard, and angry red.

"I want you to remember how this feels," he said darkly, grabbing my waist. "So when you wake up aching, you'll wonder how you ever thought I was just a fantasy."

He lifted me easily, like I weighed nothing, and impaled me on him in one savage, unforgiving thrust.

No warning. No easing in.

Just thick, full, and all-consuming.

I exploded, screaming his name into the night. My body convulsed around him, every nerve on fire.

He didn't stop.

His thrusts were relentless, brutal. His hand on my ass moved me on his cock, forcing me to take him deeper. My nipples dragged across his chest, sending more sparks through me.

I screamed. My head fell back. Every muscle in my body locked down as he filled me; deep, hard, perfect.

Vareck hissed through his teeth, holding still, buried to the hilt. "You're so godsdamn tight," he groaned. "So fucking perfect."

"Move," I gasped, nails scoring his shoulders. "Fuck me like you mean it."

He did.

He fucked me like it was his mission. Like this dream was the only place he could ever touch me, and he was going to make it count. Every thrust rocked my body, the sound of skin on skin echoing through the quiet, mist-laced air. The water churned around us as he drove into me over and over.

I wrapped my arms around his neck, holding on as he claimed me. His hand slid down, cupped my ass, lifted and dropped me onto his cock like he knew it would wreck me further. And fuck, I loved it. I loved every brutal second of it.

"I can feel you clenching," he growled, lips brushing my ear. "You gonna come for me again, Meera?"

"Yes—fuck, yes—don't stop," I cried out.

He reached between us, thumb finding my clit, circling it with ruthless precision.

Harder than the first time, I went over the edge. I convulsed around him, crying out his name, trembling as my orgasm tore through me like wildfire.

He didn't stop.

He pulled out, turned me around, and bent me over the ledge, my hands bracing on the stone. His hand fisted in my hair, yanked my head back, and then he slammed into me from behind.

I sobbed with pleasure, legs shaking, the position deeper, rougher. His other hand slipped around my waist, fingers sliding down and finding my clit again, tormenting it as he thrust harder and faster.

"You feel that?" he snarled. "That's mine. This body, this pussy, this dream—it's all mine."

I was incoherent—gasping, whimpering, shattering

again as he pushed me into a third orgasm with ruthless efficiency. My body was nothing but sensation, a vessel for the overwhelming, soul-deep pleasure he dragged out of me.

And then I felt it.

The shift. The unmistakable heat blooming low in my belly as his rhythm faltered, as his breath hitched against my neck.

He was close.

"I want to come with you," he panted. "One more, Meera. Give me one more."

I moaned his name, pushed back against him. Then his fangs pierced my neck.

White-hot ecstasy exploded through me. I shattered around him again, screaming. My legs locked tight as he fucked me harder, chasing his own climax.

But it still wasn't enough.

"Need. More," he growled.

He pulled out and rolled me over, like I weighed little more than a rag doll. I loved the way he could move my body. Water sluiced down his body as he lifted himself out of the water and onto the ledge. He pulled me onto his lap and suddenly I was straddling him, riding him, chasing another high. I ground my hips, fucking him deep.

"What do you need?" I purred.

"Bite me."

His hands gripped my thighs, bruising. I leaned forward and dragged my tongue up his throat.

"Bite me," he demanded again.

I sank my fangs into his neck . . .

CHAPTER 19

MEERA

I woke up from the blissful haze of my dream to the weight of a fat cat on my chest.

"About time," he said lazily, shifting his body and making it harder for me to breathe.

"Off," I said through a strangled groan, and I rolled to the side as he reluctantly toppled over, before sitting up. I turned my ankle to see if it felt better. It was tight, but it wasn't throbbing anymore. That was a good sign.

Sadie was braced against the cave wall, asleep, axes in hand. Damon rested on the other side of the cave entrance, sleeping in a similar fashion. Vareck lay next to me, his breathing steady and soft. A rush of panic surged through me. We had all screwed up on keeping watch.

As though he could read my mind, Corvo sauntered around and sat next to me. "I took the last watch. They've only been asleep for a couple of hours."

"You did something nice for Damon?" I asked, raising a brow at him.

He snorted and wiggled his whiskers. "Uh, no. I did something nice for you. And I expect payment in return."

"Well, I'm fresh out of tuna, so I don't know what you want from me."

"You can get me some fresh salmon." His little tongue darted out, licking up the front of his nose and then off to the side. "I've had a craving lately. I found some canned, but alas, I need a human can opener."

I looked around the cave. "Corvo. I'm stuck in hell, in case you haven't noticed. Unless you happen to bring me some, I can't help you."

"Oh, I did. The canned one, anyway. That'll hold me over. You owe me a big, giant fresh filet when you get home."

"If I ever get home," I muttered, wiping the sleep from my eyes.

"Oh, about that," he began, then he trotted to Vareck's ear and let out a long, loud, obnoxious meow. Vareck's brows scrunched and his eyes shot open.

"Gods, you stupid cat," he groaned, sitting up. "Why do you do that?"

"It amuses me," he said with a feline shrug. He shrunk down into a loaf and curled his tail around himself. "It's also payback for that pill you crushed into my tuna three months ago. Don't think I didn't notice."

"It was medicine, you twat. You may be a god, but you're stuck in a cat's body. You can get worms and other parasites.

"He is a parasite," Damon grumbled. He and Sadie were apparently awake, giving death glares to Corvo for his loud performance.

"Now, now," he said, flicking his tail in annoyance. "You keep being mean to me, and I won't tell you what you need to know."

"Stop," I begged, reaching over to scratch him behind

the ear. "It's too early in the morning, or night, or whatever time it is."

"It's a doozy, right?" he purred, closing his eyes and leaning into my hand.

"What is it we need to know?" Vareck rubbed at his temples.

"The plan!"

"Devil cat," Sadie said quietly, shaking her head. She stood up, reaching her arms above her head to stretch.

"Thank you." Corvo looked as though he were smiling. "But enough of the compliments. This is about the plan."

"Stop saying that," Vareck growled.

Corvo took a breath in what seemed like another attempt at annoying everyone in the cave. Before he could be an asshole further, I stopped petting him and just said, "Didn't you say you brought canned salmon for me to open?"

His golden eyes lit up, and he dipped his head pointing at a pile of things he'd brought. "Yes. Breakfast is a good idea. I always do better when I've been fed."

"History would suggest otherwise," Damon said as he also got up. "I've fed you plenty, and yet . . ."

I ignored all of them. Corvo was a cat, and I had no idea how long he'd been that way. God he may have been, but he fully embraced the lifestyle of a pampered house pet. As such, he needed to be treated like one so he would be at least somewhat agreeable.

I tossed a piece of fruit and a protein bar to Sadie and then the same to Damon. Vareck got up and grabbed breakfast for himself and I made sure to open the can and set it down for Corvo. The moment he got wind of it, his little pink nose began to twitch as he scented the air. Hopping up, he ran to the can and began to gobble his precious treat.

Sadie began to talk around a mouthful of food, but I held my hand up to shush her while I shook my head. She shrugged, and we all ate in silence, waiting until his royal pain-in-the-ass was finished with his fish.

After smacking his lips and licking all around his mouth, Corvo let out a little sigh. "That hit the spot. My stomach thanks you. Which reminds me . . . what does your food supply look like?"

"Slim. Some basic protein bars, fruit, and bread are all we have left. We need something shelf stable and light-weight." I hummed in thought, considering what would work best for him to bring.

"What about those survival meal kits?" Sadie asked. "Like military supply stores have."

"That's a good idea. Corvo, can you bring us some? If you can find one of my brothers, they can show you where to go. They'll be at our gym. And bring another sturdy back-pack. We should have more than one."

"I can figure it out," he said, and he started to sound sleepy. "Might be after a post-breakfast nap though."

"Corvo," I said firmly, raising my brows at him point-edly. "No napping. We still need to know where we're going."

"Ah, yes. The plan." Vareck rolled his eyes. "You need to head in the direction you've been going. There will be a portal waiting for you in the Fold. You'll find it just beyond the purple waterfall."

"That's not even remotely helpful," Damon argued. "Is the water purple? The rocks? The trees?

"It can't be that hard to find. How many purple water-falls are there, water, rocks or otherwise?" Sadie asked, winking at Damon. "You telling me you can't find something that's obviously different from its surroundings? That's so disappointing."

Damon huffed in derision, and I just sighed. "I need more information, Corvo."

"Fae just have no sense of direction, do you?"

"I think you're confusing us with humans."

"Oh yeah? Which direction are you heading now?"

None of us could properly answer. We had two moons guiding us, and I had yet to figure out any measurement of time or moon cycle. The truth was, I don't think any of us knew how many hours had passed, much less how many days. And worse, we could be walking in circles, and we wouldn't know it. We had been mostly hoping our gut instinct was leading the way, and we felt like we were heading in the opposite direction of the things that wanted to eat us. I needed to start paying better attention. Half-assed measures weren't going to work.

"That's what I thought. You're heading north right now. Keep doing that."

"Genuine question, Corvo. How do we know? This is the land of eternal moonlight. No setting and rising here."

"Finally, an intelligent question." He waited for me to pet him, and when I did, he finally continued. "The blue flowers that grow here in Evorsus? They face north. Always."

"Why is that?" Sadie asked.

"They're looking to Noxathra. It may not look like it to you, but they are facing that way. As long as you keep an eye on those flowers, you will know which direction you're going. Just don't pee on them. They take it personally and release a smelly mist that sticks to you like sap." He wiggled his whiskers and flared his nostrils in disgust. "Ask me how I know."

"You didn't mention this earlier," Vareck said, crumbling his wrapper and stuffing it in the backpack before he took out a canteen and drank from it. He seemed to quickly realize he needed to amend his words, so Corvo didn't go off track. "Not about the pissing on flowers. About the flowers facing north."

"Nobody asked," he replied simply. "Besides, I didn't know you didn't know. You've been here before. Meera here is the one who asked the good questions. I left and told you all not to get eaten. You've done a fine job of it. Congratulations. Now keep heading north."

"For how long?" I frowned, wondering how long it had already been. I sort of didn't want the exact answer.

"Hard to say. I can check in on you from time to time. Bring you food as you need it. Some canned salmon too. Drayden won't open them for me, the stooge." He mumbled in cat, clearly displeased. "The passage of time is weird here, as you've noticed. You've got a few days at minimum, assuming the land doesn't go topsy-turvy on you."

"The Fold is dangerous. I wonder if there was any way to bring the portal to us," Damon mused, crumbling up his protein wrapper and stuffing it in his pocket. Sadie looked at him curiously. "What? It feels weird to litter. Just because this is hell doesn't mean I need to leave my trash here."

She shook her head and shrugged. "I got nothing. I actually agree with you." He smiled cautiously, right before she added, "Probably won't happen again any time soon, of course. Sort of shocked that a princeling knows how to throw away his own garbage."

"There she is," he muttered.

Corvo tsked. "Damon. I see you reading in the libraries. I'm assuming you read and aren't looking for picture books." Vareck studied his nephew intensely.

"Libraries? Plural?" he questioned, crossing his arms. "You've been in *my* library?

"Is this really the topic of conversation we need to be having right now?" Damon shot back defensively before he addressed Corvo. "I understand the complexities of this realm. I was just thinking out loud. Problem solving? Wondering if the portal can be made to follow you, the demon god cat, so you can bring it to us, but obviously we cannot."

"Portal magic doesn't work like that. It's a doorway, ding dong. And you're stuck in a realm that doesn't exactly have a map of its terrain. It's not like I can give them coordinates. A—a witch made the portal. They said it must be in the Fold. Something about the ley lines converging there. These realms don't exist on the same timeline, and as you discovered, they aren't mirrors of each other. What's here isn't there. The Fold exists on both sides. All things considered, a waterfall sounds pleasant. Be glad the Fold doesn't exist in the thorn fields of Eversus."

There was so much to process. I had no idea why Damon would feel the need to guard himself over being in the library, and I also had no idea why it mattered to Vareck. Books were for everyone. But I had to agree with Damon. This wasn't what we needed to be talking about, and Corvo had given us a direction. There was comfort in knowing this location didn't move around on us. I placed my hand on Vareck's arm, feeling the tense muscle. "He's right. We need to get to the portal."

"Listen to your woman, Vareck," Corvo advised. "She knows what she's doing."

Well that was a lie. I knew jack all about surviving here. I had no idea what I was doing. I had proven that enough already. I just wanted to go home.

Sadie barked a laugh. "She knows about as much as the rest of us. No offense, sister."

I snorted in return. "None taken." I tapped my temple twice and then pointed to her. "Same thought."

Corvo tilted his head, his golden eyes standing out starkly against his black fur. "Oh, she knows far more than she realizes. You'll see."

"What is that supposed to mean?" Vareck asked.

"Well, time for me to go. Head north. Drayden and Kaia will be waiting. Probably. Assuming he doesn't get eaten. Honestly, he is such a grumpy fucker, you'd better hurry up or else he just might leave you all here."

Then Corvo winked out of existence, leaving us all with his cryptic comment and half-assed goodbye. Three pairs of eyes looked at me. "What? I don't know what he's talking about either."

Vareck growled softly, putting his arm around my waist and pulling me closer to his side. "I don't want you getting too far from me once we head out."

His body felt warm against mine and I nudged him with shoulder playfully. "C'mon, Vareck. It's Corvo. He likes to be a pain. Do you think he really meant anything by that?"

"I don't know. This realm already wants you. I can feel it."

"But it's not like Corvo's being serious. He doesn't want me to get hurt. He's just fucking with you because he knows he can."

I said the words, but I wasn't sure I even believed them. Something about this place continued to make me increasingly uncomfortable. The land was supposedly sentient. It was watching us. Following our every move. The Nameless were out there waiting for us. Hopefully the murder bears weren't tracking us. Gods knew what else lurked in the shadows. We were all on edge to an extent, but I felt this current of uncertainty just beneath my skin. Something far more than danger. It was a fear I couldn't yet name, and it followed me as we trekked our way north.

"I half expected you to rub two sticks together," Sadie said, bickering once again with Damon while we all sat around a small campfire in the middle of nowhere.

"You knew I could start a fire. I had one before you dropped into the cave. Are you always this bitchy?" he shot back while he prodded the kindling, stoking the flames.

"I'm saving it all for you, dumpling."

"You spend most of your time alone, don't you? No man in his right mind would stick around long." I winced as soon as he said it. Our sisterly conversation about the past was still a freshly picked wound and he unknowingly just rubbed salt in it. Sadie could talk a big game, but she'd been hurt something awful, and her inability to be in a relationship was proof of it.

Her jaw set and she narrowed her eyes. "I hope you step on a nail and get tetanus."

"You see any fucking nails around here?" Damon dropped his stick and threw his hands up.

"Only if we're lucky!"

"What is it you want? What have I ever done to you?"

"I don't know. I can hear when you chew. You walk like you've never tracked a thing in your life. You breathe too loud. You snore."

"Do you think you don't snore? Besides, what do you care? It's not like I'm inviting you to sleep next to me after we leave this place."

"Get fucked, pretty boy."

"You offering to climb on top, warrior princess?"

Vareck groaned beside me, but I watched in curiosity as the two of them argued with each other. My sister was no doubt feisty and hotheaded, but this was something different. It was almost as if this place was changing her. Bringing out a heightened version of her qualities . . . especially the more difficult ones.

Corvo had so kindly popped in while we were trudging along, quite literally dumping a full backpack of food for us, before he quickly disappeared, telling us it was dinner time in Faerie and he didn't want to miss it. No pleasantries, no conversation, nothing. Just showed up with the backpack, turned around to show us his asshole, then popped right out of Evorsus all over again.

I couldn't even be annoyed with him. I didn't want to stay here either.

I rummaged through the bag and picked out four food pouches to warm up. They were your standard survival kits. Bland, shitty nutrient-packed food that was made just to keep you alive. You'd certainly never eat it for the taste.

"Do you know how to stop this?" Vareck whispered, flicking his eyes to Sadie and Damon. "We're all going to end up mad if this goes on for much longer."

"I had a thought about that. You said this place is sentient." He looked at me curiously, nodding in acknowledgment. "Do you think the realm is messing with their heads? I don't know Damon, but Sadie isn't usually this bad. I mean, she's a lot to handle, but this version of her is bigger. Meaner. More explosive. Could the realm be blowing up their emotions? Maybe trying to break them mentally, or even break them apart somehow?"

"Breaking them mentally makes sense. I don't see the

purpose of breaking them apart. They barely wanted to be together to begin with," he mused, scrubbing his fingers through his beard as he considered the possibilities. "Unless it's as simple as strength in numbers..."

I nodded along, wondering if that was what was happening. The land either wanted us to lose our minds, or to separate so we couldn't fend off whatever Nameless or murderous teddy bears or cannibal mutant rabbits it wanted to throw at us. I hadn't seen those, but my mind had wandered enough that it was starting to create things that weren't there. "We need them to chill out."

"If you have a plan to shut them up, I am all ears," he said.

After handing Vareck his pouch, I stood up and tossed one to Damon. He caught it quickly, pausing long enough for there to be a moment of beautiful silence between them.

"Hey, Sadie." I tossed her a pouch and when she caught it, I smiled. "Truth or dare."

She grinned, and the murderous look in her eye disappeared. My sister looked like herself again. "We don't have liquor," she pointed out.

I shrugged. "Getting drunk here wouldn't be my first choice anyway."

"Fair enough."

Vareck raised a hand. "I'm sorry, what's 'truth or dare'?"

"A drinking game we play with our brothers." I launched into the whole explanation of how the game was played between us. You pick truth, you tell the truth and take a shot. You pick dare, you complete the dare and take the shot. Refusal or incompletion equals forfeiture, and you lose the game. The last man or woman standing wins.

"Wait, you have to drink even when you complete your turn? It's not a situation where you take a shot because you refused?" Damon asked, his brows scrunching, looking around as though he missed part of the rules. "I don't understand the point."

I scoffed, smacking my hand over my heart in a mocking gesture of shock. "Bragging rights, of course." I looked to Vareck for encouragement, but even he looked slightly dubious. "Look, we don't have a drink, but we can still have fun."

"Is it fun?" Damon whispered to Vareck.

"Sadie is the reigning champion," I added. Damon's back straightened and his jaw muscle tightened. "If that matters . . ."

"Too scared, princeling?"

"I'm in," he said. Damon turned to Vareck and nodded like they were teaming up somehow. Vareck looked at him, craning his neck back and turning to me for an explanation. I just shrugged.

"All right, sister. Truth or dare."

I knew my sister's answer. She only ever took a dare, and this time I was going big. It was a calculated risk, but it was dangerous all the same. For days on end, I had been listening to Sadie and Damon make snide remarks and snap at each other. Yes, it was getting out of hand, but I truly thought that was the realm just amplifying bad behavior. An outsider wouldn't realize it, but my sister had a crush on this man. She didn't know how to act on it, so instead, she was scared shitless and decided the best course of action was to be obnoxiously mean. He was everything she wasn't, and the antithesis of everyone she had ever dated. Damon was cultured, had clean fingernails, chewed with his mouth closed, didn't beat people's faces in for a living, and he didn't own a motorcycle. What she didn't see was the way he looked at her too. The way he held her eye contact even when she was bitching at him. Or how he watched her when he thought no one was looking. There was a subtle curl to his lips when she said something flirtatious, albeit still a little mean.

She smirked, tearing the seal off her food pouch. "Dare, of course."

I took a breath, then exhaled through my nose slowly. "Kiss Damon for thirty seconds."

Sadie choked on air while Damon paused in the middle of opening his food parcel.

"I'm sorry, what now?" he asked, and somehow, he still made it sound polite. My sister, not so much.

She stood up, throwing her arms out, incensed. "What the fuck, Meera? What are we? Thirteen?"

I grinned, showing off a toothy smile. I wiggled where I was seated. I knew what I was doing. Waving my hand around, I said, "You can forfeit if you want to. It's okay. I won't tell Cadoc."

Sadie's nostrils flared, incensed. "Never."

"Glad to hear it. Go on and kiss. Thirty seconds."

Vareck leaned in closely, turning his head slightly so he could barely be heard. "Is this a good idea?"

Sadie tapped her wrist and tutted. "You know, we don't have a watch, so . . ."

"I'm pretty sure Meera knows how to count," Damon said as he stood up, and Sadie whipped her head around to glare at him. But there it was. A split second of heat between them. A tiny glimmer in his eye. A fire in hers.

"He's right!" I said, clapping my hands in excitement. "I do. So, kiss!"

Sadie was about to protest again, but she didn't get her chance. Damon stepped forward, reaching his hand behind her neck and pulling her face to his. Their lips met and

Sadie's sharp inhale echoed in the silence. For a brief moment, it was just shock that it'd happened, but an electric current charged the air quickly, and I wondered if I was the only one who felt the literal change in the energy around us. They went from a stiff kiss to something far more urgent. I noticed the moment her body melted against his, the tension easing. Their mouths opened, and they devoured each other passionately. I almost felt bad about watching. Wind whipped around all of us, fanning the flames of the campfire. Sadie's nails racked his back, and his hand tightened in her hair as he growled against her lips. She pressed her body into his, trying to get closer as his other hand pressed into her lower back.

"Thirty," Vareck said, and I elbowed him and mouthed "what are you doing?"

The buzzing sensation in the air fizzled suddenly, and Sadie and Damon stood in front of each other for several seconds, their chests heaving with labored breaths, their hands still tangled in hair or holding the other closely.

And then they weren't. He dropped his hands away from her, stepping back, looking down to where he had sat earlier. She did the same, blinking rapidly to process what had just happened.

I sat in awe. I had never, not once, seen Sadie kiss a man like that. I fanned myself theatrically. "That was some intense chemistry. You two have a lot to figure out."

Sadie flushed but shook her head trying to rid herself of what I assume were emotions. She cleared her throat, but her voice still wobbled slightly when she spoke. "Chemistry isn't the same as feelings."

Damon smirked, and he whispered, "So you are saying we *do* have chemistry?"

My sister scoffed, but she refused to meet his gaze as

she ate from the food pouch. "I have chemistry with every-one. You aren't special."

Damon pursed his lips, knowing he had the upper hand for once. "Something tells me you're lying."

Sadie ignored him, then turned to Vareck. She was pissed at me, but she'd also forgive me. "Truth or dare."

"I don't want to kiss Damon, so I'll go with truth," he said. I snickered, and somewhere in another realm, I knew Corvo would have appreciated that moment of Vareck's humor.

Sadie swallowed another mouthful of the survival gruel. "Tell us a secret you've never told anyone else."

I stiffened. That was the same truth she gave me when I had finally told her about dreaming of Vareck. My heart raced at the memory, and I wondered what he was going to say.

Vareck tilted his head to the side, pensive. He scratched his chin while he thought, and he shifted as though his spot on the ground was no longer comfortable. Sadie was eating it up. She loved making people squirm, and right now, she would be out for blood after I'd just made her kiss Damon and face some of her feelings about him. "This is a tough one," he said softly. "I've never said it out loud."

"Thems the rules, Your Majesty. Or forfeit."

"Fair enough. No one can repeat this, understand?" He looked at each of us, pointing at us individually as we nodded. Damon leaned forward, completely taken in. Vareck sighed. "I hate peas. Not all peas. Green peas, specifically."

I snorted, and Damon laughed. Sadie chose to shout as her medium. "What? That's not a secret!"

Vareck sat up straight. "It is too. Who are you to decide what is a secret and what isn't?"

Sadie looked to Damon for help but he just laughed again. "I actually think it's a secret. I didn't know it, and the chef makes a ham hock and pea soup once a fortnight." Damon leaned back, tilting his head back as he cackled. "Because the stewardess thinks you love it! That's why she has the chef make it."

Vareck nodded. "And that is why you can't say anything. Imelda is the kindest, most gentle, hardworking woman. The castle runs smoothly because of her. She'd be crushed if she knew how much I hated it. I won't do that to her."

I rubbed his arm. "That's really nice of you."

Sadie grumbled, crossing her arms. "That's a bullshit secret."

"That secret would hurt feelings, Sadie. Feelings of someone I care about. That's not bullshit. But is it what you were looking for? No. Because you weren't specific." Sadie narrowed her eyes at him.

"Well played, Your Majesty." She inclined her chin.

Vareck dipped his chin in return. "It's my turn, yes? Damon, truth or dare."

Damon shrugged. "I've already been a party to a dare, so I guess I'll go with truth."

"Good. I've been wondering about something for a while now." His nephew gestured for him to carry on. "I know you've snuck in my chambers and fucked in my bed. I don't need that answered." Damon paled, his eyes darting over to my sister quickly before looking back to Vareck. He shook his head slightly, but Vareck either didn't notice or didn't care. "How many women did you bring into my room?"

Damon closed his eyes, breathing out. He was miserable. This was the same man I had kidnapped by enticing him while he was already on the way to sleep with another woman. Everyone knew he was a playboy. He didn't hide it. The only reason he would want that swept under the rug now was because he caught feelings for my sister, and now he would either have to back down and forfeit or give away the answer. Both of which would cause my sister to lose respect for him, if she had any to begin with.

Vareck groaned. "Fucking hell. How many?"

"Sixteen," he answered softly, opening his eyes and looking at Sadie. She held his gaze for what felt like an eternity before she sniffed once and looked away, taking a drink from the canteen.

"For fuck's sake, Damon!" Vareck started, but I put my hand on his leg and tried to subtly show him that now wasn't the time to bring it up. I angled my head over toward my sister and looked again at Vareck with wide eyes, just hoping he could read my mind.

"Vareck, it's not–"

He held up a hand, cutting Damon off. "That's enough. I don't want to hear details."

Damon's jaw clenched and cleared his throat. "You're up, Meera. Truth or dare."

"Truth."

"You sure about that?" he asked.

"Oh yeah. I'm not much of a dare kind of girl when I'm playing a game. My job is daring enough." I thought for a moment before adding, "And I usually play this while drinking, so my uncoordinated ass doesn't fare well in the dare department."

"Are you going to accept the mate bond with my uncle?"

Time stopped.

The sound of white noise filled my ears as I tried to

swallow the thick lump in my throat. I should say yes. I should know the answer, and it should be yes. Right . . . right? I wanted to say yes. Why couldn't I say it with confidence? Why couldn't I say it with certainty? I tried to speak, but no words came out. Instead, I just floundered, my lips moving, but no sounds forming a coherent answer. I may as well have been a fish out of water, gasping for air.

"Are you serious right now?" Vareck growled under his breath as he turned his head to look at me. The pain in his eyes was barely masked by pure rage. "This is how you answer? With nothing? No words at all?"

"Vareck, I—" My voice broke as I tried to hold back tears. "I don't know. I don't know what to say. I . . ."

"You said you were trying. But I guess that was a lie?"

I felt like I had been slapped, but then my own anger surged forward. "What? You're accusing me of lying? Are you high? I am trying! I thought we were on the same page! Or did you just pretend like we were so we could fuck around in our dreams?"

"I would think you know me better than that."

"Right now I'm not sure I know you at all."

"Are you going to accept the mate bond or not, Meera?"

"Why are you pressuring me?"

"Answer the question."

"I don't know," I blurted out, but somehow it didn't even feel like the truth. It just felt like words that needed to be said by someone, even if they weren't my own. Teardrops fell fast, coating my cheeks as I tried to breathe. I wanted to take the words back and stuff them into a place where no one could hear them.

"I need some air." He got up and started to walk away.

"We are literally outside, but sure, walk away. It's what you're good at!" I shouted as I got up to follow him, but

Damon held my arm gently. There was a look of concern in his eye, and it gave me pause when I remembered the story of Vareck's mom losing control.

"Let him rage for a minute," he said softly while watching Vareck storm off. "He'll be okay."

"We can't split up." I crossed my arms, not out of annoyance, but self-soothing and comfort. Everything felt wrong. "It's not safe."

Sadie gave my shoulder a squeeze before she jogged off in the direction he'd gone. "I'll go get him."

"I'm sorry, Meera, I know you two haven't completed it, but I really thought you were just waiting to be out of this. I don't know why I asked that," Damon said, motioning all around us. I believed him. He had no idea what Vareck and I had been going through. "Guess you have some things to figure out as well."

I sighed. "We were doing better. We talked in the cave, and I thought we were okay. I just need time. I thought he understood that."

"He will." Damon turned when he heard a noise in the distance. A soft rumble miles away. "I didn't mean to get him riled up like this. He doesn't usually lose his temper so fast. It's like the place just puts us all on edge. I don't know, maybe it's the food." He kicked one of the empty food pouches into the fire. "Sadie had a better disposition when the tiny monsters were feeding her."

I snapped my head up. "What'd you just say?"

He frowned. "About Sadie being better when she's fed?"

I shook my head. "No . . . this place . . . we're all on edge. It wasn't just you and Sadie, but me and Vareck too . . ."

Damon narrowed his eyes, searching for more information. "I don't know what you're getting at."

"The realm is sentient. And it's almost like . . ." I swallowed, barely able to get the words out from the dread coiling tight in my throat. "It wants to split us apart." My whispered revelation seemed to click with Damon immediately. "I told Vareck I was suspicious, and he said maybe it was trying to break you and Sadie apart because there is strength in numbers. What if . . .?"

"*'Like calls to like,'*" Damon repeated, his eyes widening as he spoke. "I don't think it's us the realm wants. I think it's trying to separate you," he muttered in horror, checking our surroundings just as a thundering crack rent the air.

The land shifted hard, and I nearly toppled over. His strong arms wrapped around me protectively, and he held me tight. In panic, I held him in return. "Do not let go of me," he ordered, placing a hand over my head as he pressed me closer. "Do you hear me?" I nodded harshly, closing my eyes and curling my face into Damon's side as my body was rocked by the twisting and turning of the landscape. Wind whipped around us, cocooning us in a tiny vortex as the ground trembled then broke apart.

Through all the noise, I heard Vareck scream my name. I saw him in the distance with my sister, running toward us, one arm outstretched. Every second counted. He was almost to us when the violent haze of a mirage clouded my vision. He wasn't going to make it. As I called out to him, the roar of the land shift swallowed my voice, and he was gone.

The realm got what it wanted. As the land split, so were we, and the last words I said to Vareck came from a place of anger that may not have been my own.

The twin hells played their games just as we played ours.

And we just lost.

CHAPTER 20

VARECK

The cold always helped.

At least, that was the lie I told myself as I stormed away from the fire, from the game, from her. The air was heavy and humid, trickling into my lungs like sap from a tree as the realm's magic thickened it further. Each breath weighed me down, and yet it wasn't enough to distract me from the very real possibility that Meera might reject me. Reject *us*.

Her voice played on repeat in my head.

"I don't know."

Three godsdamned words. That was all it took to unravel something in me I hadn't even realized was tightly wound. Hope. What a stupid, fragile thing.

I clenched my fists and let out a slow exhale. My muscles twitched as the fury beneath my skin shifted, dangerously close to the surface.

I knew she wasn't ready. I knew the bond had shaken her, same as it did me. But I'd been ready to try. Ready to reach across the unknown and trust it meant something. That *we* meant something.

But she wasn't sure.

That burned more than I could admit.

Footsteps crunched behind me, deliberate but unhurried. I didn't turn.

"Gonna break a tooth or something if you keep clenching your jaw like that."

"Go away, Sadie."

She stepped up beside me, arms crossed. "Look, I'm not here to argue. I just didn't want you to walk into a monster's mouth because you were too busy sulking."

I glared at her sidelong. "I'm not sulking."

She snorted. "Sure."

We walked in silence for a few breaths. The trees thinned, the jewel-toned foliage slowly giving way to something darker. Rot clung to the edges of leaves. The moonlight, what little there was, began to bend in strange ways.

Sadie finally sighed. "She's scared, Vareck. She didn't mean it the way it sounded."

"She meant it exactly the way it sounded." I shoved a low-hanging branch out of the way. "She's unsure. I get it. But I've been patient. I've given her space. And all I needed was for her to say she wanted this. That in the end she would choose us. Even if she wasn't ready to right now."

Sadie didn't argue. She knew I wasn't wrong.

"You need to cut her a little slack," she said after a pause. "Meera is crazy about you, but this thing you guys have is permanent. It scares her."

I ground my teeth. "You think I don't know that?"

"Intellectually? Almost certainly," Sadie said. "But the way you're acting doesn't exactly scream *understanding,* if you know what I mean."

"I've been understanding," I snapped.

She raised a brow. "You sure about that?" I opened my mouth to say as much but she held up a hand. "She's twenty-five, Vareck. In an ideal world she'll live over five-hundred years. How long have you known each other?"

"That's irrelevant—"

Sadie barked a laugh, cutting me off. "It's entirely relevant. Look, I get it, my sister is pretty fucking awesome. She's not perfect, though. Give her time to figure it out, *please*."

I stopped, turned to face her fully. "You think I'd walk away? You think I'd give up on her?"

"No," she said without hesitation. "But I think you're about to do something reckless that may make the decision for you."

My fists clenched. "She doesn't understand what she means to me, Sadie. What this bond means. I've already chosen her. There's no going back. But she's still deciding if I'm worth the risk. That"—I broke off, swallowing past the tightness in my chest. "That hurts."

Sadie's expression softened just a little. "You are worth it and I think she knows that. Her heart is yours. I just think her brain needs some time to catch up."

"What if time isn't on our side?"

"What do you mean?"

I sighed heavily. "I mean that bonds break down. They decompose just like these trees if left incomplete for too long."

Sadie stepped in front of me, planting herself firmly in my path. "Then you hold out as long as you can. For her. Because she's worth it. If you push her now, she'll run, and not because she doesn't care, but because she does. That's the messed-up part."

I exhaled slowly. "I'm not going to push her. I'm not going to punish her. But gods, I'm allowed to be angry."

"Then be angry. Just don't let it cloud your judgment where Meera is concerned. She'll come around. I really do believe that. But you have to give her time."

I didn't know what to say to that, so I said nothing at all. I just nodded in agreement. When she pointed behind me, I accepted her quiet, yet firm, instruction to return to our camp.

Silence stretched between us as we walked back, and I noticed for the first time how strange this landscape was compared to what I expected it to be. I had stormed off so quickly, I wasn't paying any attention to it. What should have been lush forests with jewel-toned leaves was steadily turning to jagged ground with scattered trees. The air warmed . . . as if heated by the light of two suns.

I stilled. My pulse quickened.

Sadie stopped, turning in circles, looking for the source. "Do you feel that?"

Everything was *wrong*.

Beneath us, something thrummed with rhythmic anticipation. Like a second heartbeat underneath the land.

"Is that—" Sadie broke off suddenly when the air around us warped inward, turning hazy like a mirage.

"It's shifting." My eyes narrowed. "Eversus is coming." The name left my mouth like a curse.

Sadie spun around again, eyes scanning the horizon. "We need to run." I didn't need to be told twice. I snagged her wrist and took off at a dead sprint in the direction we came from.

In the distance, a flicker of motion caught my eye. Two figures, one embracing the other.

Meera and Damon.

My breath caught as I saw the panic in her features. Her copper hair whipped around her face like fire in the wind. She was calling out something—my name, maybe—but the wind had swallowed her words, and the steady drum of my own heartbeat galloping was the only thing I could hear.

"Meera!"

The land twisted beneath our feet, shifting between realms. The oily hues of the forest stained red. Trees fell away one by one like an earthquake was rolling through and flattening everything.

Meera shouted again. I was close enough to make out the shape of her lips, but the sound was swallowed by the roaring of the wind. My name. She was calling to me.

I put everything I had into reaching her in time. With Sadie at my back, I reached out while closing in on Meera and Damon. Her eyes locked with mine and everything else fell away. The rolling terrain, the reality that our world was tearing itself in two—none of it mattered in that moment.

Only her. Only getting to her.

In a moment of horror, the mirage shimmered harshly, and I realized I was too late.

We were feet from each other.

And then the ground betrayed me.

My boot caught on something jagged—a rock that hadn't been there a second ago, jutting up like a spear from the cursed soil. Pain tore through my ankle. I tried to right myself, but I was moving too fast.

I fell hard.

The impact knocked the breath from my lungs. My shoulder hit first, then the side of my head cracked against the ground. I tasted blood.

Meera's scream pierced the chaos.
Darkness surged in like a wave, cold and unrelenting.
I didn't have time to reach for her.
It was just the echo of her name in my chest.
Then nothing.

CHAPTER 21

VARECK

I came to with a groan, the world around me little more than a haze of gray and blinding light. My senses filtered in slowly. Pain first. My head throbbed with an intensity that made it feel like someone had taken a chisel to my skull. Again. And again. Every breath scraped down my throat like broken glass, sand clinging to my tongue and coating the inside of my mouth.

"Meera," I rasped, my voice barely more than a whisper.

I blinked rapidly, trying to see through the grit crusted in my lashes. The last thing I remembered was her face—fearful, determined, fierce. And then the land shifted and swallowed her.

Now, where her coppery red hair had once shone like fire against the jewel-toned forest, there was only sand.

I forced myself to lift my head, pain screaming through every joint, but I had to see for myself. The twin suns of Eversus beat down on my back, their heat making my breaths ragged as my lungs shuddered with each inhale.

"Hey there, big guy."

I turned my head slowly to see Sadie crouched

beside me. Her head blocked out the red sun, making it possible to see her pinched expression. She looked exhausted but relieved, likely because we were both still alive.

Objectively, that was something.

Emotionally, it didn't mean a damned thing.

"She's gone," I said, the words scraping like sandpaper up my throat.

Sadie nodded grimly. "Yep. Damon too. So at least they've got each other?"

She said it like a question, unsure if it was a comfort or a concern.

I let out a harsh breath. *Yeah. I'm with you there.* That pompous prick is a giant pain in my ass, but if there's one thing he's good for, it's staying alive. I rolled, wincing when my swords dug into the muscle of my back. My head was pounding with the weight of it all. "I shouldn't have walked away."

"Probably not," Sadie snorted. "Not gonna claim it was the smartest plan you've ever had. But hey, could be worse."

I turned my head just enough to glare at her. "Could be worse?"

"We could be dead," she said with a shrug. "And if I know Meera—and I do—then her odds of surviving are probably better than ours at the moment."

I wiped grit from my eyes and stared up at the twin suns. "Evorsus wants her."

Sadie laughed dryly. "Yeah, I gathered that when a rock shot up from the ground to trip you right as we would have reached them." I pressed my lips together. "How often do you reckon the land shifts like that?"

"What?"

"How hard did you hit your head?" I scowled at her tone. "I said, how often does the land shift?"

"I don't know."

"So helpful," she muttered.

I scrubbed a hand down my sweat-slicked face. "It doesn't matter. She's gone."

"With that kind of thinking, it's a surprise you haven't ended up dead by now," she snapped. "Yes, she's gone. She's in Evorsus, the sort-of-sentient hell realm which low-key has a thing for her, but she's not dead, Vareck. And unless you think that delicate alabaster skin of hers can handle two suns, I'd say she's better off over there than baking like bread out here with us."

I grunted in response, but Sadie kept going, undeterred. "Look, if we wait for the shift to happen again, maybe it'll pull us back together."

"It won't work like that."

She frowned. "What do you mean?"

"Do you remember Corvo talking about the Fold?"

"Yes. Time is weird, which we already gathered. Ley line convergence. Same on both sides. Blue flowers face north."

"It's more than being weird. Time moves differently between Evorsus and Eversus," I said, forcing myself into a sitting position. "What's hours here could be weeks there. Or vice versa."

Sadie blinked. "Come again?"

"Your plan is flawed," I told her. "It could be weeks before the land shifts here again. Longer, even. And if something comes hunting them in that time—which it will— they'll be running, not waiting, as they should."

I sighed. When we fell through a portal to the twin realms, I didn't think it could get much worse.

Apparently, the universe thought otherwise.

"So what, we just keep moving? Toward the Fold?" Sadie rocked back on her haunches, crossing her tan arms over her chest.

"That's what they are doing. And that is what we will do.."

Her eyebrows inched up. "I'm not opposed, but we don't have any rations, and the walking will dehydrate us faster. All of them were with Meera and Damon."

"Corvo," I muttered.

Sadie threw her hands up. "How would he even know how to find us? We're in the middle of a desert."

Speak of the devil and he will appear.

My familiar popped up a second later, perched on a rock, blinking lazily like this was his afternoon nap spot.

"So, where's the saucy redhead and the nephew?" he asked casually.

"Evorsus." I spat its name like a curse. "The land shifted and separated us. Intentionally."

"Intentionally?" Corvo blinked again. "Why are you lying on the ground? Did you hit your head?"

"Yes, but that's not the point."

"He's telling the truth," Sadie cut in. "We were running. We would've made it if some rock hadn't just sprouted up out of the damn ground and tripped him."

Corvo hummed. "That's . . . concerning."

"No shit, Corvo."

"Hey, don't look at me," he said. "It's not my fault your lady love is trapped with the playboy prince. You don't think he'd try anything, do you?"

I didn't think. I lunged.

Pure instinct.

If not for Corvo's feline reflexes, I would've had him by

the throat. As it was, he leapt back just in time, ears flattened.

"Damon. Would. Not. Dare," I growled.

Sadie raised her hands. "And Meera's loyal. She might be unsure about the whole forever bond thing, but she'd never cheat. Besides, Damon's not really her type. She likes the kind of guy you settle down with and have babies and all that."

The silence that followed was loud.

She blinked. "What?"

Corvo and I stared at her.

I rubbed my jaw. "Good to know."

"Well," Corvo drawled, brushing imaginary dust off his leg with a paw. "You and Lady Love have been separated. Naturally, you want me to find her."

"Yes."

He sighed. "It's like I know you or something." Corvo flicked his tail. "But as much as I'd like to help, no can do. I'm only bound to you."

"And I'm bound to her," I said.

He paused, considering the implications.

"I know it's a stretch, but with you being bound to me and me being bound to her, that has to amount to something where magic is concerned. We tried a blood oath, and it didn't work. Now that I know we're mates, it makes sense. Only one bond can exist between beings. The stronger one supersedes everything else."

Corvo cocked his head. "Maybe . . ."

He didn't sound convinced. His golden eyes squinted in thought, then blinked slowly as if his brain had just buffered through a realization.

"Whatever was blocking us from recognizing each other

before, it's gone," I said again, more firmly this time. "The bond snapped into place, whether Meera's ready to accept it or not."

Corvo sat upright, tail flicking. "You're thinking if I'm tethered to you and you're tethered to her, then by the transitive property of magical bullshit, I might be able to find her?"

"It's worth a try."

Sadie scoffed. "Yeah, or he ends up sniffing his own tail in circles."

"I'm not a dog," Corvo scoffed. "And as magnificent as I am, this bond isn't a trail of enchanted perfume. If you're expecting me to sniff my way across realms, lower your expectations."

I leaned forward, elbows on my knees, fingers steepled. "Can you at least try?"

Corvo groaned, his tail flicking with indignation. "Try? Sure. But if my spirit unravels like a badly knit sweater, that's on you. I wasn't designed for directional magic." He shot me a flat look. "I claw expensive things for entertainment and judge people—that's my lane. I'm a cat, not a compass."

"I thought you were a god," I countered.

"Then the judgment remains, but the form of entertainment changes."

"You're my familiar," I reminded him.

"Still doesn't mean I signed up for trauma."

"Corvo," I warned.

"Fine, fine." He stood up slowly, stretching with an exaggerated groan like he'd just risen from the longest nap in history. "Let's see what we're working with."

His form stilled. The fur along his back lifted slightly,

and the air around him grew thick with static. His body vibrated with restrained magic. The gold of his eyes shifted to molten amber, glowing as they unfocused on the material world.

"I might be picking up something," he said in a voice that was no longer casual. "It's faint. Like a frayed wire."

Sadie leaned in. "You mean like magical residue?"

Corvo didn't answer. His entire body had gone eerily still.

I stood, my knees groaning from the movement. "Corvo?"

"Shhh." He lifted one paw as if listening to a distant frequency. "Be right back."

Then, without another word, his body vanished in a shimmer of displaced air.

Sadie blinked, startled. "Did he just—"

"Yeah," I said, my voice low. "I think he found something."

We stood there, the air thick with dust and silence, both of us staring at the spot where Corvo had vanished.

"Should have asked him to bring us food and water first. And maybe an umbrella," she said lightly, but it didn't mask the concern in her voice. "Do you think he'll be okay?"

I shrugged, though the weight in my chest said I wasn't sure. "He's a cat. He always lands on his feet."

She snorted. "That was terrible."

"You're just mad you didn't say it first."

Sadie gave a half-smile, but it didn't last. Her gaze turned toward the horizon. "You really think he can find her?"

"I think if there's any thread left to pull on, Corvo will find it."

"And if he can't?"

I didn't answer right away.

Because if Corvo couldn't find her, then I'd tear through both realms myself until I did.

CHAPTER 22

MEERA

The air was thick. Not just warm, but wet and viscous, like it was trying to seep through my skin and slow every breath. It clung to my clothes, to my hair, to my thoughts. Damon paced ten feet away, checking the perimeter for the third time in as many minutes. I sat on a patch of cracked earth beneath what used to be a tree—now just brittle limbs and peeling bark. Useless for coverage. Perfect for the vibe.

"We need to figure out our next move," I said aloud, mostly to myself.

Damon didn't respond. No surprise. "We need a plan," I said, trying to keep the frustration out of my voice. "Something better than 'stand here and hope the universe pities us.'"

"Yes, because that's exactly what I was going to suggest," he replied blithely. "Did it escape your notice that the realms separated you intentionally? That rock that popped up in front of Vareck wasn't a coincidence."

"No, it didn't. Rudeness. I'm just focusing on what I can control: our next move." I held both hands up in surrender.

"And as for your attitude, usually your plans involve sitting still and waiting for something bad to happen—"

"I'm deliberative and prefer not to make rash decisions—"

"But in this case I think we should stay put," I said, rubbing my temples. "Find shelter, set up some kind of marker. If the land shifts again and they're close enough, maybe we'll end up in the same realm. It's a risk, but—"

"You're assuming they'll stay in place too."

"I'm assuming they're smart enough not to wander off."

Damon gave me a look. "Sadie? Stay put?"

I sighed. "She's with Vareck. He knows . . . things."

Damon snorted. "Yeah, he knows jack all about the twin hells. That plan isn't going to work."

My brow furrowed. "Excuse me?"

He crouched and drew two rough circles in the dirt. "Evorsus and Eversus don't just swap positions on command. The time streams move at different rates. Hours here might be days there—or the reverse. Waiting here, hoping we sync up again? We could be stuck for weeks, months. Maybe forever."

I folded my arms. "So what do you suggest?"

"We stick with the original plan and head to the place where the realms converge naturally; the Fold." He pointed in a direction, though I had no idea which way it was going. I didn't see any blue flowers nearby. "That's where the portal is supposed to be anyway. If they head there and we head there, it's our best shot at reconnecting."

"Sure, but there's another problem." Nudging the backpacks with my boot, I took a breath that stuttered, hating what I was about to say. "We don't know how long it'll take, and we aren't going to make it long without food and water. Everything is with us, but Corvo can't bring us more."

He nodded grimly. "I know. We have to ration carefully."

The air shimmered beside us.

I turned just in time to see a flick of movement, light bending, and then, standing on a rock like he hadn't just crossed between realms, was Corvo.

"You're here!" I threw my arms around him and nuzzled his furry self against my chest. Corvo purred loudly, arching his paws to make biscuits against me.

"Now *this* is the kind of welcome I deserve. All you're missing is tuna."

Damon rolled his eyes, pinching the bridge of his nose between his forefinger and thumb. "Seriously? Do you *wait* for dramatic moments just to make an entrance?"

"Only when the dialogue's this bad," Corvo replied, hopping down and giving himself a shake. "Honestly, I expected more from you two."

I knelt down to give him scratches behind his giant ears. "How did you find us?"

He continued to purr loudly, clearly pleased. "The bond."

"But you've never been able to track me like this before," I said, narrowing my eyes. "Or could you? Please don't tell me you could have intervened when I got kidnapped by brownies."

Corvo's tail swished like a banner of irritation. "Let's be clear. I don't lower myself to petty mortal struggles unless I absolutely have to. I'm only here because I'm V's familiar and if *he* dies, *I* die. This is self-preservation."

I raised an eyebrow. "Oh is that it?" I lowered my hand to stop petting him and Corvo narrowed his eyes.

"I *may* have tried and failed to look for you when you were kidnapped. Then I got hungry and stopped by Irene's. Running into you was weird luck—for you. I lost third dinner that night because Irene was too busy bitching at her minions to feed me."

I smirked and returned to petting him. "I think you like me."

"I'm allowed complexity," he sniffed. "I'm bonded to Vareck. I just happen to tolerate you."

Damon muttered, "That's how all his compliments sound. You get used to it."

Corvo gave him a sideways glare, then looked back at me. "Besides, tolerating you has benefits. You keep my idiot warrior emotionally upright and you occasionally feed me. That earns you . . . mild favoritism."

I blinked. "Is that your version of a thank you?"

"Don't push it."

I grinned anyway. "So, why now? Why can you find me all of a sudden?"

"Well, now I *want* to. That's probably the difference." His eyes gleamed. "And I'm just that good."

I crossed my arms. "Corvo."

"Fine." Corvo rolled his eyes. "The bond changed. Whatever was blocking your mate bond seems to have lifted and now I can sense you through him."

I frowned. "But we haven't completed the bond?" I said, more to myself than him.

He nodded once. "Yeah well, the horizontal tango did something because you're connected now, which means we are too." He cocked his head, like a thought occurred to him. "I wonder if you die, will I die too? Oh fuck. Having one meat sack to keep alive was hard enough."

I went still.

Corvo blinked slowly and shrugged in a very human-like manner. "Who knows? Let's all try not to die and *not* find out. Shall we?"

"About that," Damon said. "Our best bet of staying alive is getting to the Fold. But we're going to run low on supplies depending on how long it takes. Can you pop in frequently to bring us stock, and to let us know where Sadie and Vareck are?"

"Ugh," Corvo groaned. "Corvo do this. Corvo find that. Corvo keep my mate alive. I'll have you know I expect snacks in return. And pets. There better be catnip crusted halibut in my dish when you get back to the castle. All this do-gooder-ing is exhausting."

"When have I not fed you, hmm? Ever since—"

"We don't need to go spilling secrets now, Damon." Corvo's eyes flashed, and he whipped his tail around. Damon just hummed in return.

Ignoring whatever was happening between them, I scratched under his chin. "Is that a yes?"

"Obviously."

I looked to Damon. "Problem solved, it would seem."

He shrugged. "Slightly better than starving to death."

"Of course it is," Corvo deadpanned. "Start walking that way," he flicked his tail in the direction Damon had motioned to earlier. "Follow the blue flowers. I'll be back in a few—"

"Wait! Are Vareck and Sadie okay?"

"Alive," Corvo said, then paused. "Sand-scorched. Possibly concussed. Emotionally dysregulated. But yes, fine."

I swallowed and nodded. "And they know we're okay?"

"Not yet," he said. "But I was just about to deliver the

good news when I heard you two and thought, what's a little detour?"

Damon took a backpack and set it down near Corvo. "They'll need rations. And water."

Corvo wiggled his whiskers and shook his head. "Keep it. It means I get to check on you less. I'll bring them their own. Saves me all this back-and-forth nonsense."

I slung my bag over my shoulder. "Can you deliver a message to Vareck for me?"

"Absolutely not."

"Corvo," I all but whined, and he winced. "Just tell him that I'm sorry about before. That I . . ." What was I going to say? That I'm sure now? That I don't have doubts? That while I was still scared, Evorsus was messing with me, and my emotions were amplified and I didn't feel like myself? There were so many things that needed to be said. "Just tell him I'm sorry. Please."

Corvo groaned again. "Fine, no idea what you're sorry about. Guilt is a useless emotion if you ask me, but what do I know? Oh right. Everything."

"Thank you, oh reluctant hero of mine." I kissed his furry face. "I'll give you all the pets when we get home."

"You better," he replied. "And don't forget the halibut. And salmon. By the time this is over, there will be a long list."

"Make sure they're safe," I said, and my voice wavered, giving away the worry I was trying to conceal.

"I'm many things, Meera, but I'm not a liar. Most of the time. They're fine. You, however, need to start moving." He paused. "Try not to get yourself eaten or anything before I get back."

He shimmered out of existence with a soft crack of air displacement.

Damon looked at me. "You ready?"

Not even close. But I nodded anyway.

"Let's go," he said, slipping the other backpack on.

We turned toward the unknown, the air heavy with humidity and silence, and started walking north—toward the convergence, and hopefully, toward the others.

Toward home.

I tried to stop it, but my emotions caught up with me. A single tear slid down my cheek, and somehow, it didn't escape Damon.

"Hey," he said gently, rubbing my shoulder. "They're okay. Corvo wouldn't lie about it."

"I know," I whispered, sniffling once and trying to pull it together. "I just wish I hadn't said the things I did."

"That wasn't you, Meera. That wasn't Vareck either. Evorsus wanted you to be split apart."

I huffed. "Yeah, well, it got what it wanted."

"Just don't leave my side. I fear it wants you alone entirely."

"Hey." I stopped walking, and he did too, waiting for me to speak. "I didn't thank you for what you did back there."

He raised a brow. "For what?"

"You realized what was happening. You protected me during the land shift. Thank you for that. I know you're stuck with me and that puts you on edge, and I know you have no reason to like me after the . . . circumstances of how we met. And—"

Damon held a hand up. "Meera, stop. You don't have to thank me. I will do everything in my power to keep you safe. I'm not on edge because I'm with you or have a grudge against you. Did we meet under ideal circumstances? No. Do I believe that you were going to search for me because you didn't think it was okay to hand over a person? Yes, actually, I do. You're a fairly easy person to read. I'm on edge because Evorsus *wants* you, and that's more dangerous than just trying to trek through this land unscathed."

The softness in his eyes was sincere. He was here because of me, and I felt guilty for that. I wished I could be more like Corvo and toss the useless emotion, as he called it, out the window. I couldn't, but it also wasn't going to do me any good. Instead of giving it more life, I pressed my lips into a forced smile and nodded. "Okay. Friends?" I outstretched my hand in a peace offering.

He grinned, accepting it and shaking. "Friends."

I turned to keep walking with him by my side. After a few paces, I said, "So, the Fold. Is that really its name?"

"Unlikely. But the real name given by the twin hells is probably unpronounceable and written in a dead language, so 'the Fold' it is."

I gave him a sideways glance. "Do you know what to expect there?"

He hesitated, his mouth tightening before he shook his head. "No. Not really. No one does."

"That's not comforting."

"There are stories," he said, stepping over a root thick enough to be a stair step. "Rumors, really. Some say it's where magic bleeds through. Others think it's another prison for something ancient and pissed off. Vareck's supposedly been there, but even he doesn't talk about it."

I frowned. "He has?"

"That's the rumor," Damon replied. "Don't know if it's true. He doesn't exactly volunteer information."

"That's one way to put it."

Damon gave a dry chuckle. "No one who's gone there talks about it after. If they come back at all."

I stared ahead into the trees, where the shadows

swirled too thick to be natural. I wasn't ready for this place, but ready didn't seem to matter anymore.

We walked in silence for a beat before I glanced over at him.

"So . . . sixteen, huh?" I asked, side-eyeing Damon subtly while trying not to trip and fall on my face. The branches, roots, and rocks were in abundance now.

Damon looked away and let out a tight breath. "Yes and no."

My brows pulled together. "Go on."

"I'd rather not talk about this."

"Why not?" I asked, gesturing to the forest. "It's just us. And we're all we have for a while. Friends, right?"

"Vareck asked me how many women I'd brought to his room," Damon said, brushing a low-hanging vine aside. "He didn't ask how many I actually slept with on his bed."

My eyebrows lifted. "Those are two different numbers?"

His chin dipped. "They are. I brought a lot of girls to his room to sleep off whatever they drank. Sometimes they thought we hooked up. I let them think that. Or they remembered and do their best to manipulate the conversation about it later making it look however they want it to. Either way, I never actually slept with any of them. Not in his bed."

"Why not bring them to your rooms and just save yourself the trouble? Or any empty room for that matter?"

He huffed a humorless laugh. "So, that gets tricky. Sometimes ladies of the court are trying to attract my attention. They're waiting at entrances to the hallways leading to my rooms. Other rooms are generally occupied when we have a gathering at the castle. Lords and ladies stay there rather than traveling back to their homes. It's standard.

"If my source tells me my rooms aren't easily accessible due to someone waiting for me, I take a passage that leads me to Vareck's. I know they'll be safe there. Vareck won't be back for a long time because he's busy working, and women aren't looking for me there."

"Why are you taking these drunk women somewhere to sleep it off? Can't you send them to their rooms, or back home or something?"

With a deep sigh, Damon shook his head. "It's all a setup. Their mothers are putting them up to it."

"Come again?"

"I'm the heir. An unwed prince. Vareck is assumed to be a more difficult target. So families looking to turn their daughters into royalty are more than happy to have a princess . . . whether it's their daughter's shared ambition or not."

My mouth fell open. "You mean . . . their own mothers get them drunk and just, send them to you so you'll bed them?"

"Yup," he answered, popping the 'p.' "And I am many things, but I'm not that man."

"But . . . why didn't you just say that when Vareck asked?"

He gave me a look. "Sadie calls me the playboy prince. You've seen how Vareck talks to me. They've already made up their minds about who I am, and when I tried to explain myself, Vareck cut me off. So why bother?"

I opened my mouth, struggled for words, and closed it again. He had a point. Vareck one hundred percent believed Damon had defiled his bed, and Sadie tended to assume the worst—especially when she was attracted to someone. Even I had made my assumptions.

"So," I said slowly, "you haven't slept with any of the

sixteen women you took to his room. Not there and not elsewhere?"

"Not a one," Damon confirmed. "Also, completely unrelated to the discussion that a mother's consent isn't the daughter's consent, is the notion of doing it on Vareck's bed. That's disgusting."

His face twisted in genuine revulsion.

"I may get around," he added, "but when I do, I still have standards."

I smiled and huffed out a laugh. "You know, there's really more to you than meets the eye."

Damon cocked an eyebrow, giving me a sideways glance. "You think?"

I shrugged, playing it casual. "Maybe just a little."

"Wow. That's high praise coming from you. Should I alert the bards?"

"Are there bards in Faerie? Actually, I take that back. Pretend I didn't ask."

Damon let out a full bellied laugh. "You're dating the king and yet—"

"I know nothing about his kingdom? That is correct," I said, fighting the tug of a smile. "I'm still wrapping my head around the idea that you're secretly a gentleman under all that . . ." I motioned toward him.

"That what?"

"You know. Swagger? Supreme self-assuredness?"

He held a hand to his chest, mocking offense. "I'll have you know my swagger is an essential part of my charm. Without it, I'd just be a guy with good hair, a title, and a tragic backstory."

I snorted. "You do have good hair."

"And a tragic backstory. That's an essential piece."

"Is getting kidnapped tragic?"

He pressed his lips together in a faint grin. "I don't know, you tell me. From the sounds of it, you got kidnapped not once but twice."

I gave him a dry look. "Okay, fair. But it sounds way worse than it was. At least when Vareck did it. The brownies were just assholes."

"They usually are, in my experience." Damon huffed a soft laugh, but there was something thoughtful in his expression.

"You're not wrong," I added. "Once I got the magic nullifying necklace off, things were looking up. Until I ended up in a brothel facing off a leprechaun who couldn't be compelled."

"Nullifying necklace? Brothel? Okay, you have to tell me this story because you left a lot out when recounting it to Sadie, not that I blame you given her temper." I proceeded to tell him the whole sordid story of how I took the job to kidnap him, not knowing I'd be going after a person. Then meeting Vareck and him showing up at my apartment after I left Damon that night. I went on to what happened at the castle, minus details I didn't think he'd want to hear about me getting it on with his uncle. I finished the tale with being kidnapped by brownies, which I still have no idea what they were after, and ending up at Irene's—where Vareck found me.

"Oh! And the cherry on top of it all was Corvo spilled pixie dust all over me and Vareck before we got away. Turd."

"That is insane enough that I actually believe you. The truth is weirder than fiction in my experience."

I laughed lightly. "Yeah, it's been more than a little crazy. I might've been out of my depth, but I wasn't help-less at least."

One corner of his mouth pulled tight. "Are you calling me helpless?"

I flushed red. "No, that's not what I meant."

Damon laughed again. "Relax, I'm not mad at you. In the spirit of honesty, I understand more than you realize."

"You've been kidnapped twice?"

"Four times, actually." he said with a shrug. "When you're valuable, people get ideas."

The air between us shifted a little, the weight of something unspoken pressing in. I didn't push, and he didn't elaborate.

"I know I said it before, but I'm really sorry about the whole kidnapping thing. On one hand, I wish I hadn't done it because then we wouldn't be here . . ."

"On the other, you wouldn't have met Vareck or gone on this crazy adventure if you hadn't."

I bit my bottom lip. "Yeah, but it sounds kind of shitty given all you have gone through because of me."

Damon shrugged. "As far as kidnappings go, I give yours a five. I totally would have gotten free if you hadn't dropped me with the leprechaun so soon."

I snorted. "Why do you think I did? Any good thief knows the best way to not get caught is to get rid of the proof."

Damon lifted both eyebrows. "Oh, is that so? And here I thought Vareck found an upstanding woman." I slapped his arm playfully and he snickered.

After a beat, I asked, "So, all that swagger, that's just covering for what? The trauma of being kidnapped a billion times?"

Damon smirked faintly. "No. That's just who I am. But it helps keep people from asking too many questions."

We walked a bit farther, the silence between us easy

now, more pleasant and comfortable than before. I didn't know what waited for us at the Fold—or if we'd even make it that far—but this? This felt okay.

"So," I said, casually, "if you didn't sleep with them, why not correct Vareck? He may not believe you, but that's his problem. As it is, he's going to hold that grudge for a while now."

Damon's smile faded slightly. "Because it's easier to let him hate me than to try to make him like me."

My chest tightened. "He doesn't—"

"I know," he interrupted, voice low. "But it doesn't change the fact that I've always been the reminder of his brother. Of what he lost. Of what he has to protect."

I frowned. "I don't understand."

Damon blew out a tight breath then ducked under a branch. "My father was a shitty person. When my grandfather tried to take over the realms, he helped him."

"Oh . . . I didn't know that."

Damon smiled sardonically. "It's not exactly something Vareck is proud of. While the mad king was siphoning power from Maeve, my father compelled Drayden and Vareck so they couldn't intervene. Drayden's rage broke the compulsion, and he killed him for it. Unfortunately for my aunt, he was too late. Maeve was already dead."

I swallowed hard around the lump in my throat, lips pressed together. "I'm sorry."

"It's not your fault."

"I know that, but I can still be sorry you went through that and that the legacy your dad left behind is a burden you have to bear."

Damon smiled faintly. "Thanks, Meera. I didn't really have to go through it, though. Mum was pregnant with me when all of this happened, so I never knew my father, or Maeve. I only have the stories and memories of others."

"That in itself is a loss," I said quietly.

Damon didn't say anything for a while, and I didn't push. The forest rustled around us, full of distant sounds and unseen movement, like even the trees were listening. There was so much history between us all—some of it tangled, some of it bruised—but this moment felt simple.

"I'm not my father," Damon said finally, voice low. "But sometimes it feels like I'm paying for who he was and what he did."

I glanced over at him, but he didn't look at me. Just kept his eyes on the path ahead.

"I know you're not," I said.

The corner of his mouth lifted, subtle but real.

We kept walking, the path uncertain, the Fold somewhere ahead. But with each step, the silence between us didn't feel quite so heavy anymore. Maybe we were all just trying to unlearn what the world had taught us about pain.

Maybe, somehow, that was the point.

"In fact, as far as being stranded in hell with someone—so far, you've been pretty good company. There are a lot worse people I could have ended up here with."

Damon glanced at me, the icy blue of his eyes thawing in that moment. "Same. I don't have many . . ."

"Friends?" I said quietly with a gentle smile and a playful elbow to his side.

He smiled, and the way it crinkled near his eyes felt true. "Friends."

As we headed toward the Fold, I kept him close. While he operated with the idea he was going to keep me safe, I moved with another thought in mind. Evorsus had already taken Vareck and Sadie away from me. I wouldn't let it take my friend too.

CHAPTER 23

MEERA

"You should eat something." Damon sat on a broken tree limb. He nudged me as I stretched in front of him, holding out a dehydrated survival kit and a canteen of water.

I scrunched my nose on instinct but accepted it all the same before I plopped down on the log next to him. I groaned in slight relief, but it was short-lived. My feet ached. My back was sore from sleeping on the ground or leaning up against a tree. My scalp itched. Damon and I hadn't bathed in days. We wiped down the best we could, and I had deodorant in my backpack, but that only worked for so long. The one thing movies and shows never accurately depicted was how everyone looked pretty and clean, even when the world was ending. Sure, they had a smidge of dirt here, and a smudge of blood there. But they had clean hair and shiny lips, with just a touch of perfect mascara to brighten their eyes. The last time I saw my reflection in a pool of water, I looked like a swamp witch. I smelled like one too.

"What I wouldn't give for real food," I murmured. At

this point, I'd eat a squirrel if I saw one. "Something that didn't have 'just add water' as directions before eating."

"You can always ask Corvo if he'll bring you something else" he said while pouring water into his own before stirring. I followed suit, grimacing at the smell.

"He's moody enough as is bouncing between the realms." I sighed deeply before taking a bite. It looked disgusting. "What is this one?"

"Beef stroganoff," he mumbled around a mouthful before swallowing thickly. "It's not a food I'm familiar with, but if this is anything close to the real thing, I think we could serve this to the hounds at the castle and they'd be thrilled."

"It's not my favorite meal in my real life. I wouldn't bother trying it once we're out of here if I were you."

"Hate to break it to you," he began, pointing his spoon at me before gesturing to our surroundings, "but this is, in fact, real life."

I grumbled, chewing as quickly as possible. "Believe me, I'm well aware. My body is done with it. Nature. Hiking. The outdoors. Fricken done." I finished my food and set down my empty parcel before I ran my hands through my greasy hair. "We've been heading toward the Fold for about three weeks, and I have no idea when we'll actually get there."

"How do you figure it's been three weeks?" Damon waited, curious for my answer. "I stopped asking how many days we'd been here after Corvo said time was a useless construct and he threatened to piss in my closet and shred everything I owned."

"I didn't need to ask him. I'm a woman," I said, raising my brows to him knowingly and motioned with my hand in a circular fashion so he would connect the rest. He waited for me to elaborate, and it was obvious I needed to spell it out for him. "I have a period."

Damon smiled softly. "I didn't realize you could track the time with it."

I shrugged. "I'm regular, so that helps. I mostly get cramps in the mornings. My body does other things throughout the six weeks in-between. Periods are the worst, but at least it's good for something here."

"Your scent changed a while back. I assumed it was your courses—"

"What?" My stomach twisted and my heart shot into my throat as it pounded. I jumped up from the log we were sitting on and turned to face him. "You can smell when I'm on my period? Oh my god! Why didn't you say something?"

Damon barked a laugh and rubbed his palms on his pants. "Would you have preferred me to mention I can smell blood in that exact moment? Really? That isn't polite in Faerie, and I would think you'd be appalled if I said something."

"I'm appalled now!"

"Why, exactly?"

I stared at him, not wanting to speak all the thoughts racing through my head. Because we *know* there's a scent. We just don't want others to smell it. It's just part of the package and we deal with it, but we still try to be as hygienic as possible. Had I not been? Taking a moment, I breathed in deeply to calm myself. "It's difficult to explain."

It was the vague way of saying I was embarrassed. Sure, periods were normal. Yes, it was completely natural to have one. But something about it just made me feel icky knowing Damon could smell it.

"Periods are natural," he said, echoing my exact thoughts. "It's okay. It's just a little blood."

I blinked rapidly. "Are you trying to mansplain a period to me?"

He chuckled. "I suppose I am. Look, I'm not trying to be a dick here. How about I stop talking and wait until you tell me what I should do."

"You sound like Atlas right now," I said, crossing my arms and suddenly feeling a longing for my family. Atlas was always the voice of reason. The calmest of them all. Maybe it came with being the firstborn. I don't know. But something about Damon's demeanor and the composure of his voice reminded me of my big brother. Realizing that, I lost some of the stiffness in my shoulders.

He pressed his lips into a smile. "I'll take that as a compliment." I looked at him curious and he answered, "Sadie told me about your family, when she wasn't griping at me for existing."

"Ah." I sniffed, feeling awkward and not knowing what to say next. "It is a compliment, I guess. He's a born leader. Level-headed." I smiled, tilting my head to Damon. "Very much not a dick, most of the time. Not to me at least."

"Sorry I made you uncomfortable. We don't have to talk about it. Forget I said anything." I waved him off, letting him know it was fine. We packed our things up in silence and cleaned up the mess we made. "Can we circle back to what you said, though?"

I groaned. "Which part and why?"

"You said you could track time." Damon put his hands on his hips and craned his neck back, looking at the sky. The two moons glowed, beaming down on us and illuminating the landscape of Evorsus. He then looked down, pointing to a bush of the blue flowers we followed. "I haven't been able to. We're headed north. I know that much. But I haven't been able to find a way to track time at all. We eat and sleep based on our body's needs and instincts here, and the best I'd hoped for is that we were following some type of pattern similar to life in our realms. But time moves so differently here, that was the best I have come up with and it's nowhere close to your estimate."

My hackles rose instantly in slight defense. "Are you saying you think I'm wrong?"

He held his hands up in surrender. "The opposite actually. I trust your ability to read your own body better than my ability to guess how much time has passed based on how much I sleep and eat."

"Sorry. I made an assumption there." I huffed a laugh and started to head north. Despite being able to dream walk with Vareck, wherever he was in Eversus, we weren't sleeping at the same time. I hadn't seen him, and my heart ached because of it. I was tired all the time, but sleeping all the time was also counterproductive. "How many days did you think had passed? I don't think I even paid attention to that. Hunger has just been weird. I know I need to eat, but I just don't want to."

"Might have something to do with the quality of our meals." He sighed, walking beside me. "I thought we'd been here about two weeks."

"I had to ask Corvo for pads and some wet wipes about a week ago, give or take," I mumbled. "I had a few in my bag, but my emergency backpack wasn't meant for a long-term hiking trip through the jungles of hell."

"He brought them to you? I'm shocked."

I snorted, thinking about Corvo's reaction when I asked. "Well, he wasn't thrilled about it. He told me he wasn't a general store. Or a pharmacy. And then he brought me pads that may as well have been pillows. So I had to beg him, open a can of tuna he brought me, and then he finally gave me what I asked for." I pointed at Damon's pants. "He brought us clean underwear. It's not that shocking, is it?"

"Cats are very transactional. Especially Corvo."

"Well, he was adamant that he wasn't a trash can either so there was no transaction I could make there for garbage disposal. I've just been burying my trash whenever I have to stop."

"We do what we have to do here."

Yeah, we did. Still felt like littering which is an asshole thing to do but I wasn't carrying around used feminine products and food wrappers.

A thought occurred to me. "Do you think it's been three weeks for them as well?"

"For Sadie and Vareck?" Damon asked.

"You and Corvo said that time isn't the same here on each side. So three weeks have passed here, that's three weeks in our realms based on my body's cycle. But time moves differently in Eversus from Evorsus. Do you think that they've been there for three weeks too?"

"I think your question can't be answered," Damin sighed, not in annoyance but at the impossibility of it all. "The way that you're describing time is in reference to how time passes in Faerie or on Earth. That time is linear. Eversus and Evorsus don't move with the rules or laws of time and space that we're accustomed to. If three weeks' time have passed for us, then three weeks Earth and Faerie time have also passed for Vareck and Sadie. How they've spent it and what it feels like is probably very different from us. I wouldn't be surprised if to them it's only been a few days, or even months. It's impossible to know without talking to them."

"This place really is hell in every which way," I grumbled.

"It's possible that's why you haven't been able to sync up when you're dreaming," Damon said a few minutes later. "We know the realm was trying to separate you from him, and it's also very likely to be interfering with whatever magic lets you share dreams. If you're on radically different timelines, one person would be dreaming for the equivalent of minutes to the other person's hours."

"That's better than the alternative I suppose."

"Yes," he agreed. "I suppose it is."

While I had been able to tell overall time well enough, I couldn't measure the minutes. The hours. They just dragged on. Sometimes Damon and I talked. Sometimes we remained silent. I complained about my feet, and we thankfully found softer ground, but it didn't stop the overall ache that throbbed in my body.

Damon, scratching his head. "A bath would be great right about now."

"Ugh, don't say the 'B' word. I'd kill for a proper soak."

"And a mattress with a feather pillow."

"And some of that stew I had in the castle. With fresh baked bread." I began daydreaming about being 'kidnapped' by Vareck again. I'd be a fricken liar if I said I hadn't dreamed of it a dozen or more times these past few weeks.

He hummed. "The one with root vegetables and thyme? That's my favorite too."

Damon stopped, drinking from the canteen and handing it to me. I glanced at a bush, checking for the direction of the flowers. A large, lavender tree stood next to it. After I took a drink, I knelt down to tie the lace on my boot that had come loose. When I finished, I stood up, looking at the bush again. Only this time, the blue flowers weren't facing the same tree.

"Did you see that?" I whispered, feeling a creeping chill crawl up my spine.

Damon was oblivious, but he was instantly on guard when he heard the fear in my voice. "See what?" He looked around, assessing the trees and waiting to see if we were being watched.

"The flowers. I swear it changed direction."

He surveyed the blue flowers, gesturing for me to follow him. I did, slowly, while looking for any other thing out of the ordinary, but nothing stood out.

"Are you sure? Corvo said the flowers always face north."

My lips parted, and I took a breath but stopped before I spoke. "Maybe I was wrong. . ." I began to question myself. Was I seeing things? This was a hell realm, and even though I was in it and living it, I needed to remind myself. I had to be careful, and I knew it was going to play tricks on me.

"I hope so," Damon murmured. I cast him a curious glance, and he sighed. "If you're right, then the realm is taking us fuck knows where. That's worrisome, especially after it made a point to separate you and Vareck." With a grimace, he added, "I know we've given each other space to go to the bathroom, but, um . . . we're going to need to stay closer to each other. We can't risk it. We've been unprovoked and have not come across any creatures, but we've let our guard down because of it. That stops now."

Now I had to go to the bathroom in front of Damon? This was the worst. I knew it wasn't, but losing that privacy kind of felt like it at the moment. I wouldn't argue, though, because I knew he was right. We hadn't been attacked, and we'd been alert while we trekked through the trees, but we had accepted this false sense of security.

"Why do you think it wanted to separate us?" I asked

quietly. Internally I'd asked myself this every few hours since we'd been separated. Externally, I'd been too scared to address it. Maybe bringing up the elephant in the jungle would help.

Or I'd come away more afraid. It was a toss-up.

Without missing a beat, he answered, and I could not have prepared myself for it. "My guess is that it has something to do with the Nameless."

I reared back, blinking rapidly. "What?"

"You said one of them spoke. Like calls to like. I've been thinking about it since the moment the land shift happened, and I feel like it's related."

I stumbled over a rock, nearly face-planting into the rough bark of a tree when Damon grabbed me. He helped me get my footing back before pointing to a large flat rock. "Sit. Drink. You're exhausted."

I tilted my head back and let out a slightly manic laugh. "No shit. We both are."

Damon inclined his head and gave me a look that was so much like Vareck that my heart squeezed. Would I ever see him again? I had to hope so. If not . . . I couldn't afford to think about it.

"What's that look for?"

"You know."

"Do I?" I shot back, taking a seat regardless.

"We don't know how far away the Fold is or isn't. We've gotten lucky so far that we haven't run into anything on the way. You need to rest more, because on the off chance we do run into something, we'll have to fight or run. I know you were raised by redcaps but I'm getting the distinct impression you're not exactly a professional badass underneath all *this*." He motioned to me, and I quirked an eyebrow.

"This?"

Damon rolled his eyes. "You know what I mean. You. All curves, two left feet, frizzy hair, and good intentions."

I lifted both my eyebrows. "You think I have good intentions?"

"You have a heart of gold, Meera," Damon said with a smirk. "Bounty hunter/thief extraordinaire, you are, but anyone that spends time with you can figure out what kind of person resides beneath that. The fact you are a badass in your own right hasn't escaped me, but bloodthirsty fighter, not so much."

"Gods, you sound so much like my brothers."

"Well, you're my uncle's mate. We're practically family."

I snorted. "Just don't start calling me aunt."

A wry smile tugged at his mouth as he leaned back against a tree. "Wouldn't dream of it. All that aside, you need to take it easier. Your body isn't getting a chance to recover while we're out here, so we need to build in recovery time, and you need to not fight me on it," he added when I opened my mouth to argue.

Red stained my chest and cheeks. "I don't want to be the one slowing us down."

"And I don't want you to be so exhausted you collapse under a strong breeze. You've been pushing yourself to the max since we've been separated and if you're right about the flowers changing direction, there's no telling how long it's going to actually take us to reach the Fold."

"I might have imagined it," I said. Damon didn't comment, and he didn't need to. We both knew I didn't believe what I'd said. It was real, and we knew what it meant. "Like calls to like," I repeated. "What does that even mean?"

"I'm not sure," Damon answered. "I've been wondering that myself, but everything I've come up with is speculation at best."

"I don't understand how the Nameless saying that means anything about me. And they don't normally speak, right?" He nodded in response. "Vareck said they're soulless creatures that hunt in packs. I'm not sure what I could possibly have in common with them."

"Vareck is incredibly biased," Damon replied. "He blames them for his father becoming the mad king, and because of that, he doesn't *want* to see anything other than faceless monsters."

I pulled my legs up to sit crisscross on the stone. "Why does he blame them?"

"Because they're the ones that attacked his parents and the reason his mother's fury accidentally cursed his father." My lips parted, but I didn't speak. "He doesn't know I know that, by the way. So when we see them again, I would appreciate it if you kept it to yourself."

I nodded. "Of course. I—I appreciate you telling me, but I also don't know if you should have."

Damon tilted his head. "I don't see the point in keeping secrets. Besides, you'll be queen soon enough."

"You don't know that."

He snorted. "We'll pretend I dignified that with a response."

"Damon!"

"Meera," he said, making me laugh. "You two have your issues you need to work out, there's no doubt about it. I also don't doubt that you will. Vareck, for all his faults, is a stubborn bastard. He wouldn't give up on you so easily."

I smiled softly. "I hope you're right."

"I am," he replied in complete confidence. He stretched

his legs out, shifting into a more comfortable position against the tree.

"You make it sound like the Nameless are more than what Vareck made them out to be."

Damon sighed, not for the first time in our conversation. "No one knows what the Nameless really are. There are theories, though."

I waited, the knot in my stomach tightening.

"Lots of people buy into the soulless monster concept, but there's one in particular that doesn't. I've always found it interesting. There was a woman scholar that went missing about twenty years ago. Her name was Jakarta Delarothe. In her recovered journal, she wrote that the Nameless aren't just monsters," Damon said. "They're trapped. Bound to this realm. And they're searching for something—or someone—to get them out."

My mouth went dry. "Searching how?"

"No one really knows. One theory is that they can sense magic. Others think they follow blood. Or instinct, like animals that know when a storm's coming. But Delarothe believed the Nameless are looking for a way back to what they lost. Or maybe a way forward."

I frowned. "Forward to what?"

"That's the part no one can answer yet. Maybe it's redemption. Maybe it's revenge."

I chewed on that. "So, when one of them spoke to me …"

Damon nodded. "Maybe it recognized something. Maybe you reminded it of what it used to be, or what it needs to find."

"That's not at all comforting."

"No," he agreed. "It's not."

CHAPTER 24

VARECK

The Nameless didn't bleed, which meant they didn't die. Not really.

You could hack them to pieces, set their corpses on fire, watch them crumble into ash, but they'd always come back, reeking of death and ruin. They weren't alive. Not in any way that mattered.

But that didn't mean I wouldn't enjoy killing them.

The surrounding canyon was scorched by the midday suns, heatwaves rising off the stone like steam from a forge. Red rock stretched high overhead, cracked and jagged. The air tasted like dust and sweat.

I rolled my shoulders and readjusted the grip on both swords. My fingers twitched with anticipation.

Sadie wiped her forehead with the back of her hand and smirked. Her twin axes gleamed—one darker from old blood, the other freshly cleaned and itching for a stain.

"I count twenty coming in," I said quietly.

"All right," she said, nudging my elbow. "First to ten wins."

I gave her a sideways glance. "And the prize?"

"Bragging rights and a crisp high five."

I snorted. "That's not much of an incentive."

"Spoken like a sore loser."

Movement caught my eye against the cliff wall. The Nameless came crawling down the stone like roaches, limbs cracking at odd angles, spines bowed and eyes hollow.

"On your mark," I said, spinning both blades once.

Sadie grinned. "Get set."

"Go!" we said in unison.

The first dropped between us with a hiss of displaced air. I ducked under its swipe and drove my sword straight up through its sternum. It gurgled, body jerking as ichor sprayed from its mouth.

"One."

Sadie rolled her eyes, then took three steps forward and slammed her axe into the neck of another as it leapt at her. The blade hit with a sickening crunch. She kicked the twitching corpse off the axe, spraying black everywhere.

"One," she repeated.

More emerged, crawling from cracks in the canyon floor, scuttling from behind boulders, rising out of the sand like summoned nightmares.

A Nameless lunged at me from the right. I pivoted on instinct, brought both swords across in an X, and sliced through its chest. It hit the ground twitching, and I finished it with a boot to the skull.

"Two."

Sadie was already in motion, a spinning force of steel and fury. One axe caught a Nameless in the shoulder, the other swept its legs out from under it. She kicked it in the head before it could rise.

Before she could call out the number, a second screeched and barreled toward her, claws raised.

She sidestepped, grabbed it by the wrist mid-swipe, and drove her axe into the joint of its elbow, then the side of its neck. It collapsed in pieces. "Three!"

I fought two at once, my swords flashing, movements tight and deliberate. I severed the first's leg, then opened its chest with a wide horizontal slash. The second caught my arm, claws biting in, but I spun and drove my blade through its throat, twisting hard.

"Four," I muttered.

Sadie's axe embedded in the skull of another. "Four!"

I slashed at one's throat with the tip of my sword. "That's five."

"That one was already dying!"

"They never really die, so it all counts."

"Then so do mine," she huffed, kicking her next opponent in the ribs and cleaving its head off midair. "Five!"

A Nameless leapt from the ledge above me. I caught its fall with a blade through its abdomen, then flung it into the canyon wall where it crashed into another body. They both cracked the stone, and didn't get back up.

Sadie whistled. "Nice move, but jury says that only counts as one."

"Six." I laughed, but there was no time for more.

We moved in a blur—back-to-back, breathing hard, cutting through the swarm. Sand sprayed beneath our feet and blood sizzled in the heat. My arm burned where the claws had caught me earlier, but I ignored it.

Sadie grunted, "Nine."

"Eight," I shot back.

"You're going down, Your Highness."

"Not without taking a few more with me." I arched backward, swinging the sword over my body to behead another one, putting us equal once more.

The last two came at once.

Sadie tackled one to the ground, buried both axes into its chest, and yanked them out with a roar. It spasmed once, then stilled.

I locked blades with the other, shoving its claws aside, and delivered a brutal headbutt. It reeled. I followed with a strike that split it from shoulder to hip.

I turned toward her, breathing heavy. "Ten."

Sadie wiped ichor off her cheek. "Ten."

We stared at each other, then spoke at the same time. "Draw."

But the fight wasn't over.

Something shifted in the air.

Thicker. Heavier.

A single Nameless stepped out from the canyon shadows.

This one was taller. Broader. Less grotesque and far too human in its movements.

It didn't charge. Didn't shriek.

It smiled.

Sadie lowered her axes slightly, eyes narrowing. "They always send the creepy ones last."

I said nothing.

Its mouth moved, voice like caverns; far reaching and hollow of any emotion. "You're too late, cursed king."

My jaw tightened.

The thing took another step. "We know where she is."

I didn't blink, didn't breathe.

"You can't save her now."

Sadie's lips curled into a snarl. "Shut up."

"Hail the Queen that was promised," it hissed. "Her blood—"

I struck.

Blades crossed, then split.

The Nameless's head dropped into the sand.

Still smiling.

The body collapsed moments later.

Silence.

Just the wind. Just the blood. Just the weight of what it had said.

Sadie exhaled beside me but didn't speak, our game long forgotten. I cleaned my blades on the cloth at my hip, jaw locked tight.

They knew where she was.

That made one of us. For what felt like a week we'd been traveling toward the Fold. The desert plains giving way to canyons told me we were getting close. That and the increase in run-ins we had with the Nameless. They bled through the gap between the realms, spilling out into the hellish atmosphere of Eversus.

Every spare moment, I spent sleeping, hoping to dream of her, but every time she evaded me. Even with Corvo playing go-between for us, the time never synced quite right. Sadie was exhausted taking watch so often. Meanwhile, I was a different kind of tired. The anxiety that clawed at my chest every second of every day made it hard to function.

"What do you think he meant by 'the queen that was promised'?" Sadie asked.

"No idea," I replied. This wasn't the first time the Nameless referred to her as a queen, or more specifically, *their* queen. It happened every encounter. The final monster would step forward spewing prophetic bullshit about Meera being destined for Evorsus. In the beginning I entertained it, hoping to get more information, but the Nameless picked up on that and ended its own miserable life.

If a rise was what they were looking for in me, they'd found it. Since then, Sadie or I cut them down regardless of the words they said. Meera's sister was more than admirable on the battlefield. She was a godsdamned machine, wielding axes and unlimited fury. The first time they taunted her about Meera she went into battlelust, and I had to stay back until she finished slaughtering the party that found us. Since then, we'd both been more on edge but we didn't speak of it.

"Hey," Sadie said, bumping me with her shoulder. "She's going to be okay. Corvo would have told us if something bad happened."

"Would he?"

Sadie arched a brow. "You know he would. Mercurial as that cat is, he has a soft spot for Meera. Him being gone right now is a good thing, because it means he's with her and no news is good news."

I sighed. "I hate how things ended between us before the split."

"I'm sure she does to. Instead of spending your time worrying about the worst imaginable scenarios, maybe think about what you're going to say when you see her again."

My jaw worked, but I didn't answer right away. There were a hundred things I wanted to say, and none of them seemed like the right place to start.

She gave me a pointed look. "Don't tell me you've been trudging through hell all this time without thinking about what you're gonna say."

"I've thought about it," I said finally.

"And?"

"And I don't know." I blew out a breath, watching the

dust swirl at my feet. "I want to tell her I'm sorry. That I should have been faster—"

Sadie cut me off with a snort. "You're going to waste your first words by telling her you should have run faster? That's not what she needs."

I shot her a look. "And what is it that you think she needs?"

"The truth. Your truth. And not the polite king version. You've crossed a literal desert and fought off countless Nameless to get back to her. Something tells me there is very little you wouldn't do for her." I dipped my chin, and she continued. "She knows you're sorry. Fuck wasting time on apologies. You need to tell her how you feel and then *show* her."

"Show her?"

Sadie smirked. "Yeah. You're not exactly the type to stand around reciting poetry, so lean into what you're good at. Actions. The kind that leave no doubt in her mind where she stands with you."

I huffed a quiet breath through my nose. "You make it sound simple."

"That's because it is. You've done all of this to get back to her. That's already half the speech done for you."

I let that sit between us, the crunch of sand under our boots the only sound for a few steps. She wasn't wrong, but I still had worries. "What if she's not ready to hear it?" I asked.

Sadie didn't even blink. "How would you know she's not ready to hear the truth unless you speak the truth?"

We walked in silence for a few more steps before I said, "What would you say, if you were me?"

Sadie grinned. "Easy. 'I'd cross every godsdamned

desert, cut down every Nameless, and burn the Fold to the ground if that's what it took to get back to you.'"

I huffed a quiet laugh. "It sounds insincere. Rehearsed."

"It is rehearsed and cheesy," she said again. "But you mean it."

"The problem isn't saying it. It's not even meaning it. I would end realms for her, commit unspeakable acts if it meant keeping her safe. You were right when you said there is very little I wouldn't do," I murmured as we walked. "I just don't know if it will be enough."

"Seriously, you could say what you just said to me. Don't think about it not being enough," Sadie said. "Instead of going into the conversation with the outcome you want from her, go in with honesty and an open mind. You're not the only one who's been through hell this entire time, and knowing my sister, she's done some thinking of her own."

Her words sank in, heavy but steadying, like a hand on my shoulder before a fight. I didn't answer right away, just kept my eyes on the shadowed cut of canyon ahead. The heat was still oppressive, but the air had shifted, cooler now, threaded with the faint metallic tang of the Fold.

Sadie must have felt it too. She rolled her shoulders, tightening her grip on her axes. "Almost there."

"Yeah." My voice came out low, the weight of what waited ahead pressing in.

She gave me a sidelong glance. "Then you'd better have those words ready."

I kept walking, the image of her—of Meera—burning behind my eyes. "She'll hear them when I see her."

The wind shifted again, carrying a sound from up ahead. A scrape of stone. A whisper of movement. Shadows stirred along the canyon wall, and the heat that had baked us all day bled into the chill of oncoming night.

The Fold was upon us, but we weren't alone.

CHAPTER 25

MEERA

"Godsdammit!"

The word left my mouth like a curse and a prayer all at once, just as a golden snake slithered across the ground beside my boot. I yelped, stumbling backward and, in a moment of sheer panic, launched myself toward Damon like he was a lifeline.

Spoiler alert: he wasn't.

The air whooshed out of his lungs in an exaggerated puff as I collided with his chest. Rather than catching me gracefully, he staggered backward, our combined momentum carrying us both down.

"Ow," he grunted, pain coloring the single syllable.

"Sorry!" I cried out, but my attention was still half on the snake, which had vanished into the underbrush. "Did you see it?"

"What, my life flashing before my eyes?" he asked dryly, rubbing the back of his head.

"There was a snake!" I gestured wildly to the area, even as I climbed off him, brushing dirt and leaves from my body. "You didn't see the snake?"

"Nope," he said, still seated as he eyed me with a mixture of amusement and wariness. "Just saw you run into me like a damsel in distress."

"Take it back," I said, feigning my offense. "I am no damsel." I bent at the waist, offering him my hand.

He looked at it, then pushed himself up without taking it. "And risk falling again? Nah."

I rolled my eyes, muttering a few creative curses under my breath. "Whatever. Let's just keep going."

I turned back toward where the snake had disappeared, only to find the forest still and silent again. Dark green foliage and twisted roots carpeted the ground, dotted with the trailing vines of little blue flowers we'd been following for weeks.

"Ah, shit," Damon muttered, stepping closer.

"What now?" I asked warily.

His hand caught my wrist, lifting it gently. That's when I saw it; my right palm, scraped raw from our fall, blood welling at the edge of the wound.

"It's fine," I said with a shrug, tugging it back. "Just a scratch."

He gave me a look that said I was full of it. "We need to get supplies from Corvo. I don't want it getting infected—"

He broke off as I rubbed at the wound with the edge of my shirt, staining it red. When I pulled my hand away, there wasn't a mark to be seen. Only a smudge of blood on otherwise unblemished skin.

"Okay, wow," Damon muttered. "You heal really fast. Even faster than Vareck."

"That's . . ." I wasn't sure what words I was looking for, only that I was having a hard time finding them. "I've never healed that fast before."

He narrowed his eyes, watching me like I was some kind

of puzzle he was determined to solve. "Do you think it has something to do with Evorsus?"

I snorted. "You're crazy."

"I'm serious. You've been here for over a month now by our estimation, and weird things keep happening. The land responds to you." His gaze flicked to my hands again. "You're not *just* fae. What if something inside you is . . . waking up?"

"This again? You say that like I'm housing some sort of monster." I laughed at a borderline hysterical pitch, waving the comment off. "Nothing is waking up. I probably just . . ." My voice faltered. I didn't have a good explanation. And worse, part of me thought he might actually be right.

We kept walking, the silence stretching between us for several long strides.

The path narrowed, brush pulling at my legs until the trees opened into a moonlight-dappled clearing. A wide river cut through the middle, its current fast and foaming where it hit submerged rocks.

"Well, that's inconvenient," I muttered.

Damon stepped up beside me, squinting downstream. "We'll need to find a shallow crossing. Or a fallen tree."

"I should probably mention I'm not exactly the strongest swimmer."

"You did okay after you jumped off a cliff," he teased.

"Okay, that's fair. I am a decent swimmer, but I don't like dark water."

His lips curved. "Afraid of snakes *and* water? You're just full of surprises." He smirked, stepping toward the bank. "Come on. Let's find a way across."

As we walked along the edge of the river, I stole one last glance at my hand. The skin was still flawless. But that wasn't what made me uneasy.

It was the tugging beneath my ribs, low and pulsing like something—I just didn't know what.

Maybe I was crazy. Maybe Damon was crazy.

But gods help me—I was starting to wonder if he was right.

We walked until the trees thinned and a wide log stretched from our side to the other, moss-covered but seemingly stable enough, assuming neither of us slipped.

Poor assumption, given my shitty balance, but I wasn't going to chicken out when we needed to cross.

Damon tested it with one foot, then the other. He jumped a little to test the give and when it held he said, "It's solid. I'll go first."

He didn't extend his arms like I would, or any person who was vertically challenged. He prowled several feet across with the ease of a silent predator before turning back to me.

"Coming, damsel?" he called over his shoulder.

I flipped him off, but he just grinned.

With a huff, I stepped onto the log. It was slick, damp from the misting air above the river, and my boots squeaked with every movement.

Unlike Damon the unflappable, I extended my arms outward in a tee formation and slowly started to shuffle across. As I neared him, he reminded me to go slow and keep close, as though I had any intention of doing otherwise.

The current rushed beneath me, loud and wild and untamed. I really did hate dark water. It wasn't necessarily a fear of swimming or water—it was not knowing what was beneath the surface.

A splash sounded to my left.

I flinched, eyes scanning the roiling surface.

Nothing.

"Meera?" Damon called from in front of me. "You good? You want me to slow down?"

"Nope. I'm good," I mumbled and forced a step forward. Another.

Then something cold wrapped around my ankle.

I screamed. Blind panic overrode all sense of reason as I swayed on the log, trapped in my own fight-or-flight response.

A hand, pale and bloated, its nails blue and cracked, like it had been drowned long ago and forgotten, held my ankle like a shackle. It reached up from the water like a corpse risen from the deep.

A splitting pain clouded my vision; an electric shock went through my body as I felt every muscle tense.

Everything went white—my sight, my mind—an emptiness that swallowed everything around me.

There was no sound. No river. No Damon.

Just me.

Floating.

Drifting.

Then, as if lurched from one place into another, my sight returned, and a vision appeared. It was . . . me? And Damon?

I watched from an outside perspective as I screamed and launched myself into Damon's arms. It was the snake incident from earlier, except I wasn't seeing it as myself. It was from somewhere or someone else. An unknown third person that had been watching while Damon and I were none the wiser.

I felt my feet move as my body in the vision creeped forward. Everything blurred except the blood on my hand.

Drip.

Drip.

Drip.

My knees hit the log. Damon's hands grabbed my shoulders as I fell forward, yanking me upright before I could hit the water.

"Meera!" His voice sounded distant, like I was underwater. "What happened? Talk to me!"

I blinked, vision slowly sharpening.

The hand was gone. The river roared as it always had. I looked down at my ankle.

Nothing.

Not a scratch. Not a bruise.

But something inside me was *screaming*.

"I—you saw that, right," I asked quietly, breathless. My heart pounded a million miles a minute.

Damon's grip tightened on my arms. "Saw what?" His voice was taut. Alert.

"The hand. There was a hand," I said, scanning the river, even though I knew I wouldn't see it again. "It grabbed me. Gods, it touched me. I wasn't just imagining it."

He looked me over carefully, his eyes flicking from my face to my legs to the water. "There was nothing there, Meera. One second you were crossing, the next you dropped like someone cut your strings."

I opened my mouth. Closed it. My chest heaved as I struggled to find the words. "It showed me something. A memory. Not mine, though. Not exactly. It was mine—*ours* —but from the outside. Like someone was *watching* us earlier when I fell."

Damon's expression turned grim. "Evorsus?"

"I don't know," I said, shaking my head. "It didn't feel

like it. Or maybe it did. I—gods, I don't know what I saw now. Maybe . . . maybe I imagined it."

"Don't do that," he said. His jaw tightened, a muscle flexing in his cheek. "Don't pretend. If you say there was a hand, then I believe you. In this vision, did it say anything?"

"No." I hesitated, then added, "But I felt like it was trying to show me something. It was focused on my hand. On the blood."

He let go of my shoulders slowly, but his eyes never left my face. "We need to get off this log, and preferably, out of this realm."

"Agreed."

We crossed the remaining few feet quickly, neither of us daring to look down. My legs trembled as they hit solid ground again, the pressure in my chest lessening, but not gone.

Damon reached for me instinctively. His hands skimmed my arms, checking for injuries again. "You're sure it didn't say anything?"

"Positive. It just touched me." I trembled, wrapping my arms around myself.

Damon gave me a hard look. His mouth pressed into a thin line, his eyes sweeping the shadowed edges of the riverbank before shifting to the dense woods beyond. Whatever he was thinking, it wasn't good.

"I think we should stop and take a longer rest," he said, voice low and clipped.

I blinked. "What?"

"You're shaking, something just reached out of the water and hijacked your mind, and we're still in the middle of nowhere with no idea what direction the flowers are actually pointing." He stepped away, already scanning for a decent place to set up camp. "You're spooked, with good reason. We're stopping. I'll take watch while you sleep. Maybe we'll get lucky and Corvo will show up."

"All right." I didn't argue. For once, I didn't have energy, or the will. "Let's just get further from the river. I'm not comfortable being so close to it."

Damon dipped his chin in agreement, then held out his hand. I took it for what it was, not a romantic gesture but a protective one. With all that had happened, it was obvious the realm had an interest in me. Now something had just grabbed me. It happened right in front of Damon, and yet he saw nothing. I was going to hold on to him for dear life.

He found a shallow rise just beyond the tree line where the ground curved slightly upward and offered a view of both the river and the path behind us. It wasn't ideal—nothing about this situation was—but it was defensible.

I sank down onto the forest floor while Damon pulled two dehydrated food kits from his pack. He worked fast, creating a small fire pit with a flick of the lighter and a little air magic, coaxing embers to life. I was grateful for the distraction, even if the warmth hadn't touched my skin yet.

"Here," he said quietly, dumping some water into one of the packets and handing it over. "You're pale."

I stared at him. "I'm always pale."

"You're *paler*." His tone left no argument. "I wish I could give you something more substantial than this—"

"It's all right. We're both stuck here and doing the best we can. Thank you," I motioned with the bag of barely edible food. "I appreciate this."

Damon sat opposite me, the flicker of the firelight painting shadows across his face. "You want to talk about it?"

"No." I didn't even hesitate.

He nodded once, then tossed another stick into the flames. "Okay."

Silence stretched between us. Not uncomfortable. Not quite.

"I didn't think it was possible to see my own memory from someone else's perspective," I finally said. "And yet, there it was. That moment with the snake—like a vision but twisted somehow. I could feel emotions that weren't mine in reaction to what I was seeing."

His gaze was steady. "And you said it focused on your blood?"

"Yeah." I looked down at my palm again.

"I don't like it."

I snorted, but it lacked any humor. "Tell me about it."

"Maybe Corvo will have some answers for us," he said with a tight smile that didn't meet his eyes.

"Maybe," I agreed, equally unenthusiastic.

"Sleep, Meera. I'll keep watch."

I wanted to argue. To say I didn't need watching. But the truth was, I didn't feel safe. Not from what was out there . . . or from what I had seen.

So I lay down and stared into the flames until the warmth finally found its way to my bones.

But even then, I didn't close my eyes.

I wasn't sure what I'd see if I did.

CHAPTER 26

VARECK

The body hit the sand with a wet thud, its limbs twitching once before finally going still. The sound was swallowed by the canyon's walls. The air hung heavy with the stench of rotten blood, cloying yet foul, and just thick enough to taste. Flies were already circling; their buzzing just audible under the slow wail of wind between the cliffs.

I dragged both blades across my pants, the black smear vanishing into layers of older stains, marks from the countless fights, before sliding the swords home. The motion was muscle memory now.

Sadie rested one axe against her shoulder, the other hanging loose at her side. Her breath came in steady bursts, though her face glistened with sweat. "That's the last of them?"

"For now." My gaze tracked along the jagged walls, searching for the flicker of movement in the cracks. The Nameless had a habit of coming back when you thought you'd won. But this time only the wind answered, low and constant, carrying with it the faint scent of salt and minerals.

We started forward, boots grinding the grit and sand underfoot. Shadows stretched long in the dying light, reaching ahead of us toward the darker parts of the canyon. This was quite literally the edge of a world and the only place on Eversus that shadows existed.

The air shifted, cooler now, the breeze picking up a foreign yet familiar scent.

"There's something you should know before we get there." My voice carried low in the narrowing space. "The Fold—it isn't just a doorway, and it's more than a converging of the ley lines. It sits directly on a ley line. A big one. one of the few stable crossings between worlds."

Sadie tilted her head, flicking ichor from her axe with a sharp twist. "And?"

"And the ley line doesn't open for free," I said. "To step through, you have to give it something it can feed on. Something that matters to you."

Her brows drew together. "Feed on?"

"It's alive," I said, my tone flat. "In its own way, of course. Like everything else in the twin hells." My hand brushed against the canyon wall as we walked, feeling the subtle pulse beneath the stone. "The ley line takes a piece of you in exchange for passage."

Sadie's mouth twisted into a humorless smile. "When you say a piece of you . . .?"

I didn't smile back. "It's not always the same. And what it asks of you may be different from what it asks of me."

The canyon bent sharply, and the space ahead widened. The walls drew back, revealing a jagged gap in the stone—a black seam cutting deep into the earth. Even from here, it seemed to breathe, the shadows shifting in rhythm like the slow inhale and exhale of some buried god. The air spilling from it was cooler still, with an edge of damp that smelled faintly of rain on stone.

We both slowed.

"What kind of stuff does it ask for?" she asked quietly.

"Blood. Secrets. Sacrifice," I said. "Sometimes memories. Sometimes worse. The severity depends on the mood of the ley lines."

She blinked several times, processing. "You're shitting me."

"I wish I was."

"Do Meera and Damon know about this? I mean, I feel like this is really important information that you've kept to yourself until now."

I trailed my fingertips along the stone as we moved closer. The wall was cold now, and beneath my palm I felt it: a faint tremor, as though the stone was listening.

We were nearly there.

"It wasn't worth mentioning yet. It was only important that we made it here. And yes, Damon is aware of what will happen. Corvo made sure to tell him. Whether or not he told Meera, I don't know." I hoped it wouldn't matter. I hoped that whatever Sadie and I could give would be generous enough.

"Right. So your way of thinking was this was a 'future us' problem?"

"Correct. And now it's not."

The path pinched tight until the canyon walls pressed in like closing jaws, swallowing what little light remained. Every step forward dimmed the world until we passed under a natural arch of stone and into a darkness so deep it felt older than time.

Then, without warning, the space opened around us.

We had stepped into a cavern so vast the ceiling was lost in shadow, the walls stretching away into black. The air here was cool—unnaturally so—pressing against my skin like damp fingers. It carried the faint scent of wet stone and something metallic, sharp enough to sting the back of my throat.

A low hum threaded through the silence. At first it was so faint I thought it was just the ringing in my ears from the earlier battle, but the farther we walked, the stronger it became; vibrating in my teeth, my ribs, the marrow of my bones.

Sadie slowed until she was nearly matching my pace. "Feels like it's breathing," she muttered. Her voice carried farther than it should have, bouncing off unseen walls, coming back smaller and more distorted.

She wasn't wrong. The hum wasn't steady. It rose and fell, a rhythm that wasn't quite random. Inhale. Exhale.

The hairs along my arms lifted.

A light shimmered ahead, faint but steady, not the warm flicker of fire or the clear gold of sunlight. This light was soft and cold, shifting in strange ways as we drew closer. It pooled at the heart of the cavern, illuminating a pedestal of smooth black stone that rose straight from the ground as if it had grown there.

Atop the pedestal sat an obsidian bowl filled with liquid the color of molten silver. The surface rippled, though no breeze touched it.

The hum deepened, the sound curling into something almost like words—low, resonant, and indiscernible in direction.

"The cursed king returns, once broken, now whole. Ask what you desire, for the ley knows your soul."

The voice was in my head and all around me, sliding under my skin, brushing against my thoughts like cold hands rifling through drawers, looking for things that weren't theirs to touch.

Sadie froze mid-step. "Tell me you heard that."

I nodded once. "Yeah." My voice came out tight. "I heard it."

The hum thickened, pressing down on my skull until my vision wavered. The voice came again, heavier now, like stone grinding against stone.

"To walk the Fold . . . you will give what is owed."

Sadie's grip on her axes shifted, her knuckles pale in the dim light. She took a slow breath, her eyes scanning the cavern's edges as if the voice might have a shape. "It's not asking," she said finally, her voice low. "It's telling." She glanced at me. "And my gut says this thing doesn't let you walk away if you refuse."

The hum seemed to pulse at her words, almost like agreement.

I stared at the bowl, my stomach knotting. This wasn't my first bargain with ley lines and their demands, but I'd never had much to lose before. Now I had everything.

The silver in the bowl rippled, though no breath stirred the air.

"To pass where shadow births the light . . . you must pay the price."

The words slid through me like cold iron, heavy enough to settle in my bones.

Sadie tilted her head slightly, listening, though her jaw was clenched tight. "You hear how it says that? Like it's already decided what it wants."

"It probably has," I said.

The voice returned, each syllable dragging like chains across stone.

"The road is bought with what you cannot replace . . . to walk the Fold and look upon her face."

"You speak in riddles, old friend. Tell us what you want so that we may be on our way," I said, attempting to reason with the voice of power. Whatever this was, it was ancient. Perhaps just as old as the Fold and the worlds it bridged.

"The toll is what you hold most dear . . . pay it now or remain here."

I stepped closer to the pedestal, stopping just at the edge of its cold light. "What if we refuse?"

There was no pause.

"Then you will fade . . . lost to the stone, your debt unpaid."

The air shifted with those words; colder now, as if the cavern was angry and we were feeling its icy wrath.

Sadie's hand flexed on the haft of her axe. "So much for negotiating a price."

I glanced at her. "Would you like to take over?"

"Yes, actually." She turned toward the cavern and spoke to it. "How about a secret instead? I'm sure the king has some pretty juicy ones—"

"Seriously?"

Sadie shrugged. "Seems safer than whatever you hold most dear."

"The price is set, the key in your hand . . . yet only in loss will you understand."

Fear prickled my spine. I slowly stepped backward, only once, but it was enough to trigger the ley line.

A screech of stone followed.

"What the fuck?" Sadie asked. "Vareck did you—" She turned and froze, her eyes locked on something over my shoulder. "The door is gone. The cave sealed itself."

The grinding echo still rolled through the cavern, rattling the air in my lungs. I turned just enough to see it. Where we'd entered was now nothing but seamless rock, the arch we'd passed under was gone as if it had never existed.

The cold deepened. The shadows seemed to inch closer.

Sadie's voice was a rasp. "Yeah. I'm officially hating this."

The hum swelled, drumming against the inside of my skull.

"The price is set; the toll must be paid . . . or here in the dark your bones will be laid."

My gaze fell again to the bowl. The silver surface wasn't just rippling now. It was churning, thick swells rising and falling like the breath of something living beneath.

A faint, almost imperceptible steam lifted from it, catching the cold light and fracturing into pale shards in the air before vanishing. The scent coming off it was sharp, metallic, and wicked.

The hum rolled through the cavern again, deeper this time, vibrating in my ribs.

"Drink, and the Fold shall open. Refuse, and the dark will claim its token."

I looked around again, searching for another way forward but I already knew there was none. Ley lines were fickle but their demands were clear. If death was the price, then we'd be entombed in this cavern for eternity.

The air pressed down heavier now, like the cavern itself was leaning closer.

Sadie rolled her shoulders, then stepped toward the pedestal. "Fine. I'll go first."

"Sadie—"

She whirled on me, speaking in a hushed whisper as

though the ley line wasn't listening to our every word. Feeling and knowing what we were deep inside. "It's not like we have a lot of options. If we don't drink, it kills us. If we do drink, it takes something."

"Something we can't replace," I said, my voice rough. It wanted what I held most dear. I couldn't give that.

The hum deepened once more, final and absolute.

"*The toll must be taken before the gate will turn . . . the choice is made, now drink, and learn.*"

She cupped her hands and dipped them into the silver liquid, the ripples warping the surface like molten moonlight. No testing. No sniffing. Just one smooth motion—she tipped her head back and drank.

I tensed, waiting.

Nothing happened.

Sadie wiped her mouth with the back of her hand and gave a crooked grin. "I feel fine, but I really thought something crazy was going to happen."

I didn't return the smile. "You're sure? Nothing is off?"

"I think so." She rolled her shoulders like she expected something to hit her and came up empty. With a few hops, she tested her legs and her body. "Maybe it likes me."

"Or maybe you just don't know what it took yet," I muttered.

She raised a brow, but I wasn't focusing on her anymore. I was staring at the ley line.

It hummed again, deeper this time.

"*The toll is taken, the way prepared . . . one more debt, and you may be spared.*"

"The price was paid," I said quietly.

Sadie shrugged. "Then I got off easy."

I didn't say what I was thinking. It would do no good at

the moment to tell Sadie nothing in the Fold was easy. And no one was left untouched.

I turned toward the bowl, fury tightening every muscle. "I don't trust it."

Sadie snorted. "You don't have a choice."

"There has to be another way . . ."

"You are the one who told me about this, so you know there's not. Like it or not our choices are you drink, or we die here."

I hesitated, the hum in my skull growing louder, insistent, as if the ley line itself was leaning in to listen. My pulse thundered.

"What if it takes something from her?" My voice came low, almost a whisper. "What if it hurts Meera? Or it takes her?"

"Meera is a person, and it's *your* sacrifice, not hers. Right? It wouldn't take a person, would it?" Sadie's gaze was steady.

"I don't know."

"It said it wants us to learn something. I'm not dying here, Vareck. Drink it."

I hesitated one heartbeat too long, and the shadows stirred, inching closer. Cold pressed into my spine.

I dipped one hand into the bowl, the silver clinging to it like mercury. My reflection warped on the curved surface, dark-eyed and grim.

I raised it to my lips. The liquid was colder than ice, slicing down my throat in a rush of fire and frost all at once. My chest seized. The hum became a roar.

For a second, nothing happened—then a tearing sensation ripped through my chest, clean and merciless.

The bond. The thread that had been there—warm, unshakable—snapped.

I staggered, gasping, reaching for it instinctively, but there was only emptiness.

Meera was gone from me.

The ley line's voice rang through the hollow it left behind, satisfied.

"Once whole, now broken . . . and the gate opens."

CHAPTER 27

SADIE

Magic surged beneath my feet. I barely had time to curse before a wave of power swept through the cavern. The ground shuddered, then rolled as the ley line bucked, spitting us out with all the grace of a landslide.

I hit the grass hard, the softness doing nothing to cushion the blow. Air left my lungs on a tight exhale.

I pushed up onto my elbows, coughing, and then froze.

The Fold was unlike anything I'd ever seen.

Cliffs hung in the air, weightless. Waterfalls spilled from their edges in purple streams, free-falling into pools stacked one above the other. The cliffs moved slowly, deliberately drifting across the sky like islands pushed by an invisible current.

Everywhere I looked, the world was packed with color. Deep greens, sun-drenched golds, a sky so blue it felt unreal. The air was heavy with mist and magic. Warm. Alive. It smelled like crisp autumn air and felt like something older than time.

A place like this shouldn't exist.

But it did.

And somehow, that was more terrifying than anything we'd left behind.

Behind me, something broke the spell.

I spun.

Vareck was on his knees, head bowed, hands buried in the grass as if holding on could stop him from falling apart. His shoulders trembled, slow and uneven, like each breath was a fight he wasn't winning. His breath was harsh and uneven, like each one cost him.

Low, ragged, and damaged. Like the air had been ripped out of his lungs and replaced with nothing. It wasn't a scream. It wasn't a roar.

It was pain; raw and unshaped.

I crawled toward him. "Vareck—"

"She's gone." His words rang hollow, a deep emptiness emanating from them.

I reached for his arm. He didn't flinch or pull away or react in any way. It was like he wasn't here at all. Not mentally, at least.

"What do you mean by gone?"

"I can't feel her." His eyes lifted to mine, and gods, I almost wished they hadn't. The despondent look on his face was a man undone. "The bond's *gone*, Sadie."

I gripped his shoulder hard. "It's not gone. You're just cut off—"

"No. This is different." His voice was flat, but the way his fingers curled deeper into the grass told another story— one of fury barely leashed.

"Vareck . . ."

He shook his head, the movement sharp and final. "You don't understand. It's not distance. It's not interference. It's *gone*." His breath hitched, and for a second, his gaze darted past me, unfocused. "It's like someone took a blade and cut it clean. No fray. No thread.”

The muscles in his jaw flexed so hard I worried he might crack his teeth.

“We’ll find a way to get it back,” I said, trying to keep my tone level.

His laugh was quiet and without humor. “You don’t just ‘get it back’, Sadie. A bargain with the ley lines isn’t something you can go back on . . .” He trailed off, shaking his head again, slower this time, like he was still trying to convince himself it wasn’t true.

“Vareck.”

He blinked, and when his eyes came back to me, there was a spark there, explosive and unstable. The grass rippled under my knees, though there was no wind. Warm mist slid against my skin. The Fold was listening. Watching.

The air thickened, the kind of subtle shift you only notice when you’ve been in dangerous places before.

Vareck’s shoulders drew tighter, his whole body taut like a bowstring. “I can’t—” His breath came shorter now, and his hands left the grass, curling into fists. “I can’t breathe without feeling her there.” His voice cracked again, the anger and grief colliding into something volatile.

“Then you breathe *for* her,” I said sharply. “Until we find her.”

“And if we don’t?”

I shook my head. “Don’t talk like that. We’re going to find her. They’re on their way here. The bond may be gone for now, but Meera isn’t—”

“You don’t know that.”

“You don’t either!” I snapped back. I was trying to be encouraging, but guilt and frustration bled into every word. Vareck was right. I didn’t know shit when it came to bonds or ley lines. All I knew was that I couldn't afford to think my sister wasn't okay. I pushed him to drink because we had no choice, and it wasn't fair that I got away scot-free while Vareck had to pay the ultimate price. None of that changed the fact I refused to believe Meera was gone.

A low chuckle slid from between his lips. Uneasiness ate at me as I watched his descent.

"This is what I get for the things I've done."

The darkness in his voice sent ice through my veins, and I stood there frozen. "What the hell are you talking about?"

Vareck didn't answer immediately. He kept his eyes on the horizon, jaw still clenched so tightly it looked like it hurt. Magic rippled faintly around him, the Fold responding to emotions he wasn't even speaking aloud.

"Vareck," I said, more forcefully, wishing I could compel him to pay attention. That power resided with the high fae, of which I was not. "What do you mean about the things you've done?"

"Faerie was starving. Children were dying in the streets. I didn't know what else to do . . ."

I stayed silent, waiting for him to continue.

"My father plunged Faerie into eternal winter, and I didn't know how to fix it, but I had to try. I had to do something . . ."

Everything in me stilled.

This wasn't just the breaking of the bond talking. In this madness there was something else. Remorse. Shame. Sorrow buried so deep it had become a part of him. It terrified me.

"What did you do?" I whispered.

"I came here once before," he said quietly. "To the Fold."

My brow furrowed. "And?"

"There are ley lines in every realm, but none are as

powerful as this one. I needed it to destroy something for me." His hands flexed against the grass. "A god-forged artifact. One that never should have existed."

"Why?"

"I thought," he choked out, taking a breath before he could go on. "I *hoped* that it would end the winter. I was a *fool*."

"What type of artifact?"

"Amoret's necklace. The amulet. My father gave it to Drayden so he would gift it to Maeve. No one suspected that it was cursed. No one thought he'd hurt her." Vareck swallowed hard and shook his head. "Maeve was his favorite. She was the heir apparent."

I felt so lost. There was a story here I didn't know. I wasn't sure I was *supposed* to know. "Maeve was your sister?"

"My sister. Destined to ascend."

"Ascend?" I asked, a chill creeping down my spine. "Ascend to what?"

"Her place amongst the gods."

A fae becoming a goddess? Was that a thing? I knew about gods and demons, how they were basically one and the same. In all the legends and stories passed down, I'd never heard of someone ascending to godhood.

"You're not making a lot of sense, Vareck." I moved my hand slowly, not wanting to startle him while I checked for a fever. His skin felt normal, but nothing he was saying did. "What does your sister and father have to do with a god-made artifact you asked the ley line to destroy?"

"The necklace was the key. He used it to drain Maeve of her power and kill the furies. The winter was brought on by him—by *it*. I couldn't let it remain. If the necklace gave him the power to curse Faerie, then maybe destroying the necklace would undo the curse."

I tilted my head, taking it all in. This was really personal information, and I wondered if he was in his right mind telling me all this. "All right, I'm following. Seems logical enough. Except Faerie is still frozen over. So something didn't go as planned?"

"It didn't work," he said, curling his fingers harder, piercing the compacted dirt beneath us as he dug them in. Nails cracked, and blood smeared his hands like an offering. "We brought the necklace to the Fold. We asked the ley line to do what we could not . . . and it still didn't work."

"It wouldn't have done that for free."

Vareck swallowed again and lowered his eyes. "It didn't."

The air turned heavy. The ground beneath us hummed, a feeling of satisfaction that was not my own emanating from the ley line.

I leaned in. "What did it ask for?"

"I thought I was doing the right thing. People were starving," Vareck started, falling back on what he was saying before. Despite the manic edge, there was an awareness in how he held himself that told me the king wasn't completely gone. Not yet, at least.

"What did you give it?" I asked again, harder this time.

His lips parted, but no sound came out at first. Finally, he whispered, "Fate."

I frowned in disbelief. "Fate?"

"*Take what is forged by immortal hand, and leave in kind what fate once planned. A thread for a thread, a bond for a bond —unravel the heart where souls respond. What was eternal is now gone, severed in silence, yet ever lived on.*"

It wasn't hard to recognize the cadence. Despite the

lack of emotion in his voice, the whispered words of the ley line's demand settled over me as though I had been there with him.

"I still don't understand . . ."

"It unmade true mates. Every bond. Every thread. Fated love. Gone."

I stared, my brain processing the words too slowly. "You can't be serious. . ."

Vareck nodded. "Fated mates vanished. No one knew why. They blamed the curse, and I let them. But it was me. I was the catalyst."

I swallowed, trying to make sense of it. "But Meera—"

"She was the exception," he whispered. "I thought the Fold had missed one thread." He shook his head again, digging his bloodied fingers into the roots near his scalp. "Maybe it did. Maybe it didn't. Either way, it corrected its mistake."

"But it wasn't your fault," I said, trying to reason through the madness. "You didn't know what the ley line would take."

His eyes met mine, dark and hollow. A slight sheen glazed over them. "I did."

My words dried up as I stared at him. I opened and closed my mouth, searching for the right thing to say. He beat me to it.

"People were starving. Faerie can't import enough food. The famine was—*is*—a crisis. The way I justified it was that you can't miss what you didn't know you had. No one is guaranteed they'll find their true mate. We only hope. But chosen mates happen all the time. I thought it was better to take that bond away from the world than to let them starve. What I didn't bet on—what I didn't let myself consider— was that it wouldn't work."

"You were trying to save people," I said softly.

"And I *damned* them." Threads of dark brown hair tore away from his scalp. I grabbed his hands with my own, trying to force him to stop. "Do you know what it's like to wake up knowing you took fated love from an entire world? That you stole soulmates from the very people you swore to protect?"

"I don't."

"No," Vareck agreed. "You don't. And now—now the only one I've ever loved is *gone*. That's not chance, Sadie. That's the Fold collecting its due."

A horrible silence stretched between us.

"But she's not gone," I insisted. "The bond might be, but Meera is still alive and kicking. She's fighting her way back to us—to you. Bond or no bond."

"You don't know that," he mumbled.

"Stop it." There was no room for arguments. "My sister was in love with you before she knew you were real, before she had a fated mate bond. Nothing has changed."

"Everything has changed."

"Nothing that *matters*," I said. My fingers wrapped round his, gripping them fiercely to stop him from hurting himself more. "So what if the bond is gone? So what? You said it yourself that chosen mates happen all the time. Fate or no fate, you can still choose each other."

Vareck laughed, and I knew that was the moment I lost him. The unhinged sound coming from his chest made my own stomach twist. "In what world does she choose a man who sacrificed fated mates for *nothing*?"

His laughter faded, leaving only ragged breathing and the restless hum of the Fold, as though even the ley line was waiting for my answer.

I tightened my grip on his bloodied hands. "This one," I

said fiercely. "This world. The one where Meera never once looked at you and saw a crown or a curse—only you."

His jaw clenched, but his eyes flicked toward mine, desperate and broken.

"You think she won't choose you?" I pressed on, heart pounding. "She already did. Long before you two had a true mate bond. You can't undo that. Not even the Fold can undo that."

"You're wrong." He shook his head, but the motion was shaky now, unconvincing.

"The Fold may have taken fate, but love by itself was never something it could claim. It can unweave a thread, but it has no power over choice. And Meera chose you."

For a heartbeat, something flickered across Vareck's face; something fragile and unbearably human. "You truly believe that?"

I dipped my chin. "I do."

I'd seen Vareck furious, ruthless, cold. I'd never seen him like this—stripped bare, raw enough that I almost felt like I was trespassing just by looking at him. His eyes closed, lashes trembling, and when he opened them again, the devastation was still there, but so was something else. A fracture in the grief. A space where hope could bleed through, if only he let it.

"Liessss," a voice hissed. Out of nowhere, a golden snake appeared. "You don't sssseriously believe that, do you, Ssssadie?"

CHAPTER 28

VARECK

Sadie stumbled back, crab walking as fast as she could, her hands digging into the grass in a frantic scramble to put distance between herself and the serpent.

"What is it with talking animals," she muttered under her breath, panic sharpening her voice. "You. Snake. Go away. You're not wanted here."

The creature slithered forward, silent and sinuous, the golden sheen of its scales catching the sunlight. It stopped just short of my knees and rose, its long neck arching upward until its face hovered inches from mine. Its black eyes burned bright, soulless, and endless.

"I can't believe," it hissed, "after all you've been through, you can sssstill hope."

The words landed like a whisper, but they cut like a blade. Behind me, Sadie's breath hitched.

A shadow of doubt flickered through me, brief as a heartbeat, but enough. Enough for the serpent to feel it; to smell it like blood in the water.

"Shut up," Sadie snapped, pushing to her knees.

"Vareck, don't listen. In every story *ever*, the snake is deceitful—"

"Ssssilence."

The word rippled with magic. A pulse of unnatural energy crackled through the air. Sadie gasped, then clutched her mouth with both hands. Her eyes blazed, but no words followed. Only muffled, furious sounds as she fought to speak through the spell.

"Be sssstill."

She looked at me.

I didn't look back.

The serpent had me. Its gaze was like chains, cold and binding. It saw too much. More than I wanted anyone to see. All the wreckage I carried inside; Meera's absence, the way her laughter had once filled the hollows of my soul, and the aching silence that had replaced it. The serpent looked at me like it *knew*. And worse, it *understood*.

"The Fold has tessssted you," it said, almost gently now. "And you've been found wanting."

Sadie snarled behind her gag, desperation bleeding through every twitch of her limbs. She would've lunged if she could.

I didn't move. I couldn't. The serpent's voice had wrapped around my mind like a coil, tightening, drawing me in.

"You got what you dessssserved, Vareck. You desssstroyed the balance. You shattered the bond meant to endure time, war, death itssssself. You took away your people'ssss fate. Yet you were ssssurprised when the ley line took your own?"

My fists clenched. The bones in my hands cracked.

"What would Maeve think had she not perished?" it whispered. "You were gifted a true mate, and sssstill you chose to ssssever that bond. You walked willingly into the ley line, knowing the rissssk."

"That's not true," I said, but the words felt thin. Flimsy. My voice cracked on the second syllable.

"Isssn't it?" The serpent tilted its head, slowly, like a puppeteer studying his marionette. "You made the bargain. You knew what it had taken before. What wassss to sssstop it from asssssking again?"

"I didn't know it would be Meera."

"But you did. In your heart of heartssss, you knew." It slithered closer, unblinking. "You felt the tension in the bond. You felt her sssslipping through your fingerssss. And you let her go."

Did I?

A single thought, but it stopped me cold.

Had I truly known the magic would take what I loved most, and I bargained anyway? How long had I suspected as we trekked our way toward the Fold?

"She fightsss for her life," the serpent crooned. "To return to you, the cursssed king. But she doesss not know, doesss she?"

I tensed. "Know what?"

The serpent's tongue flicked out, tasting the air.

"What you have done?"

The weight of those words crashed into me, harder than any blow.

I said nothing. Couldn't. My throat closed.

"No . . ." I whispered. "She doesn't."

The serpent nodded like it had expected as much. "And when she findsss out?" it asked softly. "When she learnsss that it wassssn't your father nor sssome cursssse that sssstole your bond, but *you*—will she sssstill choose you?"

"I was doing what I had to, to survive," I snapped. My voice trembled. "For me and Sadie—"

The serpent's body coiled tighter, its presence suffocating even in the open air.

"Do you not feel the ache?" it hissed. "The emptinesssss? The pain of a bond ssssevered . . . I hear it'ssss agony."

"It *is*," I growled, louder than I meant. "Of course I do."

The words ripped out of me like blades. My chest burned. The fury under my skin threatened to surface.

"You musssst not truly feel it," the serpent said, almost pitying. "Or you would do *anything* to regain the bond."

I swallowed, wincing against the dryness. My mouth tasted of sand and ash.

"I *can't* bring it back," I said, but even as I spoke, doubt began to grow. "The ley line took it. There's no going back."

"But there issss," it whispered. "There *issss* a way to bring it back."

It slithered closer, so close now that I could feel the magic bleeding off its skin like steam. "The amulet. You sssstill have it, don't you?"

"I don't," I lied.

The serpent laughed. It wasn't a sound. It was a sensation, dry and papery and empty. It reminded me of dead leaves cracking underfoot. Of things that would never grow again.

"Liessss," it hissed, tightening its body again, its golden scales undulating like liquid. It flicked its tongue to taste the air. "Lying doessss not become you, curssssed king. You know where it issss. Even if you don't carry the piecessss, they are sssstill yourssss. Hidden. Bound. Masssssked by blood magic. Forever your burden to bear."

I stared down at it, my breath catching. I could hear the

thrum of my blood in my ears. Every part of me felt too loud. Too still. Too *full* of grief and guilt.

"How do you know this?" I whispered.

"I am of the Fold," the serpent whispered. "Undo the glamour. Find the piecessss. Repair it . . . and bring back what wassss losssst."

I hesitated.

"You don't understand why . . ." I said, voice barely audible.

"But I do. The Fold knowssss everything; I am of the Fold. A bargain to end the endlesssss winter," it finished, with a slow nod. "And did it work?"

The words struck like a blade driven through the center of my chest.

I faltered.

"No," I said finally.

The serpent hissed, triumphant. "Becausssse the amulet wassss not the ssssource."

"I didn't know that then."

"Then why keep it sssseparated?" it asked, wrapping its body tighter, rising as though it were ready to strike. "What have you protected, Vareck, king of winter and death? *Nothing* changed. The curssssse sssstill sssstrangles the land. Fatessss are losssst. Your mate"—its voice curled into something cruel and sweet—"issss sssstill gone."

My shoulders sagged under the weight of it. I shut my eyes.

And for a moment, I let myself *want*.

Want her back. Want the ache to end. Want to undo the one mistake I couldn't fix with blade or magic or will.

Even if it came with a price I shouldn't pay.

"Ressssstore it," it said. "And perhapssss the old wayssss

will return. Perhapssss *she* returnssss. Whole. Yourssss. Again."

A dangerous hope cracked open in my chest, and I hated how good it felt.

"She would be mine again?" I asked, my voice a whisper. "If I restored the necklace?"

"Wouldn't it be worth the rissssk?" A fire flashed through the serpent's eyes, hues of orange and reds dancing in the black depths.

A tremor ran down my spine. The amulet had been more than symbolic. It was pure power given form. An artifact forged by the threads of life and fate. That was why my father had used it. It's what made its mass destruction possible. Kaia, Drayden, and I were all there that day. Forever bonded by our grief, we used the amulet and tried to right the wrongs. When I failed, we glamoured the severed pieces, then scattered them; hid them across the realms, all to prevent people from finding it and attempting to use it again one day.

My mistake had cost everyone.

My fear of the amulet itself led to its dismantling. I could reverse it all.

If the amulet was also the key to restoring the bonds . . . if I could feel *her* again . . .

I didn't notice Sadie moving until I heard the scrape of steel. Her hands were free. She had broken the gag. One of her twin axes was already in her palm.

"Vareck, step back!" she shouted.

"No!" I snapped. "Wait—"

She lunged forward in a fluid blur, axe raised high. The serpent didn't move, and Sadie didn't swing. She froze, and then her eyes went wide. Her mouth fell open, as if stuck in silent horror.

"I can't see," she whispered. Her weapon clattered to the ground, and she touched her face, searching for an obstruction that wasn't there. "I can't see!"

She stumbled back, hands outstretched, blinking furiously at a world she could no longer sense.

"What did you do?" I roared at the snake.

It slowly turned toward her, unconcerned. "Nothing. Twassss the ley linessss."

I darted toward Sadie, catching her as she swayed.

"Shh," I murmured, pressing a hand to her cheek. "It's okay. You're okay."

"I'm blind, Vareck," she whispered harshly, breath shallow. "I can't see *shit*."

Several moments passed where Sadie hyperventilated. Then her eyelashes fluttered. She blinked rapidly. "I can see again."

"What was that?" I asked.

"I don't know," she breathed, then narrowed her brown eyes on the serpent. "But you know, don't you?"

The snake tilted its head as though it shrugged. "A priccce twassss asssked. The debt twassss paid."

Sadie lunged forward, making to grab her axe. She missed the handle by millimeters and collapsed on the ground on her hands and knees.

"Fuck!" she screamed. "It's happening again! I can't see. I can't—" She broke off. A deep, full body shudder ran through her. "No, no, no," she muttered in strangled gasps. "This can't be happening."

"What? What is it?"

"The price is what you hold most dear," Sadie murmured, her voice quivering. "Most dear . . . no . . ." She sank back on her haunches into a kneeling position. I could tell the minute her vision came back because she turned to me, tears filling her eyes.

"I can't do it," she whispered, her hands shaking as she looked down at them.

"Can't do what?"

Her response was little more than a breath. I wouldn't have heard it if I hadn't been straining to listen.

"Fight."

Behind me, the serpent waited, silent and poised, tongue flicking out before retracting it yet again. It didn't need to speak.

The seed was already planted.

And gods help me . . . it was starting to grow.

CHAPTER 29

MEERA

I dreamed of a floating island.

It wasn't the first time I'd had strange dreams, but this one felt different. Weightless, lucid, and painfully real.

The sky above stretched in an endless canvas of cobalt, painted with swirls of cloud. Beneath my feet, a bed of impossibly soft grass tickled my bare soles, vivid green and almost glowing. A low breeze whispered across the terrain, though nothing moved with it. The air smelled faintly of autumn.

In the center of the island, purple water cascaded down from a shallow pool, flowing like silk over smooth, dark stone. Each level of the waterfall spilled into another, forming perfect, concentric pools that spiraled out toward the edge before tumbling into infinity. The whole island hovered above a vast nothingness. No land. Just the sky below and an endless, terrifying void.

It was beautiful in a way that didn't exist anywhere else. Majestic and haunting all at once. Enchanting and ethereal. It felt as old as time itself.

What appeared to be a place of calm and comfort, I felt nothing of the sort. Trepidation tiptoed through my psyche.

I stepped forward, drawn by a sound I couldn't quite name—until it hit me with crystal clarity.

Vareck's voice was low. Strained. Each word carried a heavy burden, the cause of which I didn't understand yet. But gods, I felt it. I felt his pain before I saw him, and it tore at my very soul.

Kneeling on the grass, shoulders hunched, he looked like a man defeated. In front of him loomed a massive serpent; golden, beautiful, and dangerous. It coiled like liquid sunlight and towered over him, its scales catching the light of both the sun and moon as they existed simultaneously on opposite sides of the sky.

This wasn't right. This wasn't real.

"You musssst not truly feel it," the serpent hissed. *"Or you would do* anything *to regain the bond."*

My chest squeezed tight, an invisible fist closing around my lungs. Each word it spoke slid over my body like oil, coating me, trying to suffocate my skin.

"I can't *bring it back,"* Vareck said. His voice cracked. *"The ley line took it. There's no going back."*

"But there issss," the snake whispered, slithering forward. Its movement was hypnotic in the same way fire and flames captivated and held our attention . *"There* issss *a way to bring it back."* It slithered closer to him. *"The amulet. You sssstill have it, don't you?"*

I didn't know how I'd gotten here. Whether this was a memory, a vision, a dream, or something far stranger I couldn't yet comprehend. I felt the pull of his soul like a thread tied to mine, taut and trembling. Something deep and old, fraying in ways I hadn't noticed until now. Tension coiled, low in my belly, nausea forming and taking hold.

The serpent laughed and hissed, *"Liessss."* It tightened its body and flicked its tongue to taste the air. *"Lying doessss not become you, curssssed king. You know where it issss. Even if you don't carry the piecessss, they are sssstill yourssss. Hidden. Bound. Masssssked by blood magic. Forever your burden to bear."*

"How do you know this?" he whispered, his voice laced with anxiety and agony .

"I am of the Fold," the serpent whispered. *"Undo the glamour. Find the piecessss. Repair it . . . and bring back what wassss losssst."*

I could feel the weight of Vareck's hesitation ripple through the dream scene. My stomach flipped over, threatening to drop me to my knees. He was in a horrible nightmare. One I shouldn't witness. One that was filled with fears and wounds he tried to keep hidden, tender and still bleeding, and wrapped tightly beneath his stony exterior.

"Then why keep it sssseparated?" it asked, wrapping its body tighter, rising as though it were ready to strike. *"What have you protected, Vareck, king of winter and death?* Nothing changed. The cursssse sssstill sssstrangles the land. Fatessss are losssst. Your mate issss sssstill gone."*

My heart pounded so loudly I was afraid he'd hear it. Afraid he would see me and know that I was invading such a private moment even though I didn't intend to. I wanted so badly for our sleep to sync. I wanted so badly to talk to him, but this was never the reunion I had imagined. Now I worried if he saw me here it would hurt more knowing he wouldn't have me when we woke up.

"Ressssstore it," it said. *"And perhapssss the old wayssss will return. Perhapssss she returnssss. Whole. Yourssss. Again."*

"She would be mine again?" Vareck whispered.

I couldn't breathe.

I was already his. Couldn't he tell? Even though I was scared and even though the realm played its tricks, he *had* to know he was mine and I was his. Damn the invasion of his private thoughts. I couldn't bear to watch any longer. I couldn't let him think this way, dream this way. Even if he didn't have me when we woke up, he had to stop thinking what we have is gone just because I wasn't there. I walked forward, but he didn't move.

"Vareck?" I said softly, but nothing happened. "Vareck."

Nothing but stillness. Sickness roiled in my gut.

The air felt suffocating. Cloying and rotten and no longer crisp like autumn.

Everything was wrong here. Something had taken hold of him. Something perverse and evil. Whatever this thing was, it didn't belong to the beauty of this place.

I moved quickly, screaming his name. Trying to tell him I was here. Trying to free him from his nightmare.

For a moment, I had hope. His head jerked slightly. His eyes searching like they were looking for mine, but he never saw me and my steps faltered.

"Why can't you see me?" I whispered, wrapping my arms around myself.

Then the serpent turned with methodical intention. Its mouth separated into a horrifying smile, its tongue again flicking and tasting the air. Blackened eyes glowed with the red embers of a dying fire, watching me with hunger.

"I ssssee you, lovely," it whispered, smug and soft.

My body froze as it stared at me. This wasn't right. This was Vareck's dream. His nightmare. "How?" I breathed out in a shaky voice.

"I am of the Fold. The Fold knowssss everything." The snake's eyes flashed with power as it coiled tightly, rising higher. The thick muscle of its elongated form twisted. "I'm afraid it'ssss not time for you yet."

Before I could move, before I could reach him, before I could even scream his name again, a wall of raw, ancient magic hit me like a tidal wave.

The ground disappeared.

The light vanished.

And I tumbled backward into darkness.

I woke with a gasp, the scream still lodged in my throat.

Pain bloomed at the back of my skull, sharp and hot, like I'd been dropped from a height I wasn't meant to survive. My limbs were heavy, leaden. As if my soul had been dragged back to my body too quickly.

I tried to sit up, the twisting of my gut threatening to spill the contents of my stomach.

Strong hands shoved me back down.

"Don't move," a voice said, low and unfamiliar. Calm, but cold.

I blinked hard. Everything spun. My vision swam, colors flickering like candlelight before settling into shapes.

When the scene came into focus, my heart began to race.

Figures stood over me. Tall. Broad. Black, jagged wings folded tightly against their backs. Their eyes were sharp, predatory. These were not Nameless, nor were they fae.

They were *furies*.

I needed no confirmation . I felt it in my blood; charged, primal, and fierce. Like the moment before a thunderstorm breaks.

Damon looked at me silently with rage-filled eyes. One

of the furies had him by the back of the neck, holding him in a headlock. He was on his knees. Magic shimmered along the fury's skin like smoke. Damon wasn't resisting, but his jaw was clenched, and his gaze was locked on mine.

Panic surged, but so did my nausea. I tried to get up, but I rolled to the side, emptying all that had been churning there since my encounter in Vareck's dream.

"I said don't move," a figure repeated, reaching for me. I tried to knock its hand away in a weak attempt at self-preservation.

What a weak fae I was, sprawled on the floor, vomiting while held captive.

"Drink this," another said, offering a skin of some unknown substance. I glared at him, wiping my mouth with the back of my hand.

"No," I rasped, trying to push it away.

"I told you she needs a moment to come out of it," one spoke to another. "She's had an encounter with a demon shadow."

Damon growled softly, a low rumble.

"Let him go," I croaked, my voice raw. Pressing my hand to the ground, I moved to sit up, away from the puddle I'd left on the floor.

A fury regarded me for a moment, then looked at the one holding Damon back. She inclined her chin and Damon was released. He catapulted forward, palms landing flat as he sucked in air in harsh gasps.

A fury offered me the skin again, but I looked at it with distrust.

"If I wanted you dead, I could have done it earlier. I don't need to poison you. Drink. It'll help you feel better."

I coughed again, accepting my fate. The fury had a point I couldn't argue. I took the skin and drank from it, feeling its cooling contents flow through me. It wasn't water, and it wasn't wine. Whatever magic it contained was rejuvenating. My shaky muscles felt stable again. The uneasiness in my stomach settled, and my pulse slowed . . .

They offered one to Damon, but he scowled, knocking it out of the hand that offered it. Several furies towered over him, leaving little room for him to attempt to stand. They may have let him go, but they weren't willing to risk him fighting, apparently.

"If you're looking for the king, I don't know where he is," Damon said, sitting back on his haunches.

"We aren't looking for the king."

Damon's brow furrowed, and he held his chin high.

A fury laughed. "We care not for a prince, either, despite knowing who your father was."

His eyes narrowed, but concern filled them quickly as he met my gaze once again.

"What, then?" I asked, my voice shaking.

The fury to my left tilted its head, regarding me closely.

"We've been waiting for you," he said. "Our Queen."

To be continued . . .
Vareck and Meera's epic love story continues in Between the Twin Realms. Subscribe to our newsletter to be the first to know when the third installment will be ready.
kelandaureliabookstore.com

If you're interested in a spicy short story about Meera's life *before* meeting Vareck, you can grab it for **free** here.
P.S. There may or may not be a sexy dream scene.
wink wink

Need something else to read in the meantime?

"Markus Del Reyes, I reject you."

He left me no choice.

I refuse to spend the rest of my life with my childhood bully for a mate. I may be a cursed shifter, incapable of shifting—but I wasn't desperate.

Not till the Alpha Supreme cast me out of the House of Fire and Fluorite for rejecting his son.

Now I'm packless.

Homeless.

No longer under the protection of a House.

Until the dark vampire king of Blood and Beryl turns his sights on me.

In return for protection from my former House, I have to become his fake mate.

I'll be a queen and a fraud.

It's a treacherous lie to live—and I find myself forgetting what's real and what's not with every stolen touch and heated kiss we share.

What starts as a business arrangement turns complicated when my heat hits, and the king insists on being the one to help me through it.

I've lost everything for doing what I know is right, but the greatest danger I ever faced was never losing my life ... it was opening my cursed heart.

START READING REJECT ME NOW

ACKNOWLEDGMENTS

Gummi bears are a comfort food.

Funyuns make great road trip snacks.

Sometimes, blow drying your hair is self-care.

Make the appointment and get a massage.

Divorce isn't a dirty word.

Found family isn't just a trope.

Therapy and medication isn't taboo.

Make time for your friends.

Find your village.

Movie quotes can make the best inside jokes.

Divorce memes and reels are hilarious.

Deadlines are bullshit.

Perimenopause is bullshit.

Go rogue and do what you want in your acknowledgments.

Lauren, you are the best and we are so grateful for you. Kayla, we thank you for being there when we need you.

Mr. Jane . . .

Jude, 14, and 11 . . .

Love. The kind of love we feel so deeply in our bones, it's sometimes hard to breathe. All day, every day. Love.

AJ & Kel

www.ingramcontent.com/pod-product-compliance
Lightning Source LLC
Chambersburg PA
CBHW021236190726
48289CB00005B/1355